THE FOURTH ARM

By the same author

Secret Army
Secret Army Dossier
Kessler

THE FOURTH ARM

A novel of the Second World War
derived from the BBC television series by

JOHN BRASON

BRITISH BROADCASTING CORPORATION

The series *The Fourth Arm* was produced by Gerard Glaister in the Glasgow Studios of the BBC. It was directed by Viktors Ritelis, Nick Renton and Andrew Morgan.

The writers were Michael J. Bird, Brian Finch, Gerard Glaister, Alfred Shaughnessy and John Brason. Devised by Gerard Glaister and John Brason.

Published by the
British Broadcasting Corporation
35 Marylebone High Street
London W1M 4AA

ISBN 0 563 20096 0

First published 1983

Set in 10/11pt Monophoto Ehrhardt and
printed in England by
Cox and Wyman Limited, Reading

For Gerry

Contents

Preface

It was Hugh Dalton in the early days of the Second World War who called for a 'Fourth Arm' to supplement the orthodox armed forces of the United Kingdom. That Fourth Arm was supplied, over the years, by many organisations: the many Commandos, the SOE, MI6 (and others), the American OSS, etc. The Fourth Arm of the television series is a separate unit that does not properly identify with any of them. It is an amalgam, and it is fictitious, though based on fact. Its activities and operations are also based upon actual fieldwork. The course of war history is followed closely.

The series also marks for me a decade of working in close partnership with my producer, Gerard Glaister. Together we have re-fought much of that war through *Colditz*, *Secret Army*, *Kessler* and now *Fourth Arm*. I would like to put on public record the pleasure it has been to work with 'a real pro'. Gerry has proved himself to be probably the most successful television producer BBC television has had. Through *Doctor Finlay's Casebook*, *Colditz*, *The Brothers*, *The Expert*, *Secret Army*, *Kessler*, *Blood Money*, and countless others he has captured the nation's viewers as no one else has. For me it has been a pleasure and a privilege to be closely associated with him for ten of those years. Few people have my professional respect as he has. But he has earned it. Hopefully *The Fourth Arm* will herald the start of another decade of collaboration and friendship.

My thanks are also due to Bill Randle, technical adviser to all of our wartime escapades. Another man I am happy to number among my friends.

J.B.
August 1982

7 March 1944

'My name is Paul Lamboit. I am a bookseller.'

The dark-haired man in his mid-thirties reiterated the statement yet again. Name, rank, serial-number of a civilian. He had told them twenty times already. It wasn't that they did not believe him. They didn't seem to care. It had become a sort of mantra to repeat at intervals when the silence demanded relief. The Milicien, a member of the French secret police, who asked the question was more concerned with the activity outside in the small square.

There, five uniformed German privates tipped box after box of books and papers into a central pile. The top books blew open in the breeze and their exposed pages flapped and turned in the morning sun. When the job was done and the last book tossed onto the pile one trooper returned with a can of petrol, poured it over the books and then threw the can on top before drawing a box of matches from his tunic pocket and striking. The match flared, and Lamboit held his breath as his eyes stared through the shop doorway out into the square, focused upon that pile of books that was his stock, his livelihood and his faith.

The pyre roared into orange flames as the light wind urged the top books to accept the licking tongues of destruction that ran back and forth along the petrol-soaked edges of the bindings. Closed books do not burn all that easily. A certain temperature is necessary to maintain combustion otherwise they merely return to smouldering and eventual extinguishing. The temperature is 451° F. The March breeze must have been enough to fan that fire for it burned for three hours. The heat could be felt at the far side of the square . . . It could even be felt inside the ransacked bookshop and down the right side of Lamboit's face, a face seemingly without reaction, without emotion. Only the dark eyes spoke of a hatred that burnt inside the Frenchman even more fiercely than did the fire outside.

They didn't take him away. They didn't decide to shoot him, or deport him. They just looked, then turned away and got into their trucks and drove out of the town.

1
THE PROBLEM

2 April 1944

Lamboit didn't take his eyes from the entrance of the police station. He sat at the table outside the café pretending to read the small volume on his lap, but keeping his eyes firmly upon that black-painted door. Inside, talking to the desk gendarme, was the Milicien who had dropped that flaming, petrol-soaked rag into his life. He waited. The rumbling noise took some moments to register before he found his attention drawn from the entrance. One by one villagers appeared in their doorways, or at windows, and stared in awed silence down the broad village street. The stone walls of the houses echoed the approaching sounds, rendering them even more metallic as the source neared the bend in the street by the butcher's shop.

First it was two outriders on cycles with mounted machine-guns on the side-cars, followed by a newly-painted Type 82 Kübelwagen in which sat a half-asleep Major with his large coat collar turned up against his neck to shelter him from the draught. The driver and the officer wore standard army grey but the arm cocked on the door of the Kübelwagen displayed the badge of a Waffenfeldwebel. Attention switched instantly to the great vehicle that was following and creating so much appalling noise. It was a four-and-a-half-tonne Bussing-Nag lorry converted to a Maultier half-track by the use of Panzer 11 suspension components under the massive truck assembly. Two infantrymen armed with Schmeissers held onto the iron grid affixed to the bonnet structure, and glared belligerently at the watching villagers. The converted lorry dragged behind it an eight-wheeled trailer, probably another four-tonne load, which moved with relative silence behind the metallic clatter of the half-track. Both vehicles were tightly tarpaulined, effectively concealing the load from inquisitive eyes. Two Opel Blitz trucks carrying bored and half-asleep infantry guards brought up the rear, followed, as a final gesture to their mechanised superiority, by a Kettenkrad motor-cycle tractor with its yellow-toned tactical markings largely obliterated.

The NCO sitting facing the rear in the Kettenkrad caught Lamboit's dull gaze and held it before he grinned widely and winked. Lamboit turned away to where the Milicien and the gendarme stood in the station doorway as someone slid into the seat next to him watching the convoy disappear down the street. It took eight-and-a-half minutes for the noise of the vehicles to subside, and many villagers showed their disapproval by elaborate movements of fingers-in-ears and feigned bouts of deafness, while two urchins drew momentary glory in kicking fallen tiles and a chimney pot which had been dislodged by the noise and vibration.

'I wonder what they've got in there.'

The voice in Lamboit's ear was gruff and low. He didn't turn to see Pierre de Grouchy. He was watching the Milicien walk down the street. Lamboit stood and started to move away after the retreating figure.

'Leave it, Paul. It does no good.'

Lamboit stopped, letting his eyes follow, before he turned to glower at the badly-shaved face of de Grouchy, the local Resistance leader.

Lamboit then turned on his heel, and made for the blistered doorway of what was once his shop. He let himself in and crossed to the chair by the unlit stove, and turned to survey the empty, broken shelving that went round the entire shop premises. It was not a big place. Two rooms with an office off the larger of the two. His book stock had never been particularly large, but it was known to scholars, rather than collectors, and university lecturers and students throughout northern France. Paul Lamboit was not merely a bookseller, he published too. Initially his interest was in making available important theses that would otherwise never get into print. That had quickly eaten up his modest patrimony, but the University Publications Board had made a grant available to him in recognition of what he had achieved in the decade since 1934. The grant had even extended into 1942 through the careful administration of Maître Laclos, but it was also the instrument that had led the Germans to this quiet backwater of obscure printing, and the supposedly subversive, decadent philosophies held therein. Philosophies that apparently threatened the very existence of the Third Reich and demanded total destruction lest the silent thoughts contained between the heavy paper covers somehow brought about that blessed event.

Lamboit sat, then walked, then stood and looked out of the

dusty window before he decided upon action. He went to the shed at the rear of the property, and grabbed his elderly bicycle.

No one had sabotaged the convoy. Even the Germans recognised that the stoppage was due to natural causes. Simply that the recent rains had softened the ground about the road that led down to the bridge across the stream. The bridge was old, but it was stone, and well-built. It would hold. The approach road was the problem. No tarmac repairs had been made since the beginning of the war. That was almost five years ago, and the sloping bank had simply slid away down the gentle slope as soon as the half-tracks' weight cracked the elderly tarmac. It meant the Bussing-Nag truck had slipped backwards and sideways, and was out of control before the driver had the sense to stop his half-tracks threshing about, and turning soft ground into slithery mud that they would never surmount.

The Major, roused from his nap, and rubbing his stiff neck, swore at the wretched driver and stopped all activity while he assessed the problem. His NCO aide, Sergeant Tupper, with his thick Swabian accent, walked beside him and fed him his ideas for getting out of trouble. The Major was not happy. He was actually very concerned. He had a delivery schedule of the utmost importance to the outcome of the entire war. He knew it. His men knew it. Their masters had been at pains to make sure they understood just that. Consequently the activity was not merely efficient, it was frenetic.

That was the way it looked through binoculars from the ridge, on one side where the copse and undergrowth gave good cover for anyone who cared to watch the performance. Lamboit cared. He knew the half-track and its trailer did not contain books, but he was astute enough to recognise that what they did contain might just be important, and might be connected in some way with the underground workings the entire district knew were going on in the old quarries. He had stuffed his bike into the hawthorn bushes and was well-concealed. He had nothing much else to do now. He could wait, and watch, and note.

The trailer had been uncoupled and manhandled to the hill side of the road without too much trouble, but it was obvious that the back-up of the Bussing-Nag four-and-a-half-tonner would be no picnic. The barked commands resulted in chains and couplings, and a portable winch being hurried to the roadside above the truck. From Lamboit's vantage point he could assess better than the Germans that there was small likelihood of the winch assisting. And so it turned out when the tracks, in reverse, broke up the wooden boards shoved between their own metal plates and the soft mud. It was simply too heavy, a fact of life that the Major of Ordnance comprehended with bitterness. He stopped the operation and sent the first of the two outriders ahead, presumably with a report on the delay, and commanded the infantry guard to lay down their weapons and set about manhandling the truck load out onto the ground to lighten the vehicle. That was when Lamboit became more than casually interested.

The stripped tarpaulin revealed a mixture of components separately crated. Some, roped together in batches of eight, appeared to be wing-sections of a small aircraft . . . yet not quite. The crated objects were openly slatted, enough to reveal the basic contents as one shining, steel ram-jet per crate. Something about the whole thing was sinister. The leaden-coloured jet-housings, the clipped wing-section argued something that Lamboit did not recognise. He watched in silence for half-an-hour as the men sweated and struggled with the tiny derrick they had rigged up, and slipped and dragged the heavy crates up towards the roadside eventually to be reloaded, if and when they managed to relocate their half-track vehicle. Lamboit had seen enough, and silently and surreptitiously withdrew his bike, carrying it for five hundred yards before he touched the road surface, and started pedalling back to the village.

De Grouchy was still sitting at the table sipping a marc, nodding to an old codger in a soft beret who had joined him and prodded the cobble stones with his walking-stick as he shook his head and grumbled about the war, the Germans, and the weather. De Grouchy's eyes noted Lamboit's arrival, his dismounting from the bike, and knew that Lamboit wanted to talk.

'Better get back to your wife, Gaston. She doesn't like it if you stay away too long.'

The old man grunted and rubbed his rheumy eyes as he straightened his back, and staggered away muttering to himself.

Lamboit slipped into the vacated seat, still warm from the elderly backside.

'The old quarries, what are they using them for?'

De Grouchy didn't look at him but took another sip from his glass.

'Did you see the Boche convoy?'

Lamboit sighed and tapped the edge of the table with his finger as if to emphasise a point.

'I want to take a look at the quarries. What d'you know, Pierre?'

De Grouchy finally turned to face him, his eyes hard, his unshaven chin firm.

'Not much. The Germans are using it as some sort of dump. For what I don't know. Why?'

'I want to go and see for myself.'

De Grouchy shook his head. 'No, it is pointless.'

Remonstration brought no softening from the Resistance man, and it was an unwritten law in their area that no one – but no one – did anything of that nature without consulting Pierre de Grouchy personally. There had been no Resistance deaths in the Chantilly/Senlis area for three years, since, in fact, de Grouchy had assumed the leadership. He did not believe in useless and pointless sacrifice merely as a gesture of defiance. The entire *réseau*, or cell, was in abeyance until such time as he – de Grouchy – deemed it necessary to resuscitate them and bring them out into the open. Dead men achieved nothing. Widows and orphans were a drain upon the community, and a constant reminder of pointless failure. If the Allies came and pushed the Germans back – well and good. There would be point to it. Until then it was a waste of life, for the Resistants, and for the hostages who would surely be taken.

'Then I will go myself.' Lamboit's tone left no doubt that he meant it, whatever de Grouchy might say. The latter looked at the retreating back of the bookseller and breathed in deeply.

'Meet me at the old barn in half-an-hour. You can't go alone. There's a minefield.'

The two men wriggled and slid forward for what seemed to Lamboit to be little short of a mile. It seemed to be excessive caution, but de Grouchy was nobody's fool. Lamboit accepted the torn trouser knee and the surface pain in his elbows. A tap on his arm stopped movement as his guide peered silently above the grass and the bracken. Long fingers of sunlight probed through the overhead foliage of the beech and fir trees. Under the conifers the brown matting of dead leaves and needles gave no cover even though it silenced the footfall better than anything else. The gorse bushes were thin and sparse. Only the bracken itself was suitable and tall enough to hide a man from watchful eyes. But there was no one . . .

Lamboit started to edge forward to the next hiding place, but a large hard hand descended quickly and grabbed his jacket. He turned angrily to confront de Grouchy's black eyes glaring at him, and then the shaggy head turned to indicate ahead. Lamboit looked once more to see the small sign-plate sticking in the ground – black with white lettering and a white skull-and-crossbones: '*Minen*'.

'Can't you read?'

Lamboit shook his head. 'Half the German minefields are just a bluff. We all know that!'

'There might be some point in laying false warnings if anyone is going to see it. Out here it would be just obtuse. And however unpleasant they may be they don't bury pin-cushions.'

Lamboit followed his eyeline to where he could see four small wire tines sticking out of the ground. As his eyes focused on the proper distance he became aware of an area peppered with them like seed potatoes pushing up metallic shoots through the moss, which he now recognised as being carefully re-laid. Again the tight grip on his arm. De Grouchy was staring to his right, and the blood had drained from his face. Lamboit caught the sight of something brown moving before he felt himself hauled to his feet and propelled back the way they had come. The explosion sent them both flying. The rabbit probably felt nothing, but the shower of earth and stones reached out for sixty feet from the epicentre.

'Run for it!'

De Grouchy didn't bother to keep his voice down. What was the point? Both men ran through the undergrowth as if the hounds of hell were after them. Within seconds they could hear the barking of guttural commands, the thudding of feet, and the sounds of weapons.

Lamboit saw only the grass tops blurring past beneath him as he ran. Branches stuck out before him, some caught and scratched his cheeks and forehead, and the pounding in his chest became loud in his ears. Pounding not from exertion, not yet, but from sheer unalloyed fear. Then shouts, and the sound of boots, an awareness of another man at his left side also running like mad, his teeth bared in a snarl as he ran. Suddenly there were shots and something whistled past his head, then a blow like that of a pick-handle thudded into his left thigh from behind and he collapsed in a heap. He felt hands grab him, and he was lifted and carried through the undergrowth before being hoisted up onto de Grouchy's broad shoulders to hang and watch the grass move past below his eyes, before it all became a blur, and he passed out.

One moment of consciousness showed blue sky above him, and the ends of gorse branches, and something dark and breathing heavily against his chest. He glanced down and saw rough hands place a smooth round stone in the groin of his trouser leg, and hands tying a handkerchief round the stone and leg, and someone twisting a stick . . . then nothing.

6 April, London, SW1

The brick office block had originally been built as superior apartments for metropolitan dwellers who fancied something in the new modern style. Modern in 1911, that is. It still had its architraves and cornices, and a smattering of Art Nouveau in the ornamental glass over the entrances and the elaborate grilles to the now shaky lifts. The railings had long since been melted down to help the war effort, but external pride was maintained in the superbly polished brass knockers and bell pushes.

Number eighteen, Chatto Place, W1, had been commandeered to house military personnel in 1939. The military had gone in 1940, and a sort of civilian/military limbo infiltrated the block, without identification, symbols and little coloured squares and pennants, sans everything, in fact, but one, armed sentry at the only unlocked door. Sandbags gave him protection from whatever the Hun chose to hurl at London, but were more effective against the cold wind that seemed to blow down Chatto Place whatever the weather. The neighbours knew nothing of the occupants of number eighteen Chatto House. They sensed it was something frightfully hush-hush, and were patriotic enough to keep it to themselves.

On the sixth floor the secretary of the Female Auxiliary Nursing Yeomanry – or FANY as it was more popularly known – opened the door into the inner office, after knocking, and spoke to the tall, greying man who looked up as she entered.

'M'sieur Gran would like to see you, sir. I think it's urgent.'

Colonel Gwillim was not in the mood for casual visitors. He was using his stereoscopic binocular-frame to examine recent photo-recce prints of the coastal areas of Northern France, and he was not amused. He didn't like the look of the curious ramp-like constructions, and he didn't think all that much of the bombing results. Bomber Command had never, in his view, justified the expense nor the cost in lives and material, that was appropriated for its use. Harris could say what he liked. Precision bombing as such hardly existed.

'All right,' he sighed audibly. 'Send him in.'

He handed his stack of prints to his aide, Whicker, who in turn slid them into a drawer as the stooping Frenchman entered. Gwillim softened as he saw the man. He had no cause to be irritated with Jacques Gran. Of all the Free French who worked under de Gaulle Gran was the most helpful, least obstructive, and genuinely 'Allied'.

'Come in, Jacques. Take a pew. Alex . . .?'

The last comment was for Whicker to make suitable motions with the one bottle of alcohol they managed to keep alive in the office to soften relations between departments.

'I have received this report from one of our people in the Chantilly area. This may be the missing piece we have been waiting for.'

Gwillim took the offered signal and read swiftly, then read it again before looking up at the Frenchman who was taking his glass from Whicker's hand.

'This man, Lamboit, is he reliable?'

Gran nodded, and kept his eyes on Gwillim, who now examined the second typed sheet under the signal. After a moment he straightened and sniffed.

'It all ties up. Those ramps in the Pas de Calais and on the Belgian coastline, the Peenemünde business. But why there? Chantilly is a long way from the Pas de Calais.'

'It is also a long way from Commando raids, from off-coast shelling. And the Pas de Calais is largely chalk and soft earth.'

The Frenchman eyed Gwillim as he said the last. Gwillim interpreted the inflection correctly.

'You mean you think it's a dump. Reasonable enough, I suppose. Logic would imply components made in several areas, assembled and stock-piled somewhere that is not the launching-site. I agree the coast is too vulnerable.

'We also have repeated reports from the Resistance of convoys of heavy lorries coming in through the Vosges, heavily guarded. It all fits together, as you say.'

Gwillim turned to Whicker. 'When's my next Joint Intelligence Committee meeting?'

'Tomorrow morning, sir.'

'Right. Leave it with me, Jacques. I'll take it up and ask for immediate priority action.'

'Please, Colonel. Stress the time factor, I think we may not have much time.'

Gwillim did not have to twist any arms at the JIC. He had used his prerogative to call upon the Prime Minister when his duties merited such a privilege. The PM had listened and agreed without hesitation to his request, which gave his subsequent talk with the RAF liaison-officer real muscle.

'We're asking for a strike, Fielding. A high-level, precision job, if there is such a thing. I have JIC approval. You'll have the paperwork in due course.'

'Very well, sir. I'll make a request for the raid, and be back to you. You do realise that HQ Bomber Command have an established list of priorities?'

'Of course, but there is some urgency on this one. Alert your masters at High Wycombe, and tell them there will be a memo from Winston in the pipeline.'

The door opened after a quick knock, and Jacques Gran entered before he realised that Gwillim had a visitor.

'I'm so sorry, I did not realise – '

'Come in, Jacques. You know Squadron-Leader Fielding, I think. All right, Fielding, draft a signal to Bomber Command for the appropriate type of attack on this target. I would like to go through the draft with you, shall we say in ten minutes' time?'

After Fielding had closed the door Gran turned to Gwillim with a sad admonishing look.

'You intend to send in bombers?'

'We try that one first. If the raid is a good one it may do the trick, at least for the moment.' He noted Gran's expression and softened his tone before continuing. 'The villages and towns are some distance from the target area, there is no real danger to French civilians.'

'That is what they always say, and always there are French lives lost. Even so, there are those who work in the complex.'

'If they work for Jerry they have scant sympathy from me.'

Gran smiled wanly and inclined his head to one side.

'It is so easy to say when you are not occupied. They do not always work willingly, Colonel.'

Gwillim realised he had been clumsy and nodded. 'I want to fly out your chap, Lamboit. We need to talk to him. Agreed?'

Gran was also grateful for a change of subject.

'Of course, but there is a problem. Lamboit was wounded in the leg. It has not been possible to have him treated openly. The Germans regard bullet wounds as confirmation of treachery . . . which it is, of course. He needs hospital treatment.'

'All the more reason to fly him out, then.'

6 April, near Chantilly

There was a perfectly good moon, and over the target area there were cirrus clouds at twenty-thousand feet, and not much else. The Luftwaffe's night-fighters did not even appear. Flak over the coastal areas was significant but not devastating. The target was correctly marked, and the saturation area cp +250. In other words – a good strike. At eight kilometres' distance, in de Grouchy's farmhouse, it sounded and looked horrific. Saturation bombing is no picnic for anyone – giver or receiver. There comes a point when fear gives place to awe, and the sense of

Armageddon creeps into even the most stalwart mind. Such were the feelings of de Grouchy and his wife who stood in the shadow of their farmhouse overhang, and listened and watched the orange, white, and blue flashes that lit up the night from Paris to Picardy.

By 1.30 Pierre de Grouchy was mentally lighting candles for all the wretched Germans under that shower of death. In his spare room the sweating body of Paul Lamboit wakened from his fever and stared at the mysterious light that penetrated the old, sprung blinds, and flashed time-and-again inside his head as he dropped back into fevered sleep.

By 02.00 hours the All-Clear had sounded, and the citizenry crossed themselves for having been spared another Allied bombing raid, and wondered who had suffered under such terrible destruction.

By 03.00 the Germans had six hundred men and Todt* workers clearing the surrounding area. The wide-eyed conscripts stared in disbelief at the seemingly undamaged complex, the great iron doors now open, flagrantly showing lights and showing a hive of industry as it righted itself and flicked off the irritating mess caused by the monsters from the sky. For that is all it was – an irritation. The vital parts of the complex remained untouched.

7 April, London

That was also the opinion of the RAF photo-reconnaissance girls who studied the following day's prints through their equipment, and passed on their concern to the powers above.

'You have the report from Interpretation, sir. There is no doubt about the precision of the bombing, but Nuneham are quite unable to give an evaluation of the result. The steel doors seem intact to us, sir, and the photos imply business as usual.'

Gwillim looked at Fielding in silence, and nodded his thanks as the RAF man made to go. After the door shut Gwillim turned to Whicker, his aide.

* The Todt organisation was an international labour force made up of willing (paid) collaborators together with slave labour from the German occupied countries, many thousands of whom were literally worked to death.

'I don't think we're going to bomb them out, and this one is not for the Resistance. It's a special job, Willy, and a damn tricky one. You'd better get me Gallagher – a.s.a.p.'

The taxi drew up at number eighteen with Hugh Gallagher already half-way out of the door. He didn't waste time. He knew the office block, he knew the fare, he knew the face of the guard on the door, and mentally counted the stairs as he went up them two at a time. He also knew the freckled face of the FANY who looked up as he entered without knocking.

'Hello, Spooner!'

The girl smiled. 'Major Gallagher.'

He was admitted immediately, and Gwillim wasted no time on formalities. They had worked together several times before and preliminaries were unnecessary.

'I'm sending you into France again. This time it's between Chantilly and Senlis. You know the place?'

Gallagher nodded. He knew the area well.

'I want you to look at this place Jerry is building and its contents. Make your own assessment with a view to taking in a team of experts and getting rid of it. We've tried bombing, and it doesn't work. My information is that it has been used as a stone quarry. Apparently there is a seam of workable stone sandwiched between limestone. I gather the stone was used to repair Amiens cathedral in 1905. We must assume that Jerry has enlarged the original and developed underground storage areas for stockpiling whatever it is he is stockpiling. We need to know *what* that is and the best way of destroying it all – quickly. How well d'you know the place?'

Gallagher looked at the top recce photo as he talked. 'I was seconded to General Vacheron in 1940 as liaison officer. Then Special Duties sent me back there eighteen months ago.'

Gwillim narrowed his eyes and looked at him. 'Anyone likely to recognise you?'

Gallagher reassured him with a shake of the head.

'Good. You'll be leaving RAF Chilham tonight. There's a brief appraisal for you to swallow. Whicker can fill you in on the way to Kent. Take the PR prints with you if they'll help. They only tell me what we *haven't* done.'

The Lysander dropped quickly through the cloud and saw the flarepath rapidly spread out beneath them as the Resistants ran to their positions. Gallagher got himself together ready to jump out quickly and vacate the space for whoever was taking his place for the trip back to the UK. The field was tufted with couch grass, and the Lizzie bounded and bounced, even though the ground was not hard and dry. As it drew to a halt and swung round to face into the wind for take-off, Gallagher saw the running figures of his reception-committee approaching the plane, and lifted the flap to get out. Once on the ground he climbed out of his flying-gear and handed it, warm, to the faceless man who reached silently for it. They did not know each other, and did not want to. Anonymity was everything.

By the time the Lysander took off again, Gallagher was walking silently behind the burly man who seemed to be in charge of the Resistant reception. When they were far enough from the pick-up zone to be reasonably safe the burly man turned to face him.

'Pierre de Grouchy.' They shook hands and Gallagher disclosed his own code identity.

'I'm here for two reasons. I want to see this underground complex the Germans are using, and I want to see Paul Lamboit. They also tell me he's got a smashed-up leg.'

'You know I do not activate my *réseau*?'

Gallagher looked coldly at him and nodded. 'London did mention something to that effect. Does that mean I get no help from you?'

'From me . . . perhaps. From the *réseau* – nothing.'

Gallagher had the chance to mull over the last remark as they made their way to de Grouchy's farm and entered via the rear door. Inside the place was deserted, but held the slightly cheesy smell that permeates so many French farms. De Grouchy lit an oil-lamp, and placed it on a large farm table. The warm light spilled across the room casting dark moving shadows before it.

'Don't you have electricity any more?' Gallagher had seen the switches and the surface double-cables. Besides any farm in this area would have mains services unless the farmer was very peculiar, and de Grouchy was not known as such.

'The Boche turn it off sometimes when they need a lot elsewhere. They've been doing it for weeks now. D'you want some food?'

'Bread will be fine.' Gallagher had no wish to deprive anyone of rations, nor refuse hospitality and give insult.

De Grouchy said nothing but took a huge round loaf from the side-board and jammed it upright in the end table-drawer, then took his clasp-knife and started cutting slices off the great bread wheel. Farm butter was on the table, butter that was almost pure white because of the wartime feed. Gallagher spread a little on a large slice, and then spoke quietly.

'What about Lamboit?'

'I am Lamboit.' The voice from the chimney corner was gruff but weak. Gallagher spun round to see the man in the shadows sitting in the open cupboard propped against patchwork cushions and covered with a tattered blanket. He was pale, and obviously a sick man.

'What are you doing here? I sent a message to de Gaulle, not the British. Why did they not send a Frenchman?'

Gallagher took a bite of the dark bread, and chewed for a moment before replying. 'Because they sent *me*. If you want to continue the Hundred Years War that's fine by me. Just let's finish this one first, can we?'

Lamboit muttered into the pillow before continuing. 'All the British do is send the RAF to bomb the caves. Might as well piss on a forest fire!'

'I'm not arguing. That's why I'm here. But it had to be tried. I want to look at the place and work out how it's to be done. Then I'm taking you back to London.'

'Huh!' Lamboit's expletive was comprehensible only to a local, but Gallagher did not miss the drift, and smiled to himself.

'Very likely. I want to go and look as soon as it is light. In the meantime while I'm eating this very good bread can you tell me slowly and accurately everything that you saw, and exactly what happened to you.'

8 April, Chantilly

De Grouchy rapidly decided that Gallagher knew what he was about, and that he was unlikely to endanger himself or a companion by untoward and inexperienced conduct. They reached the opening in the wooded area after an hour's walk, circuitously, from the de Grouchy farm. Once they stopped and crouched down as the clatter of a Kettenkrad was heard edging its way through the woodland terrain carrying surveyor and military escort. De Grouchy gave warning that from then on they would have to take care, and be alive to possible concealed guards, for they were approaching the main entrance to the German complex.

Gallagher noted the tarmac road threading through the close trees towards the bunkered entrance. Slowly they wriggled forward, using every bit of possible concealment, taking time, taking care, and constantly alert for mines and trip-wires. Eventually the ground fell away before them, and de Grouchy indicated a tangle of fallen trees and shrubs from where they might look down upon the approach to the emplacement.

It lay before them, fed by the single tarmac road and a secondary track leading off to the right. The approach was guarded by bar and sentry post, to one side of which was a block-house obviously housing infantrymen whose task was merely to sit and wait, and deal with any intruder or attacker who might materialise. Inside of the post was the perimeter wire. There was a tall, sturdy fence of timber and metal angle-iron, and heavy-duty wire mesh infilling threaded with barbed-wire to a height of six or seven feet. The whole fence being surmounted by a two-feet electrified ridge fence the wiring of which Gallagher traced to the ground level cable that presumably entered the main underground complex by the concrete and stone entrance. Four huge loading-bays jutted out into the vehicle yard, itself protected by a high brick and concrete wall. The whole structure was cleverly camouflaged to appear as simply the stone quarry from which it originated. Trucks, half-tracks, and covered lorries stood waiting their turn to unload as Todt workers and forced-labourers of various nationalities humped their loads and laboured incessantly to keep the waiting trucks moving. Despite the four bays there was evidently an internal bottle-neck which Gallagher surmised as due to old mechanisms, probably winch-and-trolleys, that conveyed the components down into the protective bowels of the earthworks.

A quick estimate implied that there was a work force of two-hundred odd on the surface. God knows how many underground. The perimeter guard probably constituted something in the region of one-eighth of the garrison, say a complement of four-hundred men overall. A sizeable force, not to be stormed lightly.

Gallagher looked his fill, and then indicated he wanted to follow the complex right round its perimeter, examining and checking every foot of the way. He was a good soldier and he was thorough. He not only catalogued the facts of the situation but he thought of its potential, and used his imagination to contrive deployment in every possible circumstance. It was necessary that he knew just what the Germans could do with whatever they had at their disposal. He knew his job was eventually to get into the place and somehow destroy it. It was not going to be easy, even if it were possible.

There was evidence everywhere of the RAF bombing. Craters, mounds of earth, tangled blasted trees, but no sign of any underground damage or piercing of the rock fault. Binoculars focused detail beyond the perimeter wire, little more than scrub, one disused bunker stuck up through the earth, and a track some ten feet wide worn by men's boots (and possible dog paws) just *inside* that electrified wire fence. Gallagher walked widely round the area, then indicated to de Grouchy that he wanted to move in and see the perimeter fence in detail. The latter warned him of the minefields, marked here and there for the benefit of German military and Todt personnel, and as a warning, real or imaginary, to anyone else. Whatever the truth of the displacement of mined areas it had to be assumed for all practical purposes that the minefield stretched every inch of the way round the perimeter. To calculate upon any other possibility was suicidal.

One third of the way round the perimeter, perhaps quarter of a mile from the single entrance to the complex, the ground rose slightly, then descended into a dell, well-wooded and giving excellent cover. For a moment this worried Gallagher. As they crawled he considered why the Germans had gone against their manual. It was not like them. Ordinarily they would have levelled that area and removed all undergrowth and trees, to give themselves unobstructed views and fields of fire. They liked it that way. It worked for them, and they were good at their job. Why had they left the woodland and scrub? The reason had to be that they did not wish to draw *any* attention to the complex or the activity therein. They had to be prepared to sacrifice ground-defence positions in order to remain as undetected as possible or – if detected – as unremarkable as possible.

Gallagher turned to de Grouchy. 'There isn't any point in wasting your time. I shall go over the whole place, right round, and see what I can. If there's only one of us to step on a mine it bothers me less, okay?'

De Grouchy nodded without emotion. He was a practical man, and saw the sense of the proposal. He had shown Gallagher where the place was. There was little else he could usefully accomplish, and he turned back to let him get on with it.

It was dark when Gallagher returned to the farmhouse. Lamboit was sitting by the wooden table paring a farmhouse cheese with his knife, from time to time sipping the acorn coffee that de Grouchy's wife had put before them in the enamelled tin pot, on her way up to the bedroom. Neither man spoke but silently champed at the bread and cheese, and dipped into the mustard-pot the leaves of sorrel that gave zest to their simple fare. Gallagher's knock broke the stillness, and de Grouchy let him in without comment. He joined them at table, looking pensive, his frown showing his sense of frustration.

'There has to be some way! I need to know what that place looks like inside.'

'There is no way you can get in. Why don't you accept this? It is not possible.'

The men ate in silence for a moment before the quiet voice of Lamboit spoke over the cheese he was cutting into fingers. It was a voice of curious quality, with a slight local accent yet educated, slight gruffness, yet not without quiet dignity.

'There is a way . . .' He looked at de Grouchy. 'Viardot.'

Gallagher looked from one to the other. 'Who, or what is Viardot?'

Lamboit took his time in replying. 'Louis Viardot is a constructional engineer of genius. The Germans asked him to work for them, the Todt Organisation, to extend their assembly plant underground. He made it work for them, or so I am told. He is, I regret to say, a Frenchman who thinks the arrival of the Germans was the best thing to happen to France. One of *them*.'

Gallagher considered the thought for a moment. 'Does he live round here? I mean, outside of the complex?'

De Grouchy grunted. 'He's unmarried. Lives in the old Perrault house outside the village. We passed it on the way to the quarries.'

'Curfew?'

De Grouchy glanced at the mantel-shelf clock, an old Second Empire design probably handed down from his grandparents.

'Until four-thirty. The Germans lift it early in the summer months. They need the farmers to work and feed them. We could go now if you like, there aren't many about, and the police are keeping out of the way.' He grinned cynically. 'When the Allies come they don't want to be seen or remembered as helping the Boches.'

'Was it the house with the yellow wash and the shutters?'

De Grouchy nodded. Gallagher stood up. 'Let's see if he's home. You get onto London. Tell them there will be two passengers for the pick-up, not one. I'll see Monsieur Viardot myself, I think.'

When Gallagher returned he was carrying an unconscious man over his shoulder. The man looked the worse for a scuffle, and the bruises on his face were beginning to look angry and throbbing. The sticking-plaster over his mouth effectively stopped any noise. Not that there would have been much anyway. Viardot was quite cold.

'What about the pick-up?'

'London has agreed 23.00 hours tomorrow evening. Two passengers. What will *you* do?'

'I'll make my own way. There's somwhere I want to call en route. Can you cope with the pick-up?'

De Grouchy nodded and cocked an eye at the sleeping Lamboit.

'He doesn't want to go, you know.'

'He doesn't have any alternative. We need him in London,

and unless he has proper medical attention his condition will deteriorate. He could even lose the leg. He's not a stupid man, make him see it. If he won't see it, encourage him.'

Gallagher handed de Grouchy his small Walther automatic. The latter pocketed it quickly lest the somnolent Lamboit should see it.

'Where will you be going, my friend?'

'Into Picardy. How're the trains behaving these days?'

9 April

Dawn was tinging the grey clouds with little touches of warmth as the train slid into the station at Saint-Amand-de-Chauny. No one else got down. No one was there to accept his perfectly valid ticket. Gallagher stepped out into the once familiar courtyard behind the station wall. It was deserted. No sign of the occupying presence and little to indicate that a war was in progress. Apart from the now distant chuffing of the little train as it made its way northward to the two remaining halts of the branch line the morning was silent. It must have been just after five that he boarded the local 'chuffer' at Amiens, and he had been looking nervously out of the window at the dark landscape for upwards of an hour. His own watch said 6.14 but was at variance with the village church clock that claimed the hour as 6.32, though the minute hand could be seen to lift and drop now and again as if contact was no foregone conclusion.

Hugh Gallagher glanced about him at the landmarks he knew and loved with a quiet, gentle acceptance of place that he found difficulty in bestowing upon his native Scotland. The Highlands did excite him and made his blood course just that little bit more swiftly whenever he left the grey of Inverness and headed across country towards his birthplace, but that was something to do with grandeur, with 'bite', with history and lore. Here it was a warmth of familiarity of days spent happily and a memory of shared moments. The history was of his own making, and contained within the last five years; the sharing was always with someone who had taken his naïve, boyish emotions by the short hairs and dragged him into a world he had not even acknowledged in his dreams.

The lane wound round the beech thicket before the top of the house could be seen above the four, tall, elm trees and the containing stone wall that surrounded the estate and terminated in a broken-down, sixteenth-century dovecote. The ten-acre field that fronted the road swept in one great, brown-green sward right up to the wall itself, to the piles of crumbling stone, and the rubble of yesteryear: rubble that fell to the earth in 1916 when the Germans were also in occupation.

The Castillon family had occupied and farmed the surrounding lands since the time of Henry the Fourth. The Manor House had been rebuilt unpretentiously in 1706, and restored in the middle of the nineteenth century. It was a lovely house, and its air of genteel delapidation was half of its charm, as was true with so much of French Provincial architecture.

At the front of the house stretched the long grass-covered terrace fronted by an ornamental balustrade, the approach to it was via a gravelled drive which led through stone gateposts onto a lane. Gallagher knew his pulse was racing, and there was a suggestion of trembling at his fingertips, but he had enough soldierly sense to make the detour up the side of the wall, and enter the grounds by the faded green doorway in the wall, next to the dovecote. He did not know if he would be welcomed with unalloyed pleasure. He did not know if the château had become billeting ground for Occupation troops, or if the premises had been totally requisitioned, though there was no suggestion of military insignia or signposting anywhere about the place.

He entered with caution, his blood pounding inside his head and his palms suddenly moist. The cold-frames against the wall spilled their cucumber and melon growths anywhere they cared to trail. The papery yellow flowers had withered but still hung by the tendrils creeping along the muddy path towards the raspberry canes. An empty puffer-can of ant-killer testified to a general lack of concern, it had doubtless lain undisturbed since the Germans swept in through Sedan and across the Belgian lines.

The sound of a throaty voice lisping and humming a popular tune stopped him in his tracks. It was Claudine's voice, unmistakably. She was always an early riser, as was her mother.

She looked as lovely as ever. The dress was simple, practical, and her skin was tanned just as her hair had bleached slightly from the auburn that was her natural colour. Every summer it became lighter on top as if the reddish hue faded with the ultra-violet light of the long summer days. The wide mouth pouted slightly as she looked at the radish bunches she had just lifted.

'Claudine.'

She stiffened visibly. The hairs on the nape of her neck stood rigid for a second before she swung to face him where he stood, tense and anxious.

She looked almost as if she had heard a voice from the dead, and a cold touch from the grave.

'Hugh?'

Both stared at each other for an eternity before something freed them simultaneously, and they rushed into each other's arms with an embrace that clutched at the very heart of life, hungry from the deprivation of years. It was the meeting of two people whose past intimacy was evident from the raw nature of the touching, the holding, the kissing. Then she pushed him away from her and looked into his face.

'What has happened? Why are you here?'

She looked behind him as if to see who had brought him to her. He said nothing, merely took her entwined fingers through his own and silently led her towards the house. She knew he was leading her to her bed, and he smiled to himself at the familiar sense of her drawing back from the encounter. Nothing had changed. But her fingers gripped his own tightly, and they walked hand-in-hand towards the side of the long terrace.

As they reached the overgrown stonework Claudine's mother came from the double-doors that led into the study, and turned to regard them. Her face brightened slightly at the sight of Hugh, but she said nothing, only lifted her face to one side in a slight smile as he kissed her cheek in passing. When they had disappeared inside the house the older woman touched the recently kissed cheek with her pale fingers, then ambled slowly across to the basket chair and the folded newspaper. She stared across the grass that had once been a lawn, and counted the moisture-laden spiders' webs that festooned the glass-topped basket-table by her side.

The relationship between Claudine and Hugh Gallagher was that of two young people very much in love for the first time. In the spring of 1940 they had become lovers in the physical sense. To each of them it was a marvellous, exciting experience, a revelation to them both of their own latent sexuality. They had wallowed and revelled in each other with the new-found abandon of children suddenly let loose into a fantastic sweet shop. Not to put too fine a point upon it, they made love like the proverbial rabbit, and could never have enough of the experience. Satiety was a word they did not understand. Exhaustion was the sole limiting factor until that terrible day when Gallagher was recalled to active duty. The Germans had broken through and were making headlong pace for the French border. Everyone with any sense knew the Maginot line was a chimera, it would stop nothing. Hugh had torn himself from the hysterically weeping Claudine, his own heart trembling at the thought of separation and deprivation.

There was also the uncomfortable thought that a newly-awakened Claudine might turn to others for satisfaction during his absence. Similar thoughts crossed her mind, and their parting was as easy and gentle as tearing apart two entwined hawthorn bushes.

Later, when he was assigned to Special Duties, he had been sent back to France, to work as a special agent/saboteur. He had asked for, and obtained, permission to attend to a personal matter after the job was completed and he was awaiting a new assignment. He had visited Claudine. Nothing had changed. She had been lonely, that was all. They made love as hitherto, and enjoyed each other's company for thirty-six wonderful hours. Then he had gone. She asked nothing, surmised everything. Now he was back, and it was just the same. Before everything was the insatiable hunger for each other, and they spent their first hours together in her bed.

It was after they had talked a little, after they had repeatedly made love, that she started to wheedle and needle. She wanted him to stay, forget the war. Remain with her and be her husband, and let the world go by. They would manage.

'I can't just go on waiting and waiting. You could take over the farm. You could pass as a Frenchman so easily. We could make love every day . . . it would be just as it was. Say yes.'

'You know I can't do that.'

'Please! I am so frightened here.'

'Frightened? Why?'

'I am frightened of becoming like my mother. I don't want to be alone. I'll soon be thirty . . . wasting. The war will go on for years and years and years. I will be a dried-up old woman . . . look at mother! She stayed at home and obeyed her father until she was nearly forty.'

'That choice was hers. No one chained her to him.'

'It was her obligation! Then she married my father, and had one-and-a-half years of life and love with him before he was killed at Verdun. She used to go to his grave every week when I was a child. She was still *married* to him . . . to a block of stone! I won't, Hugh. I have seen what happened to her. Darling, please stay with me. Don't go back! Please!'

Gallagher bit his lip. He wanted to stay, just as at the same time he knew he could not. He wanted her as she wanted him, but this could not be the way.

'Come back to England with me. I can fix it . . .'

'I can't leave *her*. That is *my* obligation.'

'Then there is no answer, is there? We're both in a trap.'

Lamboit was helped into the Lysander as it ticked over in the open field. The Resistants had melted into the night after making the flarepath with their torches, only de Grouchy and Marin remained and took their places at the end of the field facing the take-off to mark the end of the imagined runway, and give the pilot some guide as to when to become airborne. As the plane taxied forward and the engine revved into full power Lamboit glanced at the securely-bound dark-haired man at his side. Viardot's eyes were frantic and scared, as well as angry. He peered over the edge of the fuselage through the perspex panel at the darkness outside, as if willing the aircraft to stop and disgorge him. But they were airborne, and the bouncing gave way to gentle soaring. The Lizzie flew well. It was a comfortable, easily-controlled aircraft that responded to a pilot's touch. Viardot suddenly collapsed inside, and sank back into the corner of the tiny cramped space. So be it.

10 April

Claudine woke to the sound of the hall clock chiming five-thirty. She turned to face Gallagher, but the bed was empty. The covers carefully replaced so that she would not feel the change of temperature. She sat up and stared at the window. The french doors were ajar, and the curtains fluttered slightly in the morning breeze. Outside it was a cold, bright, summer morning. The chill was fast dispersing as the sun rose over the fields to the east. She got out of bed without bothering to cover her nakedness and crossed to the window, opening the door and moving out onto the small balcony.

There was nothing to be seen. No one moving. No one to watch or touch her nakedness as she turned back into the bedroom and sank tearfully onto the bed. Rooks cawed in the field beyond the house. Otherwise . . . nothing. He had gone.

Gallagher heard the rooks as they walked their patch of turf before flapping upwards into the lofty trees of the copse behind the house. He did not look back. What was the point?

13 April

Gallagher reported back to Gwillim's office at 15.00 hours to find his Colonel none too happy about the state of play. Lamboit was taciturn, and gave out information with the same ease as he might give his teeth to a dentist. Viardot refused to help at all. The threat of a POW camp, as opposed to reasonable and comfortable internment, moved him not. He was due to be interrogated yet again when Gwillim complained to Gallagher.

'Then we might have to make him talk, sir.'

Gwillim looked up at Gallagher through suddenly wary eyes.

'I won't have any funny business, Gallagher. Not while I am in command here.'

'I wasn't suggesting *we* should pull him to pieces, sir.'

Gwillim's enquiring look had to be postponed as Viardot was shown into the office by the MP escort who withdrew as soon as Gwillim accepted delivery. The latter swung round on the dark, lean Frenchman, and looked at him with concern.

'M'sieur Viardot, we are asking you again for information

about the underground installation in which you work. Surely as a loyal Frenchman you will assist the Allies and try and thwart the common enemy?'

Viardot lifted his black eyes to look squarely at Gwillim.

'It rather depends upon your viewpoint, doesn't it? Why should I regard the Germans as my enemy? There are many who believe they are the only ones who can save France from Communism. Anyone can see how corrupt and worthless the old regime had been. I will tell you nothing.'

There was a long pause before Gallagher stood up suddenly and spoke with his incisive, slightly nasal, voice of command.

'Then there is nothing to be gained by keeping you here. I will take you back, and drop you by British parachute, from a British plane, right into the compound you are trying to protect. How are you going to explain to your German friends where you have been? I doubt if they will believe you have told us nothing. We can quite easily make sure that they think you have . . . unless, of course, you trust your German friends the way you say you do. We will detain you no longer, M'sieur Viardot. I will take you back to the airfield.'

Gwillim looked questioningly at Gallagher then nodded.

'Guard!'

The MPs took out the wretched man whose own expression was no longer quite so sanguine. The black eyes just momentarily held a haunted, frightened look, before he dispelled the thought as bravado not to be taken seriously, and curled his lip.

Once the door was shut Gwillim swung round on Gallagher.

'What in hell are you proposing?'

Gallagher faced him, blandly innocent. 'Exactly what I said, Colonel. Unless my guess is wrong once he realises we mean it he will co-operate.'

Gwillim stared him out coldly. 'On your head be it. Now, before you go, let us be clear about our moves. JIC have approved, it's up to *us*. We have a minimum amount of time to get a team together capable of blowing the place to kingdom come. You will lead them. I'm putting the training in charge of Colonel Squires, but you pick the team yourself. How long d'you need?'

'Four days. I shall want about a dozen with varying skills,

some will fall by the wayside, but a team of five or six will ultimately do the job.'

Gwillim nodded as Gallagher saluted and left the office. He knew Hugh Gallagher would do the job. He knew he could rely upon him to get a team together, fresh, and geared for the job-in-hand. But could they do it in the time?

The Dakota crossed the French coast at 22.18. A clear night with good visibility. The odd searchlight probed, then decided against it. Who cared about a single aircraft anymore? The invasion would come soon, but it would not be supported by one sole Dakota. There was no need to scramble the already depleted resources, or waste ammunition. Viardot sat with his back against the metal skin, a parachute strapped to him, facing Gallagher, who looked neat and formal in his uniform. Both men were feeling the cold of the altitude. The flight-engineer staggered towards them and informed Gallagher in a hearty shout that they had crossed the French coast and ETA would be about eleven minutes.

Viardot's eyes had sunk into his head and gleamed with a deep realisation that it was just possible this mad Englishman was going to do as he said and drop him into the German lap.

Wild thoughts flashed through his mind as Gallagher maintained the calm, unflinching gaze of a man doing his unbending duty. Viardot moistened his dry lips, and the tongue almost froze onto the damp skin.

'One-minute-ten-seconds to drop, sir,' the flight-engineer informed them cheerfully as he released the lock-handle of the fuselage door and held it open against the clip fastening. The sudden rush of ice cold air, and the change of sound, shocked Viardot into renewed awareness. Gallagher stood and turned to him.

'Right, Viardot . . . over here. You are just about home. Ready?'

Viardot moved gingerly to the door hatch and stared out into the blackness. His hair blew across his forehead, and he was forced to lean into the slip-stream spill.

'You wouldn't do it!'

Gallagher smiled at him, 'Try me.'

He turned to the signal light as the red came on.

'Stand by.'

Both men stared at the domed light-covers. The red went out and the green light shone.

'Jump!'

Gallagher moved forward as if to aid the Frenchman, but Viardot's nerve had gone. He held back and shook his head.

'No, I will tell you what you want to know.'

Gallagher said nothing, nodded to the flight-engineer who closed the hatch again.

Gwillim stood by his car and watched the Dakota land in the darkness. He often marvelled how accurate these pilots could be with the minimal light guidance available to them. They all said a Dak was easy, even child-proof. Perhaps it was . . . not to him, however. The aircraft taxied to a halt at the apron edge, and the hatch was thrown open from inside. Gwillim started to walk towards the aircraft.

He watched the cold and frightened Viardot being hustled by MPs into a waiting jeep and driven away, then turned back to the Dakota as Gallagher dropped from the hatch and crossed to him. They exchanged looks and Gallagher gave a brief nod.

Gwillim sighed in relief. 'Can we trust him?'

'I think he understands we mean business. We have to.'

They turned away from the aircraft and walked towards the car.

'Would you have dropped him?'

Gallagher looked at him questioningly. 'Oh yes. He was no use to us silent.'

Gwillim sucked his teeth. 'He could have alerted the Germans, whatever their reaction to his return. Had you thought of that?'

Gallagher stared into Gwillim's face coldly.

'I don't think he would have said anything——' He slapped Viardot's parachute case into Gwillim's hands. '——He didn't have a parachute.'

Gallagher walked across to the car as Gwillim peered with awed silence into the collection of rags that filled the parachute case.

14 April
Gallagher made for the Personnel Records Office just behind Whitehall. Gwillim went back to his office where he found Professor Evans of Cardiff University waiting for him, anxious as to the outcome of the ploy. Initially satisfied, his Celtic unease began to niggle.

'What makes you so sure Viardot knows?'

'The Free French have checked him out. His standing with the Todt Organisation was good.'

'I still don't know that we can trust everything he says. What is Gallagher doing now?'

Gwillim poured them both a very poor Scotch from a very fancy bottle, and offered it with an apologetic gesture. The Welshman accepted it without a murmur and sipped absently. Gwillim reflected that the Welsh had no palate for Scotch anyway.

'Gallagher is searching for his team. Leave it to him, Dafid. He's good at his job.'

'He will need to be, my friend, or we can all consider the implications of a German Occupation. I can't speak for London but they wouldn't like that in Wales. How soon could his team be got into France?'

Gwillim sighed at the man's naïvety. 'Come on, man, they will have to be trained. Normally it would be about twelve weeks.'

It was Evans's turn to splutter into his drink.

'Twelve *weeks*! London could be flattened in that time. Jerry hasn't got the giro right yet. We have a little time, but it won't take long. They're good at that sort of thing. Once they've got it, they'll fall like rain. We can't *stop* them!'

The Hollerith filing-system worked well enough in the absence of anything better. The same assessment applied to the elderly epidiascope that had been supplied to him with the ATS sergeant clerk, a bright, rather pretty girl who brought enthusiasm to the job, which made a change. By 02.00 hours Gallagher had made his first shortlist from which he would choose a dozen or so to interview where necessary. He knew that time was the problem. He knew that the standard training period was simply not on. They just did not have the time. But already trained, experienced field-operators could be compromised, and would, in turn, compromise the operation. That risk had to be obviated by selecting new personnel who would bring some particular ability, some special quality to the job. They had to speak good French, unless their speciality was such that he could risk the lack.

Gallagher smoked one cigarette after another as he studied the cards brought to him by the uniformed girl. The latter, Sergeant Sally Birkett, sensed there was both urgency and importance about this job, and had mentally reconciled herself to forty-eight hours of unrelieved activity in dark-rooms and filing-corridors, aided only by the cups of coffee, or char, she could scrounge from the duty office by the main entrance. She also rather liked the look of the Major who went about his selection with method, speed, and apparent efficiency that had nothing of officialdom about it. That, too, made a change.

She picked up the final batch of cards and attached manilla files. 'This is the last of them, sir. They are all volunteers for Special Duties and have so far not been selected.'

'All French speaking?'

'As to the manner born, sir. Aren't we all?'

Gallagher smiled at the perky, dark girl, and rattled off a question in French to which she replied unhesitantly in perfectly good, accentless French. Gallagher looked at her, 'As you say, aren't we all? What about some more coffee? I've got a couple of hours with that epidiascope ahead of me. Does it work, by the way?'

'Yes, sir. I checked it myself. If I get the coffee d'you think you could manage to switch it on by yourself?'

The twinkle in the eyes was good-natured, not forward, and Gallagher responded lightly, 'I'll struggle with it, sergeant.' After she had gone he set out the cards on top of the appropriate files, and studied the passport photos attached. There was more than a little to be told by a face. If all things balanced it would be the face that said 'Yeah' or 'Nay', because that was the way it was in life, and probably always would be. Instinctual reaction, the final arbiter. He put out the room light, and started to lay the first selected on the glass plate for enlarged observation.

Gwillim wasted no time. Once Viardot was given a meal and some hot tea to restore a sense of normality he was taken straight to Chatto Place and to Gwillim's office. He was tired and wore the capture badly, and was unwilling to show anything but sullen acquiescence.

'We need to know everything, M'sieur Viardot, not just vague statistics. Can we start with the layout of the interior of the underground complex?'

After an hour Gwillim and Evans had a fair idea of the place in general terms, and how it operated. It was time for detail.

'This seventeen acre site, it is divided into specific areas, as you say, connected by tunnels. Can you give us a rough map, please, just to talk through?'

Viardot sighed and glowered, but Gwillim looked at him blandly and waited.

'There are nine main storage areas, here and here. This one has the corridors containing the laboratories and drawing offices, and administrative engineering quarters. The separate components arrive here, and here, they are assembled in the last area, here.'

'And stockpiling?'

Viardot said nothing but indicated with his index finger on the crude sketch map he had drawn.

'And just what *is* that finished article, M'sieur?'

Viardot hesitated before replying, not perhaps because of reluctance. The betrayal once made is made. There is no gain in prolonging the agony. It was simply not Viardot's field. He was a structural engineer concerned with the fabric of the building, not its contents.

'They refer to it as the FZG-76 . . . I know almost nothing about it.'

Gwillim looked at Evans who returned the look, with just a touch of relief in the eyes.

'That's the mid-wing monoplane we know about, isn't it?'

Evans sighed. 'It's a rocket-missile actually, in simple terms driven by a pulsating duct-flow motor, and carrying an explosive war-head. It carries about 150 gallons of fuel, and the test-firing we know about clocked up 350 kilometres-per-hour. If you consider it has a range therefore of about a hundred miles give or take a few, and you cannot electronically jam or interfere with the mechanism once it is pre-set . . . it is quite formidable.'

Evans was speaking in his dour, non-conformist, closed-on-Sundays manner, but Gwillim knew the seriousness of what he said. New fighters – and Germany was preparing and testing jet-propelled models at this moment – could be coped with. The Allies were geared to coping with it. At worst it could be a serious hiccup, but the rocket threat was real. Ever since they had learned of the Nazi V-weapons as more than wild imaginings of a demented Führer, Churchill and his advisers had taken the rumours, then the intelligence very seriously indeed. A rocket-carried war-head of great destructive power could change the outcome of the war very rapidly. There was no stopping it. The interim flying-bomb 'aircraft' could be dangerous, and have incalculable effect at a time when a Second Front was about to be launched, and a war-weary populace had grown used to *not* being on the receiving end any longer. The morale issue had to be considered as well as the loss of material and life. There was now and again a rumour of an intercontinental missile, but it was only rumour.

'Who supplies the various components, m'sieur? And where are the factories?' Viardot stared him out and curled his lip.

'They are not stupid enough to tell me that. Why should they? It had nothing to do with me or my work.'

Gwillim knew this to be likely, but thought it best to add his full twopennyworth. 'You are here now, M'sieur Viardot and at the receiving end of those missiles. I'm sure you will realise it would be sensible to tell us anything you might remember, should you think of it.'

15 April

Gallagher straightened his back as he switched off the epidiascope, and Sergeant Birkett switched on the room-light revealing the smoke-filled atmosphere and the cards on the table. One small pile plus one large pile of rejects.

'What's the time?'

'Just turned six, sir. Not bad.'

'Tired?'

'Not really. You get used to it, don't you? A couple of years ago I would've been dead if I hadn't had my eight hours. It's just habit. I manage nicely on two now, or none at all.' She paused and looked at him out of the corner of her eye. 'Did you . . . er . . . get everything you wanted? I mean . . . are you all fixed up, sir?'

'No. A few short. It's not your run-of-the-mill volunteer I'm after. Any more?'

'Just six, bottom of the barrel, I suppose.' She handed them over, and moved away as Gallagher flicked through them, stopping at the third card, and looking up with a tiny smile on his lips. The file card was that of a certain ATS Sergeant, French-speaking and not much else to offer, but volunteered for Special Duties. Her name was down as Sally Ogden Birkett, born at Eastbourne, 8 July 1922.

When he finally came out into the morning sunshine it was the dry, quiet of wartime London with a touch of snap in the not yet warm air. A light wind blew some rubbish about his feet as it was lifted from the road by the passing, almost empty red bus juddering down Whitehall on a clapped-out engine that should have been retired five years since. Two silver-grey barrage-balloons hung above the smoke-hazed city, more out of habit than necessity, for the metropolis had not heard a bomb dropped in anger for well over a year, and the throb of engines during the night hours told of our own squadrons returning from dropping their devastating loads upon other soil.

Gallagher mentally reviewed his night's work. He was lacking in several areas but he would explore other avenues for likely subjects. Several he wanted to meet face-to-face, several he would take on trust. It depended upon their skills and potential usage. He found a brown-and-black taxi standing by the driver's hut, and persuaded the man to leave his 'wad-and-a-dog' for ten minutes to take him to Chatto Place where he hoped to freshen up in the office Gwillim had lent him as an operating base, before he followed up his selectees and got down to business.

The Windmill theatre 11.08

The non-stop routine told on everyone eventually. Apart from altering the comedy acts and the vocalists as a matter of keeping the show on the move, and providing constantly changing entertainment for the war-weary punters, the dance routines varied hardly at all. The dancers could be registered as being in a reserved occupation if they so wished and thus avoid call-up and most of them did, but quite a few went into the forces or even the munitions factories feeling that 'doing their bit' in the theatre was not quite valid as 'war effort'. They were wrong. It mattered very much indeed. For those who worked day-in, day-out, at three shows out of five with a long break every fifth day, it was exhausting work. Dance routines are hard enough five times a day, ask any chorus girl who has played the Windmill, ask Bud and Chesney, who kept it up longer than most, and managed to keep smiling. But who, everyone asked, *who* came to see a leg-show in mid-morning? Simone Portales didn't know. She hadn't tried to find out. The footlights provided the wall with blackness beyond, and the intermittent sea of faces that denoted a half-house were no more than blurs that sometimes laughed, sometimes whistled, and clapped and cheered the tired, tatty show they had staggered in to watch. Simone fought off her share of stage-door Johnnies. She was dark and vivacious and very pretty, and French. The last seemed to promise all manner of liberties and delights to the wretched lonely men, mostly in uniform, who hung about the stage door and the lanes of Soho round into Berwick Street. Once or twice she had succumbed, and gone for a drink with a sadly eager soldier or airman, once with a Polish airman, a Squadron Leader he claimed, who insisted she accompany him to the salt-beef bar across the road. She hadn't been there before, didn't even know salt-beef was available (which it wasn't) off the ration. She should have been warned by the entrance where the proprietor, in a fit of honesty, had nailed a horse-shoe to the door alongside the mezuzah. It didn't really show – if it's boiled enough and tenderised with care and spices, and sliced up on a plate with yellow sweet/sour cucumbers and latkes, who was to know? There was a war on.

This morning as she danced off the stage into the wings

Jacko, the pimply-faced ASM, was hanging on the tabs and making gestures at her.

'Hey . . . Simone! There was a telephone call for you, luv. Bloke says you were to report to his office. Number's on your mirror. 'Morrow morning. Nine-firty.'

'Nine-thirty? Merde!'

'Fought you wouldn't like that. Sounded military, know what I mean? 'Ere . . . you ain't bein' called-up or noffing? We're so short on chorus line it's a bleedin' fraud, init?'

'I think they do not call you up on the telephone, non?'

'Got customers on the side, then, ducky?'

'At nine-thirty in the morning?'

Simone made a very Gallic gesture, and ran up the metal spiral staircase past the 'second troupe' on their way down. In the dressing-room the chorus used while the chorus-room proper was being plastered after the ceiling fell down in 1943, she found the telephone number scrawled in No 12 Leichner on her bit of mirror. Regent 8424, extension 169.

Gallagher was not in his office when she returned the call but the arrangement was confirmed by the FANY duty-clerk. Gallagher was in with Gwillim, having an additional member of his team handed over. One he had not reckoned upon and did not want. The young man Lovell was a boffin. An unkempt, vague, academic who was as anxious to become part of the team as Gallagher was to have him. After a stormy meeting Lovell left in a bad mood, and indeed left Gallagher protesting to Gwillim and Evans with real feeling.

'That man is going to be a pain in the arse. I don't want him. I can smell trouble already.'

Evans sighed and sat down heavily. 'I know what you mean . . . but it's just his way. He is also overworked and very tired, but he's far and away the best man for the job.'

'What job? What makes him so special, Professor? Convince me.' Gallagher needed convincing before he spoke his mind to his superiors, which they all knew he would unhesitatingly do if called upon.

'He's a sort of Barnes Wallis chap . . . not exactly a scientist, not exactly an engineer. Bit of both, and a lot more besides. Do you remember that Fritz-X last year?'

'You mean the air-to-ground bomb thing?'

'I do. It was Lovell who worked out what it was from the bits and pieces sent back from Italy . . . marvellous job! It's Lovell who has put together more than half the information we have on this ruddy flying-rocket thing. Nobody understands it better, man. I know he's difficult. He doesn't like war, you see?'

'Does anyone?'

Evans turned and looked him in the face. 'Oh yes, Major. More than ever admit to it, on both sides. Don't *you*?'

'Why do I need him?' Gallagher wasn't to be sidetracked.

'It's more than just blowing up their stockpile. We need whatever plans, specifications, anything . . . that they have. We have to *know* about it . . . to destroy it. This isn't the only stockpile, man. Did you imagine it was?'

Gallagher stopped talking. He knew Evans was right. He just had not thought about it in those terms. The paperwork was essential, and only a fool would not realise that. But it meant a change of plan already. His mind raced and he turned quickly to Gwillim.

'Could I get someone out of jail if I needed him?'

'Possibly,' was all Gwillim offered him at that juncture, but it was enough to send him back to his office to make a telephone call.

He decided to call at the hospital on his way to Brixton, and made a small detour via Piccadilly for two rather special purchases. St George's hospital needed a facelift badly, as did most of London's stuccoed buildings now peeling and falling to pieces from neglect and bomb-blast. The Georgian building was a beauty, and occupied one of the finest sites in London . . . the sandbagged entrances, the taped windows, the roof-posts for fire-watching all testified to the hostilities that occupied its doctors and nurses through all the hours God sent. This afternoon it glowed in the sunshine, and the warm, yellow colour that pervaded the pink paint made it especially attractive as Gallagher stepped from his cab and entered the side entrance. A staff nurse directed him to the first floor, past men in hospital blues, past visiting relatives, past tired interns and overtired probationers there for the duration if they survived, till he found himself at the Sister's cubicle and enquired further.

Then he was eventually shown into the private ward where Lamboit lay recovering from the minor operation that would restore his leg to normality.

'I thought you might enjoy a taste of home. "Marc" was all I could get. Haven't your Free French lot sent you any fruit?'

Lamboit glowered at him. 'No one gets grapes these days.'

'They tell me the danger of gangrene is passed. You're in the clear. Good.'

'Then I can go back to France, can't I?'

Lamboit's look was still sullen and his tone uncommunicative. He avoided looking at Gallagher, and gave his attention to the bottle of marc and the small book simply wrapped by the side of it. It was a book, and he was a bookseller, and curiosity was too much for his pride. He looked at it and his eyes suddenly went to the spine of the book, then held it as his fingers carefully opened the cover and end-papers with the almost caressing touch of a true booklover. He stared at the title page greedily, and then looked up at Gallagher . . . momentarily speechless.

'This is the 1784 *Zaïre*!'

Gallagher looked as vague and unconcerned as he could.

'Yes, I thought it might be. I just happened to be passing Hatchards. Saw the Voltaire. Seemed a pity to leave it.'

He recognised that Lamboit was more than pleased and gratified, but would be damned before he would show it. He took refuge in small talk.

'You knew I was a bookseller?'

'I knew you had your bookshop burned down round your ears. Thought something to read wouldn't go amiss, and I didn't feel *No Orchids for Miss Blandish* was quite your style. Well, I have a call to make. Shout if you want anything special.'

As he left Lamboit turned to watch him go and even managed a reluctant 'Thank you, Major,' which he prayed no one had heard. But Gallagher left the room with a tiny smile on his lips.

The taxi took him across London, through Victoria, and over Vauxhall Bridge into the nether regions of Brixton, where, outside the sombre entrance of HM Prison it deposited the army officer and hurried on its way, aware that fares would be few and far between unless he found one by the railway station.

Gallagher was shown into the Governor's office, and thence, after a brief chat and explanation, showing his credentials and his authority from the War Office, was taken to an interview room. There he waited in total silence for more than fifteen minutes. At length, without prior warning by footfall, the door was opened and a man shown in. A man in prison garb, youngish, sharp featured, and wary.

'The prisoner, sir. Number 56181, Macklin, G.'

'Thank you. I have permission to talk unsupervised. I'll knock when I am ready to leave.'

The warder was none too happy about leaving, but he had his instructions and locked the door after him. The prisoner had not taken his eyes from Gallagher, who now turned to examine him. The eyes met and held for some minutes before either spoke. It was Macklin who gave in first.

'What's this then? Who the hell are you?'

'Name's Gallagher. I've got a job for you.'

'The only job I can do in 'ere, mate, is rob the suggestion box, an' that's stuffed with bog-paper. Come off it.'

'The job's on the outside. I can get you out to do it, but there are conditions . . . even in wartime there are conditions.'

Macklin eyed him searchingly with a tiny smile about his mouth.

'If you want me bad enough to come here and talk about springing me you want me bad, mister, so don't talk about conditions without swopping a couple, eh? I don't need any medals.'

'I'm not offering you medals. I wouldn't insult them. I'm offering you freedom, and a sizeable cash bonus at the end of it.'

'How big is sizeable?'

'How good are you?'

'Best peter man in the business. Ask around. Full pardon and a clean slate?'

Gallagher nodded. Macklin waited a second then nodded back.

The Black Maria pulled up outside Chatto House and Macklin was escorted into the building by two prison warders and Gallagher himself. The latter went ahead into the office while the others waited. Gwillim was talking with another military man, a Lieutenant-Colonel of the Guards.

'Ah, Hugh . . come in. I don't think you know Colonel Squires.

'Sir.'

'Colonel Squires will be OC your training programme. I want you to go down to Masham and talk it all through with him. Tomorrow all right with you?'

'Yes, sir. If you don't mind, sir, I want you to meet someone with a view to have him join my team.'

'Splendid. Bring him in.'

Macklin was still in his prison garb when he entered, and eyebrows were raised at the sight. Gallagher hastened to elucidate.

'This is Mr Macklin, sir. I am led to believe that he is the best safe-cracker in Britain. He may be the chap I want.'

Gwillim eyed the convict with curiosity though without disdain. Suddenly he got up and crossed to his cupboard door.

'Mr Macklin, this door is locked and inside the cupboard is my safe – also locked. I would be obliged if you would open that safe for me. You have exactly ten minutes.'

He checked his wristwatch as Macklin pursed his lips and eyed the other people in the room. Then he crossed to the desk and picked up a letter-knife which he tried with his fingers.

'Can I borrow this, guv? Came out a bit empty-handed, as you might say.'

Without waiting for permission he opened Gwillim's desk drawer and then jammed it shut on the knife-blade before prising it downwards, and bending the point into a right-angle. Easily and without any rushed movement he crossed to the cupboard door, inserted the bent blade, felt, twisted, and turned the lock with a snap. The door opened slightly with the air-pressure inside. Macklin pulled it wide and revealed the elderly heavy Edwardian safe inside.

'Cor! Haven't seen one of these for a few years. Weigh over a ton these do, you know. Hope your floor's up to it.'

He knelt down and started fiddling, put his ear against the casing, and moved and revolved the combination knob. He heard the tumblers move, carried on. Gwillim positioned himself by the window to see better. Gallagher sat on the desk edge, while Squires touched his fingers together under his chin and watched with evident amusement.

Macklin heard the last pinion drop and turned his attention to the key lock. He sighed, 'Normally I'd have a tool-kit, wouldn't I? Still, see what we can do.'

He used the bent knife point again in the keyhole, and within seconds turned the handle and the safe door opened. Macklin stood up with a smile of pleasure at his skill.

Gallagher glanced at the wall clock. 'Three minutes and eighteen seconds, Colonel.'

Gwillim peered at his safe disconsolately as Macklin handed him his letter-knife. 'Good metal that . . . might even bend back again.' But Gwillim had turned away and looked at Gallagher. 'Very well. I'll speak with the Home Office. Brixton, is it?'

Gallagher nodded and Macklin was whisked out of the office and into the waiting police van before anyone spoke again. Squires stood up and grinned at Gallagher.

'See you tomorrow, I hope.'

Gallagher muttered a vague agreement realising he was being dismissed, and left the two colonels alone. Squires chuckled quietly as the frowning Gwillim glowered at his safe and cupboard.

'Better go and have some lunch. Just a minute,' Gwillim picked up the phone and waited. 'Security? Masters? Colonel Gwillim. The safe in my office is unreliable. I want it changed. Now.'

He slammed down the receiver, picked up his cap, and stalked out with Squires following behind, still smiling.

George Macklin, prisoner 56181, was released upon special cognisance that same evening. The request came directly from the Home Office and hinted at supreme authority. The only comment he received was as he was let through the door in the main gate.

'What's so special about you, George? We normally lets 'em out in the mornings.'

'King and Country, mate. Been called up. They need me, old son. Nice to feel wanted, in'it?'

The warder shook his head and grinned.

'Be seeing you, George.'

'No you bloody won't, mate . . . once is enough. I'm telling you.' And he walked away into South London with a small wrapped box under one arm, looking about him, not quite sure it was all really happening.

Gallagher had two more of his selection to see the following morning, but it was vital that he knew everything he possibly could about the German underground complex. Success was only possible with and through that knowledge, and Hugh Gallagher wasn't about to set out on any doomed mission. His request to have Viardot to himself for one whole night was agreed to by Gwillim without comment, and the reluctant Frenchman was delivered to him at 23.00 hours by the same two MPs who immediately made themselves comfortable in the outer office. They recognised a long night before it happened. They had been doing this job for three years.

Gallagher had availed himself of a recording machine so that he could have the conversation on tap for future reference, inflections and all. The microphone fed the dialogue directly into the recorder, which preserved it, newly cut into the discs supplied by the Ministry. By 03.00 both men were tired and nerves frayed. The supply of blank discs was almost exhausted.

'The German garrison is housed in this area here, right? The garrison vehicles are kept here, and the rocket transports, here. This is where the Todt workers have their quarters, here are the guard houses. Vehicles IN . . . vehicles OUT. These steel doors, who operates them? and where from?'

'I don't know! I had no reason to. They are operated for routine work from the blockhouse outside, but obviously there must be a control in the interior somewhere. I do not know where it is. There are checkpoints every three hundred yards in the tunnel complex, as I told you.'

'How many guards altogether?'

'I don't know. A company. I don't know military terms.'

'How *many*? A hundred? Two hundred?'

'About two hundred, I think, maybe more.'

Gallagher stared at the rough map of the area, thinking hard and trying to dispel his own tiredness to ask salient questions that so often get overlooked.

'Does that minefield go right round the complex?'

'Is there any point in one that does not?'

'Frequently, I'm asking.'

'I do not know!!'

Gallagher recognised that he did not, would have little reason to know. It was not his field, nor his business.

Gallagher turned away and paced as he took another cigarette from his almost empty pack and lit it from the old stub.

'I don't understand. I just don't understand! How could they build such a place without anyone knowing about it? Something that size would take years to complete. Not weeks. You can't drill through solid rock as if it was butter. It takes time.'

'They had only to enlarge and reinforce it. It existed already.'

'As a quarry? So the bulk work was half done. Corridors and rooms take time, a long time.'

Viardot frowned and seemed to recognise one point that had somehow not been made clear, or properly understood.

'It was not a quarry, not for half-a-century, that is. It was made into a huge underground ammunition dump during the First World War. The caves and tunnels existed already. Did you not know? The Germans had only to modify and enlarge slightly.'

Gallagher gasped. 'You omitted to tell us that bit.'

Viardot grunted. 'You omitted to ask. I thought you knew.'

16 April

Viardot was taken away by his guards just before six and Gallagher tried to snatch an hour or two's sleep in the chair. It came fitfully for, despite his mental exhaustion, his mind would not let go. He replayed several of the discs and considered the replies carefully. Viardot had not lied, he felt sure enough of that, but what other monstrous facts was he not aware of by simply not knowing the questions to ask. Viardot did not volunteer information. It was given, however reluctantly, as a direct answer to a direct question.

Nothing more.

At eight-thirty he was wakened by someone entering his office and moving furniture about. It was his FANY clerk. She stopped when she saw him slumped in the chair.

'I'm sorry, sir. I didn't realise. Have you been here all night?'

Gallagher grunted and stretched his back as he stood up and looked at his crumpled uniform.

'There should be a brew-up on the next floor. D'you want me to find you a cuppa?'

'In a minute, I'm expecting someone shortly.'

'I think your party is already sitting in the outer-office, sir. Shall I send her in?'

'Oh, come through, Miss Portales,' he called out as he made for his desk.

'It's me, sir, Sergeant Birkett.'

Gallagher looked up to see the filing-clerk who had assisted him with his selection.

'Sorry to trouble you, sir. It's my Section Officer. She thinks I stuck my file in front of your face or behind your back or something. What I mean is, she doesn't believe you made a genuine request for transfer. And you did, didn't you?'

Birkett's anxiety was obvious. Gallagher looked at her, then smiled his slightly quirky smile.

'We both know that you did not influence my decision in any way. Neither by bribery, blackmail, nor offer of carnal knowledge. What's her name, your officer?'

'Section-Officer Naylor, sir. Whitehall 6959, extension 282, sir.'

'Have you got your posting?'

'No, sir. It went to Section-Officer Naylor, sir, that's why . . .' She made a small face implying the whole sad tale.

'Get back to your billet and start packing. I'll clarify it with your Section-Officer.'

'Thank you, sir.' Sergeant Birkett beamed her delight, and edged forward just a fraction as if she wanted to demonstrate her thanks in an unmilitary fashion but thought better of it, stepped back, saluted, turned, and left. She almost knocked into a rather smartly-dressed young woman standing at the door entrance, waiting.

Gallagher recognised his selectee from her photograph and description. Simone Portales was a very attractive young woman. She held herself with a certain dignity which did not however conceal the implications of sexuality, not to say sensuality, contained in the face itself and the full and shapely figure. She smiled slightly as Gallagher realised he was staring at her.

'May I come in?' The French accent was there, but slight, and the warm, low voice complemented her appearance.

'Miss Portales?' Gallagher sensed how lame and gauche he sounded. 'Good morning. I wasn't too sure you would turn up. Thank you for coming.'

'I assume you would not invite me into your den if you had not considered it important enough for me to miss my breakfast, Major.'

She stood waiting to be offered a chair with the assurance of one who always was offered that chair, in whatever company. She did not have long to wait. Gallagher moved the chair with whatever degree of gallantry the early hour could muster.

'I haven't had mine either. As we are likely to be seeing a lot of each other, Ma'mselle, we might as well start amicably.'

'Most men see rather a lot of me, Major. It doesn't entitle them to special privileges.' She caught for a moment the slight reaction in his eyes, and the boyishness thawed her. 'I was being stuffy. I am sorry. You must have my file, what is there that I can tell you?'

'How well do you know the area round Chantilly and Senlis?'

She looked at him for a moment without speaking, then became quiet and businesslike.

'Quite well. I was born in St Etienne s'Allourd, as I'm sure you know.'

'D'you have relatives there? People who might recognise you?'

'I have only my mother, but she went to live in what used to be Unoccupied France. There is no one else. I do not know who would recognise me; outside of St Etienne, I doubt it. If they did, is that bad?'

'If they know you came to England it would take some explaining.'

'No one knows that, they know I left for Paris. My mother would have told them I was working in cabaret, then she went away. She does not know where I am.' Simone Portales shrugged. 'I don't think it can matter, Major.'

'Do you speak good German?' Without waiting for an answer he rattled off several questions in the language of the Occupying

Power. Portales did not turn a hair, nor blink an eye, but answered coldly and calmly in near flawless German. Gallagher was impressed and reassured by her sense of personal containment, something usually found only in experienced operators.

'There is rather a nice coffee shop in Great Portland Street. If you would care to buy me some breakfast I would answer your questions much more comfortably.'

Her eyes challenged him, and Gallagher rose to the challenge.

'If you are trying to put me at a disadvantage you won't succeed.'

She smiled in friendly fashion. 'I realised that in the first thirty seconds, Major Gallagher. If there is one thing I am seldom wrong about it is men. Besides, it is probably the only chance I will ever have of informality with my CO, . . . non?'

Gallagher smiled and put on his cap. 'Coffee for two, then.

Royal Army Service Corps, Great Whelpington, Leics.

The warm spring sunshine beat down upon the barrack square where three individual squads were suffering square-bashing to the raw-throated bawling of their respective instructors. The sound filtered through into the outer-office adjoining the CO's domain. Captain Nigel Macaulay stood by the desk of the ATS secretary/clerk who slowly and laboriously typed the indecipherable notice she had before her.

'He must have said something! Didn't he read it?'

'I don't read the Colonel's signals, nor his post, Captain.'

'Jenny, I love you dearly but there are times . . .'

He snapped to attention as the door behind him opened and his CO, Lieutenant-Colonel Cole, came out and looked over his half-glasses.

'Ah, Macaulay. What in hell is this about?'

Cole was a tired regular officer, too old and too difficult to place anywhere other than Training Command or the RASC. Macaulay wasn't, and he resented being posted to this backwater. He closed the office door as he followed his CO inside.

'I applied for special duties, sir.'

'Without consulting your Commanding Officer? You have no bloody right to do such a thing. There are channels, Macaulay.'

'There wasn't time, sir.'

'Wasn't time? What d'you mean "there wasn't time"?'

'Just that, sir, I applied for special duties some time ago, before you were OC, sir.' Which was a lie, and both men knew it. 'I suppose it simply remained on file.' Which was unlikely, and both men knew it.

The Colonel stared at him with evident distaste, and twitched one rheumy eye before he spoke. 'I know you don't think much of it here, Macaulay. But good officers are hard to come by. Even difficult ones. I suppose that is why they're good officers. There isn't much I can do about it now, it's gone too far. Major O'Rourke will take over your company *pro tem.* I see there is a travel warrant attached to your posting. Make sure you properly clear this unit. That's all.'

Macaulay saluted, relieved that he had got off without the dressing-down he had expected, and closed the door as he left, taking his papers from the Colonel's hand. He stared at the green warrant and at the photo-copy of a map section attached to it. He crossed to the filing-cabinet, and pulled out one of the elderly wooden drawers, then tried another and another . . .

'Jenny, where in hell do we keep the one-inch maps?'

'Next drawer down, Captain. Where they always are.' The tone was unmistakably that as to a child of four, but Macaulay chose to ignore implied contempt for the whole male race, and fumbled about amid the piles of grubby, torn, and well-thumbed ordnance survey maps dating from the mid-thirties.

'Where is Westbury?'

Jenny didn't even look up but peered over the edge of the typewriter carriage, and tried to fathom why the paper would not move.

'Salisbury Plain. Sheet 167. Just left of the centrefold and below the strawberry jam.'

Macaulay gritted his teeth in masculine tolerance. 'How is it you're so bloody efficient? I don't think much of your typing, but you know your maps.'

Jenny smiled self-deprecatingly. 'Not really. That just happens to be one we have to consult regularly. WD training sites, artillery-ranges, combined-ops, you know.'

Macaulay looked at her as the penny dropped. Yes, it would

be just like special duties, thinking to pull a fast one on the wretched applicants. He hadn't forgotten his London appointment with an army psychiatrist, and sitting for half-an-hour in the waiting-room chatting away with unconstrained honesty to a fellow applicant only to find the 'applicant' was the psychiatrist. All not quite gentlemanly.

'You have great talents, Jenny, don't let anyone sell you short.'

The patronising attitude was too much for the ATS girl, even from a superior officer. 'You should know, Nigel darling.'

But the effect missed its intention. Macaulay merely grinned and walked towards the door where he stopped and turned.

'Can't make it tonight, luv, "been posted".'

With an excuse-for-a-salute, Macaulay stepped out of the office leaving the girl mentally spitting, and rebuffed – as well as having lost the round.

Didcot Junction, Oxfordshire

Every time a main line train thundered through the station the bottles on the buffet shelves rattled and shook. They were all empty. The cups of tea on the counter jumped and rattled in their saucers, and walked their way across the tin-topped counter until they made contact with the chipped mahogany edge that saved them from shattering on the tiled floor. But it wasn't the cups and saucers the four travellers were watching with open mouths, nor was it the passing trains of the up-line that shook the wall and counter of the buffet, and gave the plump serving lady palpitations.

It was the sight of blood and the look in the eyes of the agricultural worker in a flat cap and blue denim dungarees as he was thrown against the corner by the empty glass sandwich-container.

The fist that had sent him flying belonged to an Argyll Highlander wearing battle fatigues and a Commando slash across the upper arm. The tall, hard-faced Scot with the full moustache wasn't much concerned about the nervous withdrawing of the civilian travellers away from the tables towards the exit, nor about the mild protests from Elsie, the canteen lady-turned buffet-manageress who was bawling at him.

'He didn't mean what he said, Mister. He's had one too many.'

But Duncan Cameron wasn't listening. He had had a skinful which always seemed to impair his hearing and make him belligerent. Cameron was volatile and fiery by nature; and the Highlander in him wore a chip on his shoulder alongside the Commando flash.

Another blacked-out train chuffed and smoked through the station sending clouds of foul fumes swirling round the island platform and the buffet waiting room. It masked the metal-edged wooden stairs that led down from the footbridge to the central island, and made the MPs who were clattering across the bridge in their polished boots stumble slightly before the slip-stream pulled away the dark billows and sooty fumes.

The Sergeant of Police kicked open the buffet door and glared at the fight going on inside. His squad fell in behind and peered over his shoulder. Cameron chose to ignore their presence as he laid into the burly farmer's lad. He didn't want his fight disturbed. He never did. But the MPs fell upon them both, and tore them apart. Cameron lashed out in all directions until a truncheon laid him low and wiped the sight of Didcot Junction from his travel-weary eyes. He had, after all, been travelling in slow, stopping, dirty, smelly trains since yesterday morning and had only sat down for ten minutes the whole way. He was sick of sitting on his kit-bag; sick of backing against the corridor wall to let some skulking civilian-who-shouldn't-have-been-cluttering-up-the-railways-anyway climb past the recumbent bodies just visible in the shaded and turned-down lighting on their way to lavatories already bunged-up with paper, excrement and foul-smelling urine and a floor covered with stamped-out cigarette stubs. Cameron didn't like wartime travel. Cameron didn't much like civilians. But he positively detested any male between the ages of sixteen and sixty who was not in uniform, and went out of his way to insult anyone who was, and by the time he had had half-a-dozen bottles of Mackeson, or whatever he was given at the bars, he was ready to show what he felt.

When he was brought before his Commanding Officer the following morning, his head ringing with the truncheon blow, the bottled stout, and the cigarette smoke, he was what is sometimes referred to as a 'sorry sight', though, it had to be admitted, he was never less than military in bearing. The colonel glared at his adjutant who had laid the charge-sheet before him.

'The man's a disgrace to his uniform, Peter.'

The adjutant was a more practical man and a total realist.

'Indeed, sir, but he's a damn good soldier.'

But the colonel was not to be put down so simply. 'There's more to soldiering than killing the enemy. You know that as well as I do. I should have the beggar on the carpet and throw everything at him. Won't do the regiment any good, but a court-martial is about all I can see.'

The adjutant handed him a signal, and tapped the corner with his forefinger. 'There may be a way out, sir. This signal arrived yesterday. I think you'd better read it.'

The colonel frowned and did as he was invited. Then he looked up at his aide, and hope flickered for a moment in his eyes.

'By God, Peter, you could be right. Gets us off the hook, eh?' He glanced at the signal again. '"Special Duties?" What the devil does that mean?'

'I hardly think it matters, sir, and, er, if I may suggest . . . there seems no real purpose in sending a personal appreciation. I can't see that Special Duties would be all that interested, can you, sir?'

The two men looked blandly into each other's eyes, and decided, without saying a word, that no adverse report would leave that office when their man was transferred.

'Send him in.'

Cameron stomped in and clattered to a salute before his CO, trying not to show that his head was coming off with that salute, and that unless the colonel was blind he would notice that Cameron was inclined forward at an angle of something like forty-five degrees, or so it seemed to the Highlander.

'Colonel, sir.' The voice was thick, and low, and quiet, but it thundered inside the Scot's head and made him wince. But the barrage to which he was subjected, in his colonel's best barrack-square voice, echoing round the Nissen hut with a thunder that rivalled the Albert Hall, was something that Cameron would not forget quickly. The raids on the enemy coast had not offended his sensibilities to such an extent. The Bofors guns behind his head on that last raid had seemed like the cooing of doves by comparison. When Cameron eventually got out into the morning air he was pale and shaking and ready to spew up his entire three-day binge, but he was 'let off'. Glory be to God! Let off, and transferred to Special Duties! He would look at his warrant and his papers when he was in a fit state to digest them. In the meantime, the hair of the dog. . . .

Lt.-Colonel Tim Squires, ex-Guards, had been OC Training at Masham Hall, an establishment for 'special' personnel, since he was brought out of Greece and the hospital discharged him as no longer fit for active service, but recommended continuation of his military career as not merely useful to the war-effort but as a necessity for Squires' mental equilibrium. He needed to work in what he knew best. He had turned into the best training officer they had. His manner was mildly eccentric, almost a caricature of the Guards officer, yet never without dignity and integrity. Even his tiny jibes and odd verbal mannerisms in no way detracted from the overall impression he gave of efficiency and authority. If anything they added to that impression, and both his staff and his trainees grew to respect and like him. When he made a suggestion it was not to be ignored, and when he implied that he thought Gallagher ought to meet and talk with someone who might prove a useful addition to the team it was a serious and considered possibility. The person he wanted Gallagher to meet was French by birth and upbringing. She had first been noted by the colonel when she initially applied for Special Duties, and her abilities had been noted. The fact that she was Free French made it almost certain that she would remain unused. A French civilian who had escaped from German Occupation would be accepted, once cleared, by SOE, by MI6, MI9, or any of the other clandestine units whose operations within enemy-occupied territory could only benefit from a useful, French national. But, those who had for better or for worse actually joined the Free French Forces now collected within the United Kingdom under one umbrella would find their way blocked into the above-mentioned organisations. They remained 'on file', unused, apparently forgotten, yet jealously guarded from British or Allied poaching. Narrow, and pointless . . . but that was the way it was.

When Lieutenant Solange Rohr walked into the office both Squires and Gallagher instinctively rose to greet the very attractive, and self-assured young woman who wore the French uniform so elegantly. Instinctive gallantry had triumphed over military protocol, and the recognition brought the tiniest of smiles to the Frenchwoman's lips.

Squires cleared his throat. 'Thank you for coming at such short notice. You don't actually know me, I'm Lieutenant-Colonel Squires. This is Major Gallagher. Do sit down.'

Squires went on briefly to say that he was one of the adjudicating officers in the initial training applications board, and so on, and then handed her over to Gallagher.

Gallagher looked calmly at her, noted the reddish hair, the grey eyes, and the few freckles that seemed to heighten the warm complexion of her skin. He noted that the elegance also implied fitness and a certain strength. He got down to detail immediately.

'I have an operation to plan and execute. I need someone who is French, who is intelligent and dedicated enough to cope with tricky situations, who is attractive enough and capable enough to handle German officers. Someone who is already a decent WT operator, but who has potential to be better than that. And one who is acceptable by her own people, again, should the occasion demand it.'

Squires leant forward. 'It's a tall order, but you seemed to fit the bill. Before we go any further I must ask you if there is any reason why you cannot leave your present unit and work . . . say within twenty-four hours?'

'I don't think so. The decision would be for my superiors, of course, but I myself am quite agreeable.'

She did not conceal that she was delighted at the prospect of being used, by anyone, and the bright sparkle in her eyes was suddenly endearing. Gallagher overcame his urge to smile back, and frowned before continuing.

'You were working in Paris when war broke out. You trained as a wireless operator and cypher clerk. You came to England, and joined the Free French Forces. Why?'

'Why should I not, Major? I am French. My country is overrun by the Nazis. I want to fight back. Is that bad? Perhaps you do not understand, but there is much shame in capitulation. Even for a woman.'

'Of course. What I was asking was "Why did you not stay behind and fight with the Resistance where it was actually happening"?'

Solange coloured slightly, and hesitated before she stiffened and the set of her chin grew just that touch more determined.

'I came for personal reasons, Major. My fiancé decided to leave and fly with the RAF. I was very much in love. I came too. There is no mystery, no heroics, just a very young woman with only herself in mind. It was a selfish motivation I admit. Nothing more. When Jacques was killed I grew up a little, and volunteered to work for General de Gaulle.'

Gallagher looked at her stonily for a long moment before he smiled.

'I think Mademoiselle Rohr is exactly what I need, Colonel.'

Squires beamed and stood up. 'Miss Rohr, you will receive your posting, travel warrant, etc., by special messenger later today. I have already cleared the matter with your superiors.' His expression implied that it was not a matter of course, but that his stick was bigger than theirs. 'I shall be OC Training so that I regret our relationship will have to be formal and military from now on. Thank you again, for coming.'

The dismissal was obvious and the girl stood, smiled, and saluted before she left, watched by both men with due appreciation. Squires continued to watch as he spoke to Gallagher. 'I've been through your selection. Seems fair enough. Most of them will have their postings by now. Shall we go down to the Hall? My car's outside, and we have quite a bit to discuss. I shall call you Hugh, and, unless you have a violent objection to using it, my Christian name is "Tim". Ready to go?'

Omdurman Street, Walworth, South-East London

George Macklin slid the key into the Yale lock and turned it silently, stepping into the familiar room with a quick glance about him, his ears intent upon any sound from inside the flat. Sounds told him someone was in the tiny kitchen. He smiled to himself and coughed quietly. A sudden silence . . .

'. . . that you, Bobby?'

Macklin stiffened slightly at the question. He knew it was only to be expected, had even urged it himself, but that 'Bobby' stuck in his stomach and ground quickly round.

'What's the matter, then? You half-cut?'

Alice came into the doorway and looked at him. She stopped as if struck, and her face expressed her shock and fear.

'Georgie! I thought you was inside.'

It sounded so lame, so silly, so pointless. She knew he was inside doing porridge, and she knew he had no business to be outside.

'You 'aven't bust out?'

He didn't reply. She would know he hadn't if she thought for a moment. If he had, this was the last place he would be visiting. He crossed to the table in the bay-window and looked out, peered through the net curtains for a moment, then turned round to smile at her. But his eyes dropped to the floor where a pair of men's slippers stood by the chair, and the ash-tray and pack of tobacco, roller, and papers lay silently accusing.

'Roll your own now, Alice? Didn't know you smoked.' He picked up the slippers and looked closely at them.

'Size ten, nice new ones.'

Alice cleared her throat and held her head higher, almost defiantly.

'I'm living with someone now, George. Well, I mean, you was inside – eight years. I'm not gettin' any younger, Georgie.' Macklin avoided her tearful gaze, and accepted what was, after all, an unwritten tenet of social behaviour for the criminal community. Many, indeed – most, wives and families remained loyal and faithful to the incarcerated spouse, but it was accepted among them that there was neither pressure nor stigma attached to one who decided to go his or her own way once the partner was mewed up. It was only fair.

'You've done the old place up nice. Why the 'ell should you wait? Eight years is a bloody lifetime.'

'Where you stayin', Georgie?'

'Hotel, all expenses paid for a couple of days. Then I'm movin' on . . . y'know.'

'Yes . . . I know.'

'Whose are the shoes, Alice?' But Alice hesitated.

'Whose, luv?'

'Bobby Prendergast. He isn't workin' much. He can't get no job, him bein' a deserter 'n that.'

She got no further in her explanation as the key in the door announced Prendergast's entry. Alice moved quickly towards the opening door.

'You'll never guess who's 'ere, Bobby. It's Georgie Macklin.'

But Prendergast had difficulty in removing the key from the sticky lock, and snorted as he fiddled. 'Don't be bloody daft! That berk's inside, got eight years an' no good behaviour.'

But by this time the key had been extracted and Bobby turned into the room to find Macklin as reported. He stopped in his tracks and he swallowed hard. Macklin was smaller than Prendergast, but no bookie would have taken odds on a favourable outcome in any vicious contest between them. Macklin's size didn't mean a thing. One sensed he would kill or maim without turning a hair, whereas Prendergast had the air of the born loser about him. For all his bounce and bravura he was basically weak and empty.

'Hello, Mr Macklin.'

'Bobby,' Macklin smiled sweetness and light, but Prendergast fell over himself trying to make a peace where there was no war.

'Look, I'm sorry you got bird. We didn't know you was gettin' out or anythin', did we Alice? I mean, we didn't know.'

But Macklin was looking at him without really seeing him, and turned his head to Alice's pale and nervous face.

'Who shopped me, luv?'

'I don't know, Georgie. It wasn't me, luv, you know that. I couldn't anyway, I didn't know about nothin', did I?'

'Who, Alice?'

His tone was still cool and calm, but the edge was there and everyone in that room recognised it for what it was.

'Saul Collins, that's what I heard, but I don't *know*, George. Honest! An' if it was, he got his come-uppance, didn't he? He was killed in the blitz, he was. They pulled him out from under the old Rose and Crown in Walworth Road, you remember, Bobby?'

'Oh, yeah, 'e was dead all right, suffocated they said.'

Macklin nodded sagely. 'Just as well, then. Didn't want to waste time settlin' old scores. Just called to see how Alice was doin'. Thought you'd been called up, Bobby.'

'Yeh, well, I didn't like it, did I? Took a powder. Did fourteen months then scarpered. Means I've got to keep me head down though.'

'Send you overseas, did they?'

'Nah, square-bashin' up in Cheshire, bit of loafin' in the top of Scotland. Elgin, it was, then they sent me to Salisbury Plain. That was *it*, mate! Bloody mad, they was! Couldn't take no more.'

But Macklin's interest was aroused and he smiled at Prendergast encouragingly.

'Salisbury Plain. Well, now, that's interesting. Come 'ere, Bobby . . . take a gander at this.' He showed his map to Prendergast and pointed to a marked area.

'Know this place?'

Prendergast snorted and looked up at him. 'Imber? I know it, all right. It's a clapped-out village in the middle of a sodding battle-area they started after Dunkirk. No one lives there. You're wasting your time there, George, no pickin's old son.'

'What's this cross? I'm supposed to turn up there and meet some blokes.'

Prendergast looked again, and his mind ticked-over quickly. Macklin was out and looking for an obscure military place on the plain, that meant he'd been 'let out' to do a job for the military, like as not, and Prendergast knew just what that place was and had seen enough to know what happened there. He turned to Macklin, not quite able to conceal what was flashing through his devious mind, nor the hardening of the cunning look in his eyes. Which was one of the reasons he was second-rate, and George Macklin was not. Macklin would not have shown anything at all.

'Sorry, Mr Macklin, can't help you there.'

When Macklin left the flat and closed the door after him he waited silently for two minutes and listened at the door as Prendergast exploded with suppressed glee to his new girl-friend.

'Clever berk! The great Georgie Macklin . . . eh? He isn't 'alf goin' to get a bloody shock is Mister bloody Macklin; oh yes! I'd give a couple of fivers to watch that lot . . .'

'What d'ye mean Bobby?'

Alice's voice held concern and that, if nothing else, warmed the heart of the listening Macklin at the door.

'Your own little Georgie is going to get the shock of 'is bleedin' life, Alice.'

Macklin had heard enough to confirm his suspicions. Once outside he turned into the Walworth Road and crossed to the telephone kiosk by the bus stop. He closed the door, and looked at his face in the cracked mirror, then ran his finger along the chromed frame to give it a bit of a shine as he dialled 999 and waited . . .

'Police.' He waited as the operator made the connection and then heard the male voice answer.

'Sergeant Harding on the desk? George Macklin.' He waited again until a gruff, south-London voice answered.

'Hello, Bert. George Macklin. No, they let me out. Honest! Listen, Bert . . . you remember Bobby Prendergast? You wanted him for knockin' over the old man at the Benson Place . . . that's right. Well, he's a deserter. Not very patriotic, is it? You can find him at seventy-six Omdurman Street. That's right. You're welcome, Bert . . . see you around, eh?'

When he left the phone booth he felt lighter and with just a touch of smug satisfaction about him. Not that Macklin was vindictive, he just didn't like Bobby Prendergast, and he *was* trying to get him into trouble, and he *was* shacked up with Alice . . . So he whistled as he walked down the street, and Walworth looked its old self, despite the war and bombing. It was good to be on the outside again, and George Macklin was not going back in – whatever happened.

Masham Hall, Wilts

Gallagher found the Training Establishment all he expected. Little different from most of the country houses taken over by the military for the duration, it presented a stone shell of some architectural merit, largely seventeenth century with Edwardian additions, out of which all furnishings, and pictures, and family treasures had been removed to storage in the Corsham area. The necessary furniture was standard, military establishment issue, mainly supplied by the secondhand furnishers from all over the country; augmented when necessary by rather awful utility furniture licensed by the Ministry as a side-product for those factories incapable of turning themselves into munitions or general ordnance manufacturers. They were battered, torn and worn, as was the fabric of the main house. Spared the more blatant forms of graffiti by a more educated officer-class, nevertheless it was an establishment that belonged to 'someone else', or the vague 'WD', and merited scant regard from temporary inmates. That was just one of the wartime diseases now rampant, like shirking, and 'knocking-off' unimportant articles . . . new names for old games, but now tarnished by acceptance where once they were properly regarded as petty crime.

Squires made his office available to Gallagher at all times during their training period, and though he was allotted a small cubicle for his private use it was obvious that the shared office was to be home for the next few weeks. The colonel gave him the run of the place but implied that he ran a tight ship, his schedule was inflexible, and – in training matters – would bow to no man, though he would entertain special requests for special circumstances without necessarily condoning them.

After inspecting the quarters for himself and his selectees, Gallagher was taken round the Hall by one of the instructors, Sergeant-Major Gidney, an old hand, and an old comrade-in-arms of his colonel, both being seconded to training after being semi-invalided from active service. He seemed highly efficient and had a pleasant, if forthright, manner that no doubt made him an excellent instructor.

Satisfied that all was as it should be, perhaps even better than that, Gallagher acceded to Squires' request that they examine the team by record before they arrived at the Hall to begin their training. The epidiascope was rigged in Squires' office and Gallagher operated the machine as he displayed the file-card and photo, and briefly introduced each selectee to Squires.

'This one is Duncan Cameron, Highlander. A Commando as from March 1943. He's one I have a slight doubt about. His record is very good. He has seen service in almost every junket the Marines have mounted, there is just something . . .'

'What did his CO have to say?'

'Almost nothing. But I got the feeling he was delighted to get rid of him. I checked with his previous CO and he came up with, again, a splendid *military* record tempered with a word of warning. It seems that our Scot actually *likes* killing.'

Squires looked directly at him. 'You mean "anybody"? Not just Jerry?'

'That was not stated. I'm not sure it matters, about which nationality, I mean. But a warning-bell is ringing. I almost discarded him, then thought better of it. I could use a rough, tough soldier, especially one who speaks decent French, which incidentally he learned at school, then in France before the war broke out where he went to equip himself to join the Foreign Legion. All rather bizarre. We'll see.'

Gallagher continued: 'Simone Portales. French national. Dancer. Born in Chantilly according to the records, and has specialised knowledge of the area therefore. Speaks good German, and we may find use for her very obvious charms. More about her later . . .

'Nigel Macaulay. Captain in RASC. First-class officer, highly unorthodox, but a good all-rounder, wasted where he is, which I gather was something of a punishment-posting for crossing his CO in a matter of training tactics in which, I am informed, he was absolutely correct and his CO wrong. Again, we'll see.

'This one is a Merchant Navy chap . . . Geoffrey Wilson . . . born in Marseilles of British parents. Grew up there when his father deserted his mother. He's been doing Atlantic runs, convoys mostly, but volunteered for Special Duties with the RN on their French coast free-for-alls because of his language potential.'

Gallagher went through each and every one of his team outlining their possibilities as well as their records. Not once did he indicate why he had chosen this person as opposed to any other, and Squires did not ask. Gallagher was a good officer, and to be trusted implicitly. Squires expected no less in the former's attitude to him.

When it was over and the lights switched on, Squires crossed to a table in the corner which held something covered by a dust sheet. It revealed a scale-model of the German complex.

'Your chap, Viardot, gave us some good drawings, after a little persuasion. I've had my gnomes run up a little toy for us to play with.' Gallagher was already studying the model eagerly and relating it to his own recollections as well as the drawings he had seen made by Viardot.

'You'll find it accurate, at least as near as can be made with the information available to us.' He carefully removed the 'top' of the model and revealed the complex layout underground.

'Are you keeping this in here?'

'Certainly. Ogle it all you want to, dear boy. I shall lock it away from prying charladies, never fear, but you shall have a key to the larder for your very own. I am nothing if not accommodating.'

Gallagher grinned to himself. He had already conceived a liking for this Lieutenant-Colonel of Guards who was to work so closely with him. He even looked forward to the training period. Squires so obviously knew his job.

'When do my lot arrive?'

'Tomorrow. It will take an hour or so to cope with the arrival clearance, formal signing of the Official Secrets Act . . . then I shall give them my little talk. Training commences the following morning. You'll do it with them?'

'I shall keep an eye on them, it's not necessary to go through the whole thing. I'm not exactly new to the game, you know.'

'Nor am I, Gallagher. You'll find your orders clearly state that I am OC Training, after which *you* take over. Until that happens you are under my command, and you will train with everyone else. It's neat, it's tidy, and it's efficient. You may find you actually do *need* a refresher, you know.'

Despite the 'old boy' familiarity there is no doubt that Squires intended to be OC Training, and Gallagher recognised this and respected it and nodded his agreement.

'Will you lay on transport to pick them up from the station, or shall I see to it?'

Squires stared at him as if affronted.

'There'll be no transport, old boy. Goodness me, no! They

have received joining instructions simply telling them to rendezvous precisely on time at a map reference which just happens to be in the middle of an artillery range. I'm afraid they will have to cross near a target area, assuming they succeed in gaining entry. Could be difficult, even dangerous, if you see what I mean.'

Gallagher started to smile slowly. 'You're a bit of a bastard, aren't you?'

Squires' hurt look was assumed. 'Not really, old man. Just good at my job. I forgot to mention that they would be collected and dropped off one-by-one to make their own way. And, er, it is quite on the cards that there may be a combined-ops exercise over part of their area at the same time, if you follow me.'

17 April: Crowthorne Research Establishment, Berks

Stephen Lovell was usually described as a sort of Barnes Wallis type chap. 'Not exactly a scientist, not exactly an engineer, but something of each, and quite a lot more besides.' He had come down from Oxford two months before war broke out, and had been whisked into gainful employment by a former research scholar at the end of that same September. Gainful, that is, to the country generally if not to Stephen Lovell. Immediately classified as 'Reserved', then specially graded into a category known only to a small coterie, he had been quickly raised to a position in the new Research Establishment at Crowthorne where he virtually controlled every aspect of research and experiment within that vital area. Eight times now he had been called out to go overseas, and either report upon or explain some military phenomenon that baffled everyone else. He had an uncanny knack of seeing beyond the facts, and also understood weaponry, ordnance, and the scientific advancement of these into hitherto unimagined realms of near-abstract thought.

It was Lovell who put two and two together from some vague photo-reconnaissance prints, and came up with rocketry as the likely answer. The Resistance news leaked via Poland about a certain experimental station in Peenemünde, and the name of its director, Wernher von Braun, confirmed his hypothesis, a theory that had first raised a titter of merriment in high places, and had now turned quickly to apprehension.

That Lovell had now been directed to report to some out-of-the-way map-reference for some ludicrous form of training, at this juncture, implied either urgent need of his services, or latent sadism on the part of higher authority. Lovell was not amused.

He was searching the bench top for some loose and evasive pieces of notebook, which were obviously defeating him, when the Establishment head came in. Henry Broadhurst, a man of mature years whose opinion of his own status in the scientific world was not shared by those that mattered, resented the young and brilliant Lovell. When Enrico Fermi and Robert Oppenheimer asked Broadhurst to release Lovell so that he could go to America and assist the team in Los Alamos, he immediately referred the request to Ministerial level with a firm indication of his own disapproval. The block had proved effective, and the request was never passed on to Lovell, who still remained unaware of it six months later. Broadhurst glanced at the lab blackboard, covered with equations and notes, cross-referenced and annotated for the assistant who would take over in Lovell's absence.

'Ah, Stephen. Weren't you supposed to be at the station at 7.15? It is now 7.12, you cannot possibly get there on time . . .'

'That train is always eight minutes late. Stop worrying. You will have to sit on Hayman, Henry . . . he's getting behind in his work. This file here is for Kitson.'

'Do you . . . er . . . know where you are going? How can we reach you if there is a problem?'

'If it is urgent I suggest you try Evans at Cardiff. He seems to be in on this one. And there are eight precipitate dishes in Lab 6 all to go to Ashurst for Mackenzie. They're for the oxidisation tests. We still can't stop that rust. The "B" team calculations are wrong. They left out the Holcroft factor which distorts the whole thing, and means melting-point is much lower. It would fall apart . . .'

'Have you been here all night?'

'There was a lot to straighten out. That's the bus passing. It is always two minutes ahead of schedule. I'll go now.'

Lovell walked across to the doorway, and fished out a small blue case from behind the door which he held up by way of explanation to Broadhurst, beamed vaguely, and hurried out to where his taxi was waiting patiently. Jack Stafford, who ran the local, clapped-out Chrysler 'airflow' saloon which served as Hackney vehicle, and wedding conveyance, as well as delivering fragile cases to the Establishment, sat on the wing of his once white car and watched Lovell come towards him carrying his case clutched to him. Mentally he thought to himself, 'What do you look like, chum? Your trousers are short, your case hasn't got a handle, and if I wasn't here to take you you'd never find the bleeding station. I don't know . . . nutcases, the whole lot of 'em!' But he said nothing, smiled, touched his trilby, and opened the door for Lovell. He always cut it fine, this one did. Have to put his foot down.

2
PREPARATIONS

17 April: Masham Hall, Wilts
Gallagher had learned already that once Squires took over the training establishment at Masham it quickly became known to the staff and inmates as 'Dotheboys Hall'. He supposed the similarity between the name 'Squires' and Dickens's 'Squeers' together with the strenuous regime the colonel offered prompted the nickname. They talked as they walked from the office, out into the damp sunshine of early morning.

'I think we should make a start. It will take us an hour-or-so to drive to Salisbury Plain. We can have coffee in the Red Lion at Larkhill on the way. What d'you say?'

Gallagher smiled. 'As you've told me already more than once, you are OC for this part of the job. As you wish.'

Squires looked happy and stepped into his car. 'Good. I'm delighted we understand each other. Saves all those wasteful arguments I have to win.' Then he sat forward and shouted out of the open window.

'Sergeant! There are only eight persons drilling in the field. Why? There should be nine.'

'Young lady reported sick after ablutions, sir. Seems it's not a propitious part of the month, sir.'

Squires avoided his direct look that said nothing most blankly, and muttered as he sat back and prodded the driver with his stick. The car moved out from the Hall driveway, and crunched over the loose gravel that led down to the guard post at the perimeter. A WD sign advised prowlers that they stood a fair chance of being shot if they snooped about. It was going to be a long day but at least the weather appeared clement.

Westbury, Wilts
As almost all station name-boards had been removed in 1940 at the same time as signposts in the lanes, and any direction-giving or implying notice was obliterated, it was necessary for travellers to keep their ears open and to stare out of train carriage windows at any railway personnel who could be seen to open his mouth.

'Westbury! Westbury!' was the intended sound. What needed to be deciphered was the drawn-out 'Wezbrie' emitted round a mouthful of sorrel, chewed by the solitary porter/guard as he stood and looked along the length of the short train.

The only other person on the platform was a red-faced sergeant, Moody by name if not by nature, whose erect posture should have told recruits a great deal when they descended from the local train and hovered uncertainly. The clip-board was held stiffly before him, and boots, shiny-black, placed in something like a ballet dancer's fifth position, head held high as if sniffing the odour of green recruits to be selected and knocked into shape.

'Green travel-warrants this way, please. Travel-warrants only.' He nudged bewildered civilians into the somnolent clutches of the railway staff, and kept his eyes keenly aware of the equally-bemused young people stepping onto the platform, holding papers and warrants before them. He sighed to himself, 'Dear, oh Lor! another lot of half-baked juvenile delinquents. Why do I get them?'

'This way, please.' He checked off the names on his list from the warrants: two missing. 'Now, outside in the station forecourt is suitable transport. You are to take part in a small exercise which is part of your selection course. You will be dropped off at intervals en route, and you will make your way unaided to the point of rendezvous, known to us as the "RV". The course is sufficiently marked to channel you through certain obstacles and devices to test your reactions. You will be observed at all times. The course is code-named "Dickens", and will be clearly marked as such. You are warned not to stray off the course, as the area surrounding is live-mined, and other areas are part of the artillery range, and you couldn't 'arf come a cropper!'

'Now follow me, if you please, to board the transport.'

They all trooped out dutifully after the quick-marching Sergeant Moody to where a battered, small, country bus stood waiting.

'Put that bloody cigarette out, driver! Not on the deck, laddie, pick it up! pick it up! This way, please, ladies and gentlemen.'

Solange Rohr wore her Free French battletop and beret, and spoke to him, quietly voicing a question they all wanted to ask.

'Sergeant. Can you tell us, please. Is it to be one of those tests that uses gunfire to simulate the real thing?'

'It certainly is, ma'am. Shellfire from the artillery, small-arms fire, as well as firecrackers and previously laid explosions to simulate the real thing. Oh yes, indeed! I might also warn you that the last part of the course is unmarked, and you will have to cross an area in which there is a combined-operations exercise in progress. You may see men charging with machine-weapons and fixed-bayonets, take no notice. Continue on your way to the rendezvous point.'

'Which you call the RV. Yes, we know.'

Lovell had spoken with cynical and bored irritation that they were to be subjected to what were, in his eyes, puerile boy-scout games, but if the sergeant understood the inflection he gave no sign.

'The ammunition used will be live, sir, but I shouldn't worry too much about it. We usually do this at night.'

He slapped the side of the bus as he stepped on after the last passenger, and the vehicle chugged and juddered out of the station yard.

As the bus moved away Captain Nigel Macaulay stepped out from the booking-hall, and looked urgently about him. An army jeep with pennant sped to his feet, and stopped with a jerk. The perky ATS driver beamed at him expectantly.

'Where in hell have you been? I haven't all the time in the world.'

The girl looked highly indignant, as well she might, for she had done her job to the letter.

'There was a military bus waiting, hanging about for stragglers like you, I should think. What was I supposed to do? Advertise your defection?'

'Yes, all right, all right! Did you get the stuff?'

The slightly irritated head indicated the rear seat on which lay a hard-board, webbing-strapped case bearing the label of a well-known London theatrical costumier. Macaulay grabbed it, and made for the station loo. When he emerged several minutes later it was as a full-blown Brigadier, displaying all the scarlet flashes of Staff, plus a chestful of medal-ribbons, which did not altogether match his obvious youth if one cared to look more closely.

Anyone boasting the First World War ribbons that shone so garishly amid the others could not possibly have been in his mid-twenties, but, then, who really does examine ribbons unless bored to death by some cocktail party where the wretched things are flaunted before the eyes? He leapt into the rear of the jeep with the case, now accommodating his legitimate uniform, and ordered his driver to put her foot down and make for the plain map-reference.

The Red Lion, Larkhill, Wilts

Squires led the way through the ornately-carved, dark-oak entrance into the faded damask of the lounge, and stashed his headgear on a neighbouring seat as Gallagher sat down by the coffee table.

'It's never been my practice to deny myself a few creature comforts whatever the circumstances, Gallagher. Lord knows we get few enough of them!' He glanced up as an elderly waiter with whisps of grey about his ears shuffled up to the table and smiled egregiously.

'I seem to remember your name was Charles . . .'

The waiter nodded a smarmy agreement, which would no doubt have been forthcoming to any reasonable Christian name offered by a customer with the right accent, and no one could deny that Squires's accent was impeccable, with Charterhouse and Balliol etched into every syllable.

'Good. Coffee for two, and I want some of those little scones your chef keeps for favoured customers. Shall we say half-a-dozen? No, don't go away!' Squires brought a silver hip-flask from his pocket, and handed it over. 'Fill this up with the best Scotch you can find in the bar, there's a good fellow. Thank you.'

Charles, or whatever his name was, toddled off to execute his orders, and Squires returned to Gallagher. 'The coffee here's no better than wartime permits. I really come here for the buns. Awfully good! Can't think how they manage it these days.' He cocked a considering eye at his companion.

'You're very quiet this morning. Hardly said a word all the way down. Everything all right?'

Gallagher made a wry face and sighed. 'Yes, no problem. Just wondering if I made the right choices for my team. It rather matters.'

Squires himself sighed and looked paternally tolerant before speaking as to a wayward child.

'What exactly are you getting this team together for?' His tone was schoolmasterish, and he held up one finger.

'To train them to be adequate sabotage agents, to destroy a particular enemy target that cannot be destroyed any other way.'

'Squires' finger came down and a second one shot up.

'Are you sure you know all about the target that it is possible to know at this stage?'

'All that is possible . . . yes.'

The second finger was withdrawn and a third took its place of elevation.

'I assume you hand-picked these people yourself . . .'

'Yes.'

'Then I can't think what you are worrying about.' And his expression said QED. 'If your chosen few can't work out the map sent to them, if they cannot surmount a few obstacles when they know full well they are on their best behaviour and under test, then they are not the people for us, and I have no time to waste on training them. You will have chosen badly, and I shall expect you to commit hara-kiri by sundown. Ah! Here's our bun-feast. Good man, Charles! I imagine that will cover everything.'

His lordly manner as he placed thirty shillings before the waiter brooked no contradiction, though it was more than adequate.

The jeep stopped. Macaulay studied the map, and worked out how to get onto a perimeter road that would lead them round to the exercise RV with as little contact as possible, but he was well aware that the military presence was not going to advertise itself, and he had to be on his toes.

'How do I look, luv?'

'Just like the real thing, darling. A shorter hair-cut might help, but then I suppose Staff can get away with anything.'

'When you finally drop me will you get the hell out of it as fast as you can? Drop this lot back onto Sammy.'

The girl sighed, and glanced in the driving mirror at the counterfeit brigadier. 'I don't know why I let myself be talked into this. We could both end up on a very nasty charge.'

Macaulay grinned into the mirror, and made a kissing mouth. 'You love it, sweetheart. Why not admit it? You haven't had so much fun since you joined up. What time have you got?'

'10.26, better start moving.'

The jeep pulled away and turned off the road across heath terrain into the trees.

About one mile further away the old bus drew to a halt, and the red face of Sergeant Moody appeared above the front seat next to the driver.

'Right, ladies and gents, this is where we start to drop you off, one at a time. I have to remind you that you are not to disclose your true identity, but must use the nicknames you have been issued with. Right, sir.' This last with eyes directed at Cameron. 'You first. Leave your kit in the bus.'

The moment Cameron's feet touched the ground the bus shot forward again in a series of jerks and coughs, and continued down the road amid the thick foliage of the plain outskirts.

Cameron looked about him and moved out of sight of the road. Then he checked his map against a small, army-issue button-compass fished from his pocket. Once oriented he made his way north-west into the thickets, and continued until, in a clearing, he found the first 'Dickens' sign and an arrow indicating the route.

Wilson was the next to be dropped, then Solange, Simone Portales, and Sally Birkett. Stephen Lovell had held his cool for longer than even he had expected, but inwardly he was fuming. This sort of thing was not for him. It was, in his eyes, puerile, time-wasting, and utterly without point. He had not left Crowthorne with fifty urgent problems unsolved to play boy-scouts in the middle of Wiltshire.

'Right, sir, if you please.'

Lovell turned to face him squarely, and spoke quietly and firmly – there was a tremble in his voice that he could not conceal.

'I have been ordered to report to a special unit for special reasons. Not play boy-scout wide-games. I expect to be taken to the entrance, Sergeant, so that I can get on with what I am supposed to do.'

The Sergeant had had shirkers before, and didn't think much of them. 'I have my orders. This is where you get down.'

Lovell knew he was not going to win this. He was miles away from anywhere, and until he could find some superior authority he was not going to make his protest felt. He gritted his teeth, and stepped down from the bus, which pulled away instantly leaving him in the silent April woods. The beech trees were just beginning to unfurl their gorgeous green leaves. Bluebells were not yet in flower, but were showing their leaves.

Wilson was one who had not thought to bring a compass, but his sense of direction was, like most seamen's, highly developed, and he soon found himself moving between 'Dickens' signs.

Squires' car turned into the leafy lane traversed by the bus not ten minutes since, and he pulled up.

'I'm dropping you here. This is an exercise to test and observe. I think you should observe your own team yourself, don't you?'

'I had assumed there would be the usual battery of observers reporting progress to central control: yourself, I imagine. Or is that not the way any more?'

'Quite accurate, old boy, but I do think you should be *with* them. They're *your* team, Hugh.'

Gallagher looked at Squires, and nodded. It was a timely reminder that in this sort of work one led from the front. Squires had again shown himself to be right and thorough. Gallagher appreciated that, and found fault with himself that he had been mentally content to let them do it on their own. The effort and irritation of the obstacle course would chastise him for the omission, and he would, he knew, be that much closer to them, and they to him, if he was seen to do everything that they did. He set off at a trot, to catch up in case he was too separated. Squires let in his clutch, and turned the car back to circumnavigate the area. He crossed the only intersection thirty seconds after a pennanted jeep bearing a Staff Brigadier and driver had roared into the exercise area.

Squires had done this course many times, and had worked out his own routine, which amused the uninitiated and savoured of the colonel's eccentricity, but was actually totally practical. It meant to encourage a proper frame of mind in all working in the tests – seriousness of purpose that was demonstrable, and enough humour to dispel irritations. Squires was, without doubt, a highly competent trainer of special people. One who managed not to cross the armed forces in doing his job. He was about the only one who did not.

The jeep squealed to a stop as an armed guard stepped out from the shrubbery and held up his hand.

'I'm sorry, sir, but this is an exercise area.'

'I *am* aware of that, Corporal. I am GSO Plans, Southern District. I am on my way to exercise RV.'

The corporal guard looked decidedly unhappy. 'But sir, I have orders to let no one through. . . .'

Macaulay bristled in what he fondly imagined was the manner of snotty Brigadiers, none of whom he had ever met face-to-face. He sensed he was doing the right thing as he instinctively disliked himself in so doing.

'Then Corporal, someone has forgotten to tell you about me. I have my instructions from General Roberts. Here is my ID. Now drive on, girl, we are getting late.'

The corporal saluted nervously, and stood back to permit the jeep to proceed. Why the hell should he stick his neck out? These Staff pricks could be real bastards when they wanted to be and he didn't know the officer's name anyway.

Macaulay felt himself glow with success as he muttered to his driver.

'Nice and easy, darling, no sudden moves. I think we carried that off rather well, don't you?'

The girl glanced into her driving-mirror, admitting privately to herself that he had done it 'rather well', but had no intention of giving him the added satisfaction of her approval.

Elsewhere the members of the team were finding their way towards the target area, subtly channelled into a relatively narrow bottle-neck by well-placed 'Dickens' signs, and by even better-placed warning signs, red and glaring, that 'Out-of-bounds' areas bordered them on both sides, that minefields abounded, and that the proximity of artillery ranges was to be borne in mind. Little by little the course became noisy, and – apparently – dangerous, and their progress was speeded up by the injection of adrenalin into their bloodstreams. Little by little, almost imperceptibly, the mayhem increased, heightened and made terribly personal by the explosions, rattles of machine-gun fire, repeating fire-crackers, etc., that shocked them at every turning. The dreaded whistle of bullets passing overhead implied the truth of the warning that ammunition was live. It made the pulse race, without actual necessity, for the live ammo was far above their heads. The explosions were laid and triggered by the Observers, who seemed to inhabit every other bush, and were distinguishable by the 'Observer' flash on the sleeveband, and by the black woollen cap they wore. Most squatted in the shrubbery and made their notes on clip-boards, but every quarter mile, or near a particularly virulent hazard, an Observer would sit on a folding seat with an RT set by his side reporting in the progress of the contestants.

That progress was relayed to the Rendezvous Point selected by Squires. There he had parked his vehicle next to the NAAFI wagon that awaited the successful contestants who managed to complete the course. The RV was an elderly cricket hut, left over from the days in the first decade of the century, when Imber village was inhabited by people who chose to play the local teams from Westbury and environs on the long summer afternoons before the world lost its innocence.

Its white painted exterior hardly covered the evidence of rapid decay, and its overgrown verandah had to be cleared every time Squires ran one of his exercises. Inside there were two rooms. One was large – the old pad-room with shuttered window overlooking the pitch out front, and a back room once used for personal gear, and bags, and what-not . . . now totally occupied by woodlice, spiders, and fungus that was making heavy inroads upon the tongue-and-grooved panelling of the walls.

Squires' RT Operator had already set up his equipment and impedimenta in the usual place. Squires looked about him.

'Have you seen my tea chest, Saunders?'

'It's outside, sir. I'll bring it in.'

'It's quite all right. You stick to your box-of-tricks. I'll fetch it myself. Are you operational?'

'Yes, sir.'

As if to prove the statement the speaker spluttered into audible activity.

'Control, please. Cadbury-Four to Control. Are you receiving, over.'

'Control to Cadbury-Four. Receiving you, over.'

'Sergeant Adlard reports six persons already on course, two latecomers joined at 10.53 hours. Major Gallagher proceeding with first batch.'

'Message received. Over and out.'

Ellen Robinson wondered what in God's name she had let herself in for in joining this team. Her application for Special Duties was intended to apply to Wireless Operating, encoding, ciphering, and generally being intelligently cooperative. She had not signed to join the Commandos! She was fit, had always been, and was determined to remain so, but she was pushing thirty-four and that did seem a little late in the day to start this sort of thing. A quick sidelong glance at the three other girls had told her enough.

They were young and active, still with the bloom on the cheek, and to add insult to injury, they were pretty. Not that Ellen wasn't, but it was a nice face and a useful figure. She was no sex goddess. If she had only thought to bring a compass! So far the route was well marked; so far the obstacles had not been daunting, but what lay ahead? And her watch told her that time was running out.

As she turned the bend in the wooded avenue she saw the reddish hair of Solange drop from the wall across the course ahead. The choice was a sloping plank, or a knotted rope. That argued the opposite on the other side: easy UP, a rough ride DOWN, and vice versa. What the hell!

Squires sat in his chair and fingered the hip-flask on the tea chest that had served as his table for more than two years of such ventures. He sensed that this bunch about to come through to him could be important. He sensed Gallagher would prove to be so, and he knew damn well that the job was. *He* had to train them to be able to cope with almost any eventuality, scale almost any obstacle, keep in contact with base, do their respective team jobs, and return alive, well, and with whatever they were sent to recover. The failure rate among agents was high. Infiltration was everywhere, and allies had an unpleasant habit of being allied to the other side. More than half of all agents were 'turned', and Squires had no use for double-agents. They were probably worth their weight in gold to other departments, but that was how they measured it . . . in gold. Tim Squires was old fashioned enough to want *his* people to do it for King and Country, as he had, as his father had, and his father's father. It had a ring of truth about it all the way back to Greece and Sparta, and he liked things to be well established. It lent substance. He checked his watch and glanced over his shoulder at the RT Operator who was taking down notes from the quiet incoming messages.

'I think it is time to alert the Artillery to stand by. Put the RT on volume and pilot-speaker.'

The swish of sound and HT came in loud and clear with the verbiage of incoming calls, and Squires cocked an ear to decipher and separate, as the operator turned the handle of the field telephone and made contact with Wentworth Battery.

Gallagher saw Wilson ahead as he jogged into the bottle-neck between the trees and gorse. He saw the pitfall and the camouflage about the same time that Wilson stumbled and dropped into it with a yell of surprise, accompanied by the rattle of fire-crackers and two puffs of explosions to his left.

'Look where you're going, man! It's no good just being awake. You have to be aware!'

He had hardly finished his sentence when his feet were whisked from under him, and he was jerked into the air, and suspended upside-down, his head three feet above the ground, swinging like a pendulum as he mouthed some abuse at his own stupidity.

Wilson crawled out of his hole and saw him dangling, and started to grin. It made his day. Once out of the pit he ambled across to the hanging man and spoke innocently.

'I didn't quite catch what you said, sir.'

'All right, smart-arse, I asked for that. Cut me down.'

Wilson looked vague. 'I don't actually have a knife on me, sir.'

Gallagher exploded. 'Then use mine, blast you!' He threw it on the ground beneath him, fuming and gritting his teeth. Wilson cut him down sharpish, but the gaff was logged by the hidden observer, also with a smile of complicity.

Gallagher set off after him, and soon passed the seaman by virtue of taking a short cut through the forbidden area.

Which was what Lovell decided to do when he saw the obstacles piling up ahead. Within seconds he was aware of the red pennants and the raked area and stopped in his tracks. He looked down at his feet and slowly sank to his haunches, fished out a heavy knife that he used for most things, in and out of the lab, and started probing the earth in a highly professional manner. In forty seconds he had found it and was extracting it when a voice made him turn.

'That's a bloody minefield, man! Don't move!'

But Lovell had quickly and expertly revealed, and removed the flat, pancake anti-personnel mine and was looking at it in his hand.

'It's a standard Mark III S-type. I designed it. Catch.'

Nonchalantly he tossed the mine at the corporal who had challenged him, and now dropped his rifle to catch the mine sailing through the air towards him. He went cold and caught it clumsily.

'You're a bloody fool, mate. That could have been a live one.'

Lovell approached him and lifted the mine from his cradled arms, and threw it over his shoulder as far as he could. The explosion rocked them both and sent earth showering through the air, followed by a second explosion presumably activated by the first.

'Jesus!'

'It *was* a live one, corporal. I thought it probably was. Now can you please take me to your commanding officer. I've had enough of wandering in the wilderness.'

Lovell was taken to a staff tent and placed under guard much to his annoyance. After twenty minutes a junior officer appeared and loftily enquired his identity, his reason for being on WD property, and generally behaved as if it were Hitler's favourite spy he held in the voluminous tent. Lovell had had enough, and lost his temper finally.

'Look! I was *told* to bloody-well report here! For God's sake! Are all you military people cretins? Can you read? At 11.30 hours. That is fast approaching, thanks to being cooped up by half-wits. The map-reference is within this WD perimeter. What am I supposed to do?'

The Lieutenant eyed him with cold, heavy-lidded eyes, and

disclaimed all knowledge of any RV, any appointment, and made the whole business sound highly unlikely. A closer observer than the indignant Lovell would have noted that an RT set behind them had been switched on and was set to transmit, he might also have become aware that no one was behaving exactly by the book, there was just 'something', most easily suggested by the slight twinkle of amusement in the eyes of the tent guard.

Just over one-and-a-half-miles to the north a moderately annoyed Colonel Squires was cocking his ear to the RT set behind him, and deciding that Stephen Lovell was a bloody fool, quite useless to them for training, and a protest would have to be made.

'All right, Dobson, tell them to get off the air. I want this chap grilled for half-an-hour, and made generally uncomfortable, then he is to be delivered to me at the Hall about tea-time.'

Squires looked at his watch. 'Wentworth to stand-by. Foskett to stand-by.' He watched the second hand move step-by-step towards the full minute. 'Open fire . . . exercise to commence.'

The RT relayed the command to 'Wentworth' battery eighteen miles away, and to Combined Ops command 'Foskett'.

The vagaries of their progress had brought Cameron, Solange, and Sally Birkett into close proximity. Ten yards away, in the bushes, unknown to them, or the observers he had circumnavigated, Gallagher crouched and watched his flock about to make their final dash. They had all stopped to consider their position for they had reached the unmarked area. Ahead of them stretched open scrubland, undulating, and marked with shell-holes and craters of earlier days.

About half-a-mile ahead the slight rise of ground made it impossible to see any sign of an RV, but Cameron's compass was in no doubt as to the direction, and the map was enough to confirm their position. When the swoosh and whistle of shells overhead made them duck and look at each other, followed by the near-sounding explosions, and then a second later by the 'brumph' of distant artillery, they all dropped to the ground, and covered their heads. By now their nerves were stretched, the adrenalin was flowing, and reactions were instantaneous, and, if anything, over-stated.

Earth showered down upon them as the barrage increased.

There was what they thought was a many-throated shout, but it could have been a trick of nature. When they raised their heads the whole thing had changed dramatically. Smoke was everywhere. Flashes and explosions – unknown to them, almost all 'planted' – were all round. Cameron knew that he had to get through that fast-growing smoke fog or he would be lost quicker than he could say 'Carnoustie', and made a sudden dash for the way ahead. Solange and Sally Birkett reacted by following suit, and were quickly enfolded in swirls of cordite fumes and smoke. All hell seemed to have broken loose.

As Solange ran forward, ducking and swerving as instinct dictated, she found herself moving among shadows. Shades of men in battledress and balaclavas, charging forward, rifles and bayonets at the ready . . . seconds later a small squad fell upon her, swore and hastily avoided her. The sound of machine-gun bursts was everywhere. She stumbled and staggered on her way until she realised her direction was constantly changing, and this would get her nowhere.

She fumbled in her battle-top pocket for the button compass given to her by Jacques, her dead fiancé, not long before he was shot down. It was his RAF issue escape-kit compass which she had kept for sentimental reasons. It was now to come into its own. Blessedly it worked, and she realigned herself and her movement forward, looking round to reassure the more nervous Sally, but Sergeant Birkett was nowhere to be seen.

At the cricket hut Squires watched the gradual increase of smoke with satisfaction. Wind was encouraging today, there would be a good positive result. The door in the rear of the hut swung open as a salvo shook the wooden structure. A small-statured man emerged looking both concerned and surprised.

'What the 'ell's going on?'

Squires spun round to see George Macklin dusting himself down in the doorway.

'Who the devil are you, sir?'

'Name's Macklin. I was told to report 'ere.'

The RT Operator glanced at his clip-board.

'He's on the list, sir. Nickname "Choucas".'

Squires stared in evident irritation at the cockney in the cramped grey suit.

'What were you doing inside this hut, Mr Macklin? You aren't supposed to be here until eleven-thirty precisely.'

Macklin sauntered over to Squires, and brushed the white dust from his arm and shoulder.

'Came up last night. Kipped in the corner, and perishin' cold it was, too! Goin' to dodge all this caper, wasn't I? I knew there was somethin' not kosher.' He ducked instinctively as a swoosh overhead, or seemingly overhead, unnerved him. 'You quite sure we're out of range 'ere?'

'I guarantee it, Mr Macklin.'

'And if the Artillery aren't accurate?'

Squires looked at him in disbelief. 'The Royal Artillery not accurate!'

Clearly there was no room for such a doubt in Squires' mind. The possibility was unthinkable.

The sound of thudding boots reaching the wooden verandah made them all turn. Cameron burst in the doorway, and stood panting and gulping air, his face and uniform muddied and stained.

'Grive, reporting as ordered, sir.'

Squires beamed. 'Well done, Grive. Take a pew and a breather. We shouldn't have long to wait. Er . . . this is . . . er . . . Choucas.'

Cameron exchanged a reluctant nod with Macklin, irritated that he was not the first to arrive, unaware that Macklin had not completed the test at all, when the door opened again and Solange entered.

'Chardonneret . . . reporting for duty, sir.'

After watching his first charges move out into the 'battle zone' Gallagher moved quickly to the marked route to see how the remainder were coping. Well enough, as it turned out, and not far behind, but all apprehensive of the mayhem that lay ahead. He remembered his own first attempt at the course, more or less tame by comparison, for, though the obstacle route was similar as are all obstacle courses, no one had had the imagination, or sadism, or whatever, to top it with the little touch of crossing a battlefield in the middle of a battle. Real or simulated, the effect was the same if you weren't prepared for it. He had to hand it to Squires. It was a good touch. One touch he was missing was the

what had befallen, were consumed with either anger or envy, and more than a little admiration.

They watched this pretending staff officer say something to his girl driver, a girl who responded with a blush of gratitude and accepted the kiss on the cheek with evident pleasure before she put the gears into reverse, turned, and drove off.

Squires drew everyone's attention by pointing to the NAAFI wagon at the side of the hut. 'If you all look behind you, you will see our NAAFI presence. I suggest you take advantage of the delights it has to offer before the bus picks you up at 13.00 hours. If you aren't on it I shall have you posted as deserters. Major . . . will you come with me in my car, please.'

Squires stalked away, and left Gallagher to glance round his team and smile. 'Well done, all of you.'

The sound of relief was obvious once he had turned his back and was moving towards the car. All of them were exhausted, shattered, and just plain glad the whole thing was over, even if a tiny sense of apprehension at what lay ahead was rooted inside them.

Masham Hall, Wilts

The bus entered the brick gateway and chugged down the drive towards the old house. The occupants looked with interest at what was to be their home for an unspecified time, noted the guards, the WD exclusion notice, the teams working-out in playing-fields, and were not slow to take their gear when ordered to dismount. Sergeant Moody was precise as ever, and expected his charges to obey instantly even if their officer-cadet status put him at a disadvantage of protocol.

'New arrivals report at the desk inside the main 'all. No discussion, if you please. No one to leave the entrance 'all. You will be shown to your quarters after registration formalities. No smoking if you please, and let's 'ave some quiet!'

One by one they moved into the main building carrying their kitbags or cases. In the entrance hall they found a large area obviously now used for multi-purpose activities, for it held a rest area and bar, as well as reception desk. To Ellen and Macaulay it held the same atmosphere, the same flavour, as the beginning of term in their old schools. Even down to the notice board peppered with bright, pristine notices.

There was no such recollection for George Macklin. Schooldays were something he chose to forget. 'Stepney Boys' had no saving grace to warm his sentiments, assuming Macklin had any sentiments to give away. He felt out-of-it already. Not his place. Not his mates. It wasn't 'him'. These toffee-nosed berks, and the bleeding officers, and all that stuff, saluting, 'sir' and 'ma'am' . . . load of old cobblers!, and it made him nervous, ill at ease. He lit up a cigarette and tried not to look conspicuous until an ash-tray was thrust in front of his nose by the omnipresent Sergeant Moody.

'No smokin' in the 'all before five, if you please, sir. Colonel doesn't like it.'

The voice was firm, the ash-tray demanding, and Macklin stubbed out his cigarette without even a mutter.

'Where can I get a cuppa, then?'

'Tea is served at five, sharp, sir. In the mess, or right 'ere. As you prefer, sir.'

He marched smartly away to where a corporal looking harassed peered at his sheet of paper through spectacled eyes.

'Next.'

Cameron put down his bag, and walked to the stairs where another corporal, who they were later to know as the mess steward, led him to Colonel Squires' inner sanctum at the head of the first flight of stairs.

Gallagher and Squires saw jointly to their recruits, made a few pertinent comments upon their report-sheets from the exercise, and stressed that from that moment they would be known only by their nickname.

'It is the practice of this establishment to group their teams undergoing training into composite headings which determine the nicknames. As you will have observed all your team has been issued with the names of birds – French names, that is. "Grive" in your case. That is "thrush" in English. The Birds will train as a unit. The "fish" are doing their stint of Parachute training at this moment . . . those you can see outside in PT kit are the "Mammals". I shall now require you to sign the Official Secrets Act. That leaflet tells you the import of that signing. Read it.'

'I have already signed it, sir.'

'Oh, where?'

'Minchinghampton, sir, before I went on an exercise, sir.'

'Right, give your nickname to the desk-sergeant, and he will issue a billet number. The corporal will show you to your quarters. Tea is at five.'

Cameron was followed by Ellen Robinson, then the others, one by one.

Macaulay waited in line at the foot of the stairs behind Wilson. They both turned as a sudden clatter of feet brought a squad of trainees in PT kit into the hall and through into the dormitory area.

'I say . . . they look a bit hard-worked, don't they?'

Wilson smiled ruefully at Macaulay who had made the comment. 'I expect I shall be agonisingly stiff for a week. You don't get much exercise on board ship, you know.'

'No potted biographies, sir, if you please!'

Sergeant Moody seemed to be everywhere, as if simply passing by at the exact moment that required a comment. But Macaulay was showing definite interest in the two females standing together talking. Solange Rohr and Simone Portales were a very delectable pair, it had to be admitted, and Macaulay was mentally weighing up his chances. 'I wonder if they object to fraternising?'

Wilson followed his gaze, and smiled with masculine understanding, making a face of distinct approval. 'I think they're our lot. Brighten the working day, I shouldn't wonder.'

Outside in the drive a military police jeep crunched to a sudden halt. The MP next to the driver got down, humped Lovell's case out of the rear seat, and dropped it onto the drive with a resounding crunch as Lovell, silently fuming and worn out by sheer indifference, climbed out and glowered at the Hall entrance. The jeep roared away and skidded to a U-turn, throwing up shingle onto Lovell's chest. He sighed, and turned towards the entrance, picking up his bag. When he was eventually shown into Squires' office he was faced with two po-faced officers who obviously had as much desire to have him join them as he had to do so.

'Mr Lovell, your arrival at the rendezvous point left something to be desired. I appreciate that you are a civilian, and that we can't expect the same natural reaction from you as from those already half-trained in this work . . .'

'I would like to sit down.'

Squires leant forward and spoke across Gallagher.

'The Major is your Group Leader, Lovell. Quite apart from military rank and discipline I should have thought it elementary courtesy to remain standing while he is.'

Lovell spoke quietly, not giving in to his already worn out anger. 'I had a highly-technical job to complete before I reported for this shindig. I haven't been to bed since Tuesday. I *am* rather tired and I had no intention of exhausting myself further by playing your infantile games out there. I'm here because I have been ordered to be here, or rather, intimidated. Can we simply get on with whatever it is I am supposed to do.'

'I did know you were tired. I am sorry, I had forgotten.' Gallagher was genuinely contrite. He knew Lovell had worked against the clock. 'Mr Lovell, I don't want you here any more than you want to be here. You are – by your own admission – unsuitable. But I need your expertise, and you need *our* expertise to remain alive while doing the job. We're interdependent. We think this job will save thousands of lives. It seems to me to be worth doing, if only for that reason.'

Lovell did not reply. Squires brought an envelope, cut open, onto the desk top.

'I understand you gave this to our driver to post.' Lovell's ire bristled once more. He recognised his letter, and was naturally furious.

'I'm afraid I can't let you do that sort of thing. If you write letters they will reach my adjutant for censoring. We have to be security-conscious, Lovell. Surely you were subject to that even in your laboratory?'

'It is nothing to do with this place! I haven't been here long enough to know anything! It's an afterthought. Instructions for the poor bastard who is taking over my job while I am here.'

'Indeed. I have already checked it. I was going to post it for you, anyway, but not in this vicinity, Mr Lovell. Thank you. I suggest you have an early night.'

Lovell did not like Squires' patronising tone. Nor did he like being cornered out of loyalty, or humanitarian motives, or anything below the belt. But he was too tired to argue.

After he had gone Gallagher glanced at Squires.

'I think we may be having trouble with that gentleman.' Gallagher sighed and shrugged. 'He was wished on me. Apparently we need his expertise.'

'Wasn't really talking about his non-military aspect. Unless I'm mistaken I guess that our technical expert has a chip on his shoulder. Red-brick rather than Oxbridge, and that's a tricky one to get over. A devout socialist, I'm sure, and there's no cure for that except decades of reality.'

'Cynic!'

'Realist, old boy. Shall we push the boat out? More than an hour before dinner.'

The two men sat back and enjoyed the house Scotch, both quietly mulling over the group they had just interviewed, weighing their instinctive reactions to people they hardly knew but in whom they would, much too quickly, have to place total trust and reliance.

18 April – 16 May

The first days came as a shock to most of them. Settling in was not part of their curriculum. There was no time. They jumped in at the proverbial deep-end, and floundered as best they could, with whatever help was to hand. Their instructors proved to be competent, hard-working and totally merciless. Squires gave them an inaugural lecture to put them in the picture, to indicate briefly the ground they would be expected to cover, to emphasise the aspects of security that were vital for any training establishment dealing with potential agents, and the dangers and possibilities of infiltration by enemy agents set upon breaking security by anticipation. By joining the agents in the trainee stages they could, if unrecognised, prove terribly costly to agents and their *réseau* contacts once planted in enemy-held territory. By 1944 SOE, MI6, MI9, OSS, and other clandestine organisations were only too conscious of the cost to be paid against one moment's slackness of security. There was little doubt that Britain was winning the 'spy' war. The 'XX' committee had

MI5 so tightly organised that enemy agents within Britain still at liberty were very thin on the ground. But then one had to make a mental balance to allow the curious fact that the German Abwehr were neither pro-Nazi, nor deeply enthusiastic about the war at all, and never had been. Admiral Canaris, the Head of the Abwehr, was even thought – in some quarters – to be actively working FOR the Allies and against his own nation. Those who knew the Admiral personally discounted such a course. Canaris was an enemy of Hitler and his party. So much was common knowledge. But he was not, and never would be, a traitor to his Fatherland.

Thus it was made abundantly clear to the trainee intake that security was, and was to be, a great part of their daily life. They would live and breathe it in such a fashion that they instinctively weighed and considered every word they heard, as well as those they uttered. They became attuned to the tiny booby traps painstakingly laid for them, gradually increasing in effectiveness, until they noticed each crease on their bedcover that was not there when they left their quarters in the morning, each inoffensive piece of string or thread, or fold in the carpet that betokened the possibility of a fire-cracker, a whoopee-cushion, or something more lethal. Within ten days their awareness had become knife-edged, yet in such a way that their nerves were, if anything, stronger rather than frayed. As a group they acknowledged that Squires knew his job, that Dotheboys Hall lived up to its reputation if not its nickname. They became used to their own nicknames, and almost forgot anything that happened to them before they were admitted into Masham. They never spoke about their past, and no one ever asked. If something accidentally slipped out it was pounced upon, and the offender slipped a day's pay into the 'Offender's Box' to buy a round of drinks at the end of the week.

They found they were not the only trainees at Masham Hall. Two other teams were half-way through their training. They were the 'Mammals' and 'Artists'. The 'Fishes' had gone. Our 'Bird' team got used to 'Hippo' and 'Baboon' just as easily as they addressed 'Rembrandt' and 'Picasso' and remembered their own 'Rossignol', 'Hibou', 'Choucas'. But there was a difference, they had names in French. That meant, by common consensus, that they were to be operational in France, whereas the others were not yet designated. They recognised that their course was shorter than the standard one, by at least four weeks, and that they were regarded in a sense as 'special', for they were being trained for a specific job, an urgent job, and – by definition – a dangerous one.

It was on the Saturday morning that the dispatch rider brought his signal to Gallagher. It was from Gwillim's office and marked both 'Urgent' and 'Top Secret'. Gallagher was with Squires when it was handed in. He read it aloud.

'Re.FZG-76. Present estimates indicate a production feasibility of two thousand man-hours within an area cost of £300 sterling. In the event of launching sites multiplying in the immediate future it is likely that Southern Britain will have to face a barrage of more than one thousand missiles per day. Stockpiling is estimated to have reached over twenty thousand missiles. Photo-recce stills of suspected launching platforms enclosed. You can see the burn marks from trial launchings. PR and ground-intelligence have uncovered nine launching sites. It would be reasonable to assume that this represents something like one-third of the true figure. French Intelligence reports the Guidance Mechanism on the FZG-76 is now perfected, and the first batch is expected from the factories once tooling is complete, estimated time twenty-eight days. Can we advance?'

Gallagher looked up slowly at Squires, whose facial reaction was equally grim. 'Well? Can we?'

Squires shook his head. 'Not by one day, Major. Not if you want to achieve what we intend, not if you want your team to survive. I'm not being stuffy, Hugh. I do know my job, as I've said before. We're already at short time. The answer is "no".'

The two men eyeballed for some moments. Gallagher sensed the desperate urgency of the situation. He had, after all, seen the missiles. For him they existed. But he knew Squires by now. He knew he was experienced and level-headed. He knew he was right.

'Shall I send the refusal signal . . . or will you?'

There was, of course, more to it than simply replying that the team was not yet fully trained. If one was concerned with merely getting the job done and not worried about the return trip. If one was not faced with the obstacle course that the German defences presented, if loss of life did not matter at all, then it might just be feasible to go in with a half-trained mob and do something to hold up the production and firing potential. That is, of course, assuming one had a plan to start with. But it was a case of one bite at the cherry, and Gallagher did not have a plan! He had not yet devised a way of getting into the wretched place that would be totally unnoticed and allow sabotage from inside the complex itself. That was the way it had to be if anything substantial was to be achieved, and there were too many problems for an easy solution. The Germans knew it – they had made it so. Gallagher knew it – and he had to find the way round the problem. One that would work, and leave nothing to chance. There *was* only one bite at the cherry!

The days of training rolled past into weeks during which time the Frenchman, Paul Lamboit, joined the team having now fully recovered and regained the use of his leg. By the time they had completed the first part they were all fitter, had grown together as a team, and become bonded. They even found that they liked each other, and began to rely – implicitly – upon their fellows. The group had become a unit. Gallagher and Squires saw, and liked what they saw. They knew that the fining-down would break the group as a unit, and moved their tasks and exercises into smaller units, never the same group twice, never the same pair as permanent operatives. Macklin quickly overcame his feeling of being 'out of it', his inferiority complex evaporated, and for the first time in his life he knew what it was to belong to a family. People he cared for and trusted, not quite in the way that there was 'honour among thieves'. That was different. These people had become the only family he had ever known who gave him anything other than rebuffs and blows. The smell of being outside, contrasted so gratefully with HM Prisons, the ability to go and do as he wished. The knowledge that what he left lying about would be where he left it when he returned, was a new experience for Macklin. He found he liked it. Even Stephen Lovell overcame his initial objection to being forced from his environment, lifted from his laboratory, and thrust into war games that he instinctively mistrusted. He found that his bad temper subsided, his tiredness evaporated, and was replaced by physical weariness. His brain came alive again after being choked with problems. He even enjoyed the companionship. They were not boffins like him, they did not talk and think jargon, and the problems he had to surmount were not cerebral.

The others took to it all with varying degrees of aptitude. It became quickly obvious that Wilson, the Merchant Seaman, was not so quick in his reflexes as one might have hoped. It was possibly due to the years of slow-moving sea travel that had allowed him to become leisurely in his ways. His Morse and enciphering were faultless, but not fast. He showed aptitude for everything, but not ease. Sally Birkett was the same, good, but without edge.

Simone Portales, Solange Rohr, and Cameron headed the efficiency stakes. Solange showed herself to have remarkable aptitude for WT and encoding. Her speed was unusual, and her mind worked in all things with speed and balance. Ellen Robinson also showed her aptitude for WT, a general ability to cope, and improvisation that was instinctive and original. But it was Macaulay who shone in military improvisation. He had dash and invention, and Gallagher sensed that he would rapidly become his second-in-command.

But that was before they went to RAF Wutherton.

The Wutherton station was used as a stand-by operational station for transport aircraft, and offered parachute training facilities for both RAF personnel (when they had time to get any). Most crews went into combat without any, after all their chances in the night raids over Germany were not good. Many survived to be picked up by Evasion Lines and returned to the UK, and in those cases the parachutes had justified themselves, but the majority did not survive. So no one bothered all that much about training. But for Special Duties personnel, it did matter, and expertise in dropping was very much part of the training. It was at Wutherton that the first cracks began to show.

2 May 1944

Macaulay knew that he was in trouble as soon as he saw the wretched balloon. Jumping inside a hangar, with harness to 'hang' from, to lower in controlled motion, to feel secure in was one thing. To jump outside in open air was quite another. His instructor sensed the problem from the moment he got into the basket, and the captive balloon was hoisted. It was not high, somewhere round about 150 feet he reckoned, sitting back in the basket, deliberately not looking over the edge so that he had not counted the markers. He did not *know* how high he was up. It didn't matter. When the time came to take his position he had worked himself into a state of terror that only those afflicted with fear of heights truly understand. He jumped. The effort of will that it took was something he had to command, or face the shame of his fear. That, if anything, was more than he could accept, so he jumped. But the point registered, and at last Gallagher confronted him with it. Gallagher knew that he had lost his frontrunner. For Macaulay it was a moment of fighting for his place in the team, and he did so with his customary skill, using reason and persuasion that Gallagher had to admit were considerable. His verbal dexterity worked strongly in his favour, for if he was caught he would need everything he had to stay at liberty and alive. The Gestapo were not amateurs, nor were the Milice.

It was on the second day at Wutherton that a report was placed before Gallagher which was serious enough to cause him to go to London and see Colonel Gwillim. The subject of that report was Simone Portales. The observations were insignificant in themselves, and even put together were no more than circumstantial, but if security was to mean anything at all then Mademoiselle Portales, alias Rossignol, might – just possibly – be not quite what she seemed. Gwillim did not show overt concern at the report, for Gwillim never showed anything in his face. He approved the standard surveillance, suggested that the girl be given enough rope to hang herself if she had the mind to, and asked Gallagher some pertinent questions about his plan for getting into the German complex. Gallagher flannelled and avoided issues before he openly declared that, so far, he hadn't a clue how to get in, and the more he thought about it the less he thought it possible to make any entry other than that by the front door.

Gwillim was not impressed. He knew Gallagher, and had selected him for the job, but to be – at this stage in the operation – without any real watertight scheme for entry was in his opinion leaving it a little late.

Viardot was brought before Gallagher once more, and once more Gwillim lent him his office for the interrogation. It was about two-thirds through the night when Viardot said something that triggered off a thought in Gallagher's head.

'What air-shafts do you mean?'

'Those originally inserted by the French Army when they enlarged the quarry site in 1917. You don't really think the Germans have built all that in the last six months, do you? They are efficient and praiseworthy, but they are not magicians. The First World War ammo-dump was one of the biggest and most permanent in the Western Front sector. It was near enough, yet safe enough – one of the few things my country's military hierarchy ever got right.'

Gallagher eyed him. 'So, all you had to do was obtain a copy of the War Department plans of their ammo-dump and work out how to utilise it for the German war effort? Mmh. Yes, I see you used your brains, M'sieur. And highly suitable it turned out to be, did it not?'

Viardot seemed happy enough to talk about his achievement, even with a certain pride in his own expertise in the conversion.

'And where are those War Department plans now, M'sieur?'

Viardot looked at him, challenge in his eyes. 'That I am not prepared to tell you.'

Gallagher recognised that he would have to torture that information out of the Frenchman, and Gwillim would not countenance such a thing, even if Gallagher could bring himself to such an end. After the interrogation was concluded he went down the corridor and waited for Jacques Gran to turn up at his office, then pumped him.

'Where would they keep such plans, Jacques? I need to know. And quickly.'

Gran knew his way about the French colony in London,

without treading on the toes of the tall General who would most certainly have blocked him. The answers came in quicker than Gallagher expected.

'The plans were with the Department Surveyor in Amiens until the Germans requested them in 1943. They were not returned, but de Grouchy reports that they are held not by the Germans but in the Town Surveyor's office in Senlis, that is, in the Hôtel de Ville. The plans of the German alterations are held by the Todt Organisation, place unknown.'

Gran looked at Gallagher questioningly. 'D'you want de Grouchy to get them for you?'

'No, Jacques. Definitely not! We don't want anyone drawing attention to the place.'

He went back to Gwillim's office and laid the whole thing on the line. Permission was obtained to send in a team of his choice to winkle out the plans of the old complex, and the RAF alerted to play their part in the raid.

By the time Gallagher arrived back at Masham the team had also returned from their parachute training. Two things awaited him: the report on Portales, and the instructor's assessment on the trainees. Squires had read them both and was in no mood to accept additional surprises, such as the idea of a half-baked raid on the Town Hall in Senlis. It was the first real row they had together, and neither man enjoyed it. Both knew the other to have a sound argument, and both knew they were on a sticky wicket which was probably going to be whisked from under their feet anyway. It was Gwillim's phone call to say that he had laid on the RAF for the job that clinched the matter. Squires accepted it as a command, and immediately took what steps he could to ensure that all was as perfectly organised as possible. Once again Gallagher had to admit that Squires was not only a good trainer, he was one hell of a good officer, and would doubtless prove to be a very dependable friend.

The team parachuting assessment was no more than one might have expected, and no less. Attention was drawn to Macaulay's lack of enthusiasm for jumping, and the fact that he had surmounted his fears by sheer determination. The others were average to good, and there were no defaulters.

But the report on Simone Portales was another thing altogether. It was not concerned with her efficiency or lack of it. It was not an assessment of her worth as a potential special duties operator. It was a résumé of her reported activities over a four-week period, with a distinct inference drawn that there was a possible security risk in the girl, possibly much more.

Gallagher squinted at Squires as he put down the report. Squires had his own copy and had read it earlier. His face showed that he was concerned.

'What exactly are we talking about? What exactly is she being accused of?'

Squires sighed and made one of his faces. 'Not an awful lot, I must confess. She was spotted first by Corporal Moffat, who made a routine report that Rossignol had made an attempt to use an office phone for an outside call. It was nothing. Several have tried this over the years, but she persisted. She was observed, never mind by whom, re-entering the grounds of the Hall under the wire, possibly after using the box down the road. Then one or two things were recalled, for instance, she knew rather a lot about German Military behaviour.'

'She could have observed that in France.'

'Indeed. But she has taken to training like the proverbial duck takes to water, almost as if she had done some of it before. Her WT is first class, yet she has no apparent previous experience. Her unarmed combat was reported by Gidney as being unusually good.'

'If I had her sex appeal I would have learned to defend myself long ago.'

'Quite so. I see you are determined not to prejudge her. That is commendable. She took a Schmeiser to pieces and reassembled it in twenty-two seconds flat without ever having seen one before, so it is claimed. The Wutherton report is lengthy as I had her under special surveillance throughout. It is possibly significant. On May 3rd, 5th, 6th she made five telephone calls to a London number, we were not able to get anything other than the exchange. A Regent number. Those calls were made surreptitiously, with every intention of not being spotted.'

'All circumstantial. If you are trying to imply she is an enemy agent, she is not very adept or she would not have been spotted.

I agree there are grounds for suspicion. I agree we should keep an eye on her. But that is all I go along with. She's potentially the best operator I've got. I don't want to lose her, she could be invaluable.'

But Hugh Gallagher was not so sanguine as his manner implied. If there was any cause for doubt, however tenuous, he was bound to regard security as of paramount importance to the task in hand. He finalised the projected raid on the Senlis Town Hall. He had to have the old plans. He had to know if there was a tenable entry to the complex, because, on the surface as he saw it, the only other alternative was the front door, and it seemed unlikely that Jerry would make entry an easy matter. Gwillim heard him out and approved. His only enquiry was a tentative one asking if Gallagher thought he had enough of his team ready for an operation.

The matter of Portales was skimmed over until Gallagher said that he intended to take her as one of the team to attack the Hôtel de Ville. There the Colonel baulked, but Gallagher stood his ground.

'Look, sir. She'll be right under my nose where I can see her reactions. If she attempts to make contact with the enemy, then we can assume she is everything that is suspected of her, and she will be dealt with. If there is no ground for suspicion then I will strike off any unpleasant thoughts we may have had, and use her as the agent she so cries out to be. She's good. Believe me, sir, I've worked with a lot and I sense she has enormous potential.'

'On your head, Hugh.'

17 May

Following the parachute training, the group was divided into two squads, picked out by Gallagher himself. One group contained the people he intended to take to Senlis, unknown to them or their colleagues. They were given an imaginary task, following the training round Imber village – an evacuated village now part of the War Department's training area on Salisbury Plain – they were briefed and issued with kit, gear, and civilian clothing, exactly as they would be on a non-simulated mission. Then, one evening, Gallagher sent for Lamboit. He told him what they were about to do, and also that there was a suspicion about Portales, and that Lamboit was to go twenty-four hours ahead to Paris and contact a Clichy *réseau* who would know of Rossignol's 1939–1940 activities, and to check her out thoroughly. He would then liaise with them, the sabotage team, at de Grouchy's farm the following day. Lamboit accepted it without expression. He never said much to anyone.

He then called Solange into his office and informed her that the raid they were planning as an exercise was for real, and that she would be going ahead with Lamboit, leaving the next evening by Lysander.

She felt her heart suddenly pounding, and her stomach turned over. She knew the pallor of her cheeks would give something away, and tried to avoid his gaze. But Gallagher only smiled with the gentle, yet rather cheeky, smile that she liked so much.

'Don't worry about it. You're not on your own. You can do it, you know. And you're the best WT operator we've got. I need you.'

Somehow those three last words gave her the courage and the determination to accept and get on with it. When her absence was noted by the team a medical excuse was invented. Lamboit was not missed, except by Ellen Robinson, and a similar reason was given, which in his case was easily accepted. His leg still played up from time to time.

19 May

They piled into the Dakota with the same cheery banter they used on every exercise, not questioning that there were only five of them, that Sar'Major Gidney was not in evidence, but that Gallagher himself was taking part in the lark with them. They crossed the French coast shortly after eleven, and heard the first flak bursts with mild surprise.

'Bloody clowns! Can't they see it's a Dak?'

Cameron had no opinion of gunners, Ack-ack or straight artillery. Gallagher decided it was about time to tell them the truth.

'The job we're going on is the one you have been briefed for. There is one difference, however. This one is for real. That is France down there, and those shell-bursts were German flak.'

It was received with a certain disbelief and uneasy silence. Gallagher reassured them he was not pulling their legs, and then left them to simmer while he helped the dispatcher with the thermos of tea. No one spoke, and he sensed a new tension in the plane interior. He glanced quickly at Portales. She was pale and frowning, reacting as if something had been left undone that mattered. Macklin was gnawing the corner of his lip.

'Suddenly it's all happening. Am I here for the ride guv, or is there a job?'

'There's a job, Choucas . . . just as at the briefing. You have to get us into the building and out again without leaving a trace of entry. There may be a safe, there may only be a padlock. In both cases you work your passage.'

The dispatcher's intercom made sounds which he passed on to the group. 'Running up. Drop in two minutes. Red light on. Move into jumping positions please.'

He moved about and checked them, muttering the same mantra to each one. 'Two minutes. Clip your static lines on, and stand by in jumping order.'

They formed their queue: Cameron, Macaulay, Portales, Macklin, Gallagher and waited.

'DZ lights in view. Stand by. Go immediately the green shows. Don't hang about.'

Their eyes fixed on the red light until it burned into their mental vision, then was suddenly dispersed as a halo and replaced by pale green. The roar of the engines and the sound of the slipstream through the open hatch made the whole thing totally unreal.

They had done it before many times, but warm in the knowledge that – even if the drop was hairy – they would land on the friendly turf of England. This time a new dimension changed it all for them. It was just not the same. They were aware of no more flak; the rushing sound was as before; the red and the green, the static line clips, the dispatcher . . . nothing new. But they all knew it was different as they stepped forward and followed the leader out into the blackness of night. Macaulay had suddenly lost his fear, almost. Another one had predominated then he was gone. Macklin licked his lips, and closed his eyes, and stepped into space. Why had he not stayed in his warm little cell and watched the war go by, unaffected, uninvolved, quite untouched by hostilities, and not very conscious that rationing had subtly changed his diet? For the next couple of days it would be French food, if he got down in one piece before the Krauts he couldn't see started shooting up at him.

Marie, de Grouchy's hard-faced wife, was standing by the stove in the kitchen when she heard the noise. A Tom cat yowling that was repeated twice in succession. She flicked the curtain the way her husband had taught her, and then flopped over to the door in her tattered slippers and waited. Within seconds there was a coded knock and she switched out the light. When she unlocked the door her husband entered followed by people she did not know and did not want to know. Probably British. She didn't much like them. The girl they sent the day before was all right. She was French anyway. Marie returned to her stewpot as de Grouchy poured out raw wine into a variety of mugs and glasses, and they all knocked it back with evident pleasure. He sensed a slight tension and nervousness in the air. There was always a touch of that, but this lot were new to the job, and he felt for them and their need to quell the twisting of their stomachs. Macklin looked about the first French home he had ever entered. Not all that different from England after all.

'I didn't think it would be so easy.'

'It isn't always. Thanks Pierre.' De Grouchy nodded and swallowed his wine. 'So far we've been lucky.'

Marie put the stewpot on the table with a few plates and some white metal spoons, and made her way out of the room. Cameron started to dish out the food, and rapidly the tension dropped. They started to talk quietly. Portales sat down by Macaulay and smiled into his face. 'You feel better now?'

'Was it that obvious?'

'Just a little . . . we were all nervous.' She put her arm through his and gave him her sexy smile. He was grateful, and pressed her arm, then tucked into his stew. Solange came in from the back room and smiled at the surprised faces.

'When did *you* get here, then?'

She smiled and said nothing. Gallagher looked at her with a friendly twinkle in his eyes. 'Everything okay?'

'Yes, of course. But I am glad you're here.'

'Good. Send the landing success signal. Better do it now. Where's your WT?'

'In the woods, just as I was taught.'

For a moment their eyes met, and smiled, and then she turned away and left the room. They heard the outside door close, and Gallagher turned back to de Grouchy who was eating his stew noisily.

'Did the containers land undamaged?'

He nodded and continued slurping. After they had eaten Gallagher took de Grouchy aside and told him of his concern about Portales. The farmer's reaction was simple and basic. 'Kill her now, if there is a suspicion. I am not risking my *réseau*, or my wife, or myself.'

'We don't know there is anything to worry about. Lamboit is in Paris checking her out.'

De Grouchy's face stared at him as if to say, 'Why did you bring him back?' but he said nothing more for some time. Then, 'The others disperse in the woods for sleeping. The girl stays here. It is safer where we can see her.'

20 May

Squires had gone up to London to see Colonel Gwillim in his office at the latter's request. Over drinks they relaxed, and Gwillim chatted broadly about the imminent invasion of France; Bomber Command's saturation bombing strategy; the unsuitability of Eisenhower as supreme commander and Montgomery's penchant for rubbing everyone up the wrong way. At length it worked round to the job in hand.

'If they get what they want tonight, how d'you rate Gallagher's chance of success?'

Squires made a long face. 'Gallagher's a very good man. I don't doubt that for one moment, but if they succeed in getting into the place they'll be lucky. He hasn't got a plan, you know. He's waiting for inspiration, and nothing is coming. I can't see a way myself . . . too many problems. What happens if it doesn't work, sir?'

'It has to work, Tim. Or we must hope to God that the invasion force succeeds in taking the north coast of France in its entirety within two weeks, which is asking a lot, but there is no more time if this country is to survive these wretched V-weapons.'

Squires did not comment. He knew Gwillim had not invited him to visit him for some inconsequential chat. He did not have to wait. Gwillim accepted that he knew there was a reason and came directly to it.

'Something rather odd has come up. That girl you and Gallagher are worried about – Simone Portales. "Rossignol" I think is her codename. We have had an enquiry about her from American Intelligence.'

Squires felt himself stiffen inside, and his stomach dropped with anxiety for Gallagher. He spoke with a dry mouth.

'What were they enquiring about?'

'Did we know her? Where was she now . . . that sort of thing. They wanted to get in touch with her. That was as much as they gave away, except that "someone" was interested.'

'Did they imply the interest was professional?'

'No. Difficult to assess, they gave so little away. Do we admit that we do not know of her existence, which implies that we are either devious to our prime ally, or totally incompetent? They have obviously traced her to our doorstep. Or do we admit that she is highly suspect, but have nevertheless sent her on a sensitive operation into enemy-occupied territory?'

Squires saw the immediate dilemma quite clearly.

'Yes, doesn't sound all that good when it's put that way, does it? You do remember that my own attitude was logged at the time?'

But Gwillim didn't seem all that anxious to shoulder the problem alone. He pursed his lips and sat back in his elderly, wooden swivel-chair.

'Oddly enough I had the feeling that it was not a security enquiry. I am intrigued as to what their possible interest could be.'

Squires put on his blandest face and spoke ingenuously.

'You don't suppose she could be working for *them*, do you?'

The thought had obviously not entered Gwillim's head, and his slightly vacant expression held unmovingly for some moments.

'Forgive me, sir, but how did they get onto us?'

'Through the Free French actually. And that in itself has raised a storm in a teacup. Why did we recruit one of their nationals without consulting a certain General first? The usual nonsense.'

'God protect us from that gentleman, unless, of course, he himself is right, and HE is God. But, forgive me, sir, the point I am getting to is . . . is the American enquiry inspired by their Intelligence, or their Counter-Intelligence? That knowledge is paramount to us. Gallagher could be walking into real trouble.'

Gwillim regarded Squires as he turned over the pros and cons in his head. To talk or not to talk. That indeed was the question. Was it necessary in his mind to force a statement of purpose from the Americans, or to simply let it ride and leave his own team at possible risk?

Lamboit arrived at de Grouchy's off the six o'clock train. His mission in Paris had been successful. The Resistants there knew him, and his *bona fides* from London increased his stature and gave an edge to their searches.

'There is nothing certain, but if you have a friend in the SD it arouses suspicion.'

Gallagher frowned. 'How friendly was this SD man?'

'It seems he was besotted, and went every night to the cabaret where she worked, and insisted she sit at his table. It made her enemies, of course, but there is no direct evidence that she was his mistress. A friend in the Gestapo is very useful if you want papers and travel permits. She came to England in the February of the following year, possibly with his unknowing help.'

Gallagher's frown had not dispersed. 'Any relatives?'

'Mother in what was the Occupied Zone. The girl stayed, claiming she wanted to get to England and fight the Boche.'

'Why didn't she stay and fight with the Resistance?'

Lamboit shrugged. 'Why didn't they all? But they didn't. There is a sizeable Free French Contingent in Britain.'

Gallagher turned away and looked out of the window at the French landscape. There had been much rain in the last few weeks and the corn was showing little sign of drying or turning gold. In the morning light it seemed pallid and starved, the way the allies thought France should look after years of Occupation, but didn't.

He turned round after a few moments. 'We'll give her a loose rein, but she must never be without surveillance. Can you manage that, de Grouchy? Without straining your Resistants too much?'

The sarcasm was not lost on the farmer, but he chose to ignore it and replied with a dead-pan expression. 'Jacques and I will follow her everywhere. If she gets suspicious then there is Justine and Gapin to take over. Leave that with me.'

When Portales returned from taking the food to the others in the woods, with Marie, she seemed in good spirits and smiled more than usual. Gallagher watched her carefully for any tiny trace of something he could cotton onto.

'You seem in good spirits today.'

'Rossignol' Portales gave him one of the big sexy smiles she used so carefully and sparingly, but this morning it was all open and without the accustomed sensuality implicit in the eyes.

'I am in France again. Oh, it is so good to be here! even like this. I was brought up not fifteen kilometres from here, Major. I know it so well, and I love it very much. Even the air smells different. I do not mean I do not like England. It has become a second home for me, but this is where I was born. There is nowhere that replaces the feeling of belonging. It is just part of me.'

Gallagher nodded. He knew the feeling very well and very personally. He was a Scot, brought up amid heath and heather. The land of the mountain and the flood was in his blood, and he knew no other home. He, too, had learned to love other places. Oxfordshire, where he had spent four years of his youth, and Picardy, which was still dear to him, not so much of itself but because it held the memory of his time with Claudine, perhaps the most important year of his life . . . or so it seemed in retrospect. Gallagher had not been either forward with women, nor promiscuous once he had tasted the fruit. His slight experience with women had not done much except relieve something he didn't choose to concern him unduly. With Claudine he became whole. Total sexual fulfilment had changed him. As a man he was now complete, yet paradoxically no longer whole, for she had been part of him and essential to him. The longing for her and no one else had disturbed and disarranged him for several months after being forced to leave her. He argued with himself that almost all the men of Europe were in similar situations, now joined by the Americans. It was all cock-eyed and heart-breaking, and the deprivation gnawed at him. Not to put too fine a point upon it, his nature had glossed over what was simple lust, and had sentimentalised it into a latter-day *Roman de la Rose*. When he had time to do so he thought of nothing but Claudine. A curious mixture of longing and sexual anxiety lent him a permanent unease in his stomach. He recognised it for what it was, but could do nothing to ameliorate the sensation.

Portales was looking at him curiously. He sensed he had mentally drifted away for some seconds and deeply resented being brought back from his sweet nostalgia and he spoke roughly to her. She turned away, and Pierre de Grouchy stared at him, also curiously.

Gallagher stood over the crude plan he had drawn on the wrapping paper on the table top. It was as they all remembered from their briefing and this gave them comfort that nothing had changed except the venue.

'If they find the drawings missing there could be a fuss, and with suspicion aroused the Germans will take whatever action seems necessary to them. So, having swiped them, the building will catch fire, naturally and without any evidence of arson. Mésange, you will plant the incendiary devices set with timer-fuses all over the building. Grive, you stay at the door and watch for German patrols. We should not be interrupted, it's a quiet place, but we must be prepared. No contact, is that clear?' Grive nodded.

'What do I do?'

Portales was pathetically eager to be of some use.

'De Grouchy tells me that the fire chief is sympathetic and a friend. You will contact him at the address you are given. Just give him, verbally, a simple message. 'Tonight there is no hurry.' He will arrange that by the time the fire engine arrives the fire will have a good hold, and the place will be gutted where it needs to be. Come back here when you have delivered the message . . . there is more to be done. Go with Pierre now.'

She smiled at them all again, bright-eyed and alive, and happy in her work, then she was gone with de Grouchy. Gallagher settled down to individual briefing in absolute detail for the umpteenth time, but there were no groans as at Masham. This was the real thing. That much had gone home, and changed everything.

Outside de Grouchy had given her a bike, an elderly 'sit-up-and-beg' with a handlebar panier, and indicated the route for her to take. He watched her pedal off down the street as the unshaven dark-faced Jacques came out from the barn with his own bike. De Grouchy nodded to him, and Jacques set out to follow and observe.

The afternoon sun had almost gone and darkness was beginning to obscure the landscape she so much wanted to see clearly. Portales had not seen Chantilly, nor Senlis since the year before the German advance when she persuaded her mother to move away into the Puy.

Jacques watched her as she savoured the French dusk and then smiled to himself. She was no hardship to watch. He hadn't seen such an attractive girl for years. He watched her as she rode ahead of him, just able to see the movement of her limbs, and the swell of her hips. Wartime clothing was not all it might be, but if a girl had the right shapes in the right places it didn't get in the way. Then he noted two German privates, off duty, walking round the town for something to do. They saw Portales with the speed of a randy buck aware of a scent, and grinned widely and called to her. She replied with her wide smile and a wave, and an indistinct comment that made the Germans laugh, and one made an obscene gesture before he slapped his comrade on the shoulder and they continued on their way. They did not acknowledge the dour Jacques, nor the sullen de Grouchy less than twenty-five metres behind. Who cared about Frenchmen?

When Portales reached the house she left her bike in the covered archway then walked out of the yard, but not into the front door. Neither did she knock, nor make any sign of doing as she was bidden. She crossed the road, walked down the street towards the town centre. Jacques dismounted quickly and followed her on foot, now alive to the possibility that suspicion was well founded. He watched her make for a reddish stone house that was occupied, as Jacques well knew, by Marcel Lecau and his mother. Lecau was a member of the Milice. Once she was admitted and the door closed behind her Jacques hurried forward to where he could see into the room. Blackout curtains had not yet been drawn, though it was almost dark outside, showing the yellow-lit interior. The street was semi-deserted, only a cart loaded with farm-muck rumbled towards him behind an emaciated and stumbling horse which spent its meagre energies in drawing the old wagon, urged by the switch of a teenage girl. In the room Simone Portales was seen talking rapidly and intently with Lecau himself, who frequently gesticulated to show his displeasure and his situation. At length she handed him a sealed envelope, and seemed about to depart.

Jacques hurried back to his bike where de Grouchy himself now waited frowning.

'Where is she?'

'In Marcel Lecau's house. She has given him a letter addressed and sealed. I think he intends to pass it on.'

De Grouchy's face went grave and his eyes shone with a black hatred. 'Right. You take care of him, I'll look after her.'

They watched her leave the house and return to where she had left her bike. There de Grouchy was waiting for her.

'There's been a change of plan. You are to come with me.'

'But what about the Fire Chief?'

'You haven't seen him yet?'

She lied expertly. 'He wasn't in, they told me he was down the street, but I did not find him . . .'

'Just as well. Come on, let's move.'

When Jacques knocked on Lecau's door he already had his knife open in his sleeve.

He pushed Lecau into the house, and dropped on top of him before the latter had a chance to regain his stance. He did not mess about, there was the old woman in the house somewhere, so when they fell Jacques fell with his weight on the knife as it entered Lecau's body. It was well done. The blade entered the heart and severed the valve instantly. Within three seconds Lecau was gasping in shock and realisation, and life left his body before ten seconds was up. Jacques knelt on top of him, listened, and waited. Then slipped off the shuddering corpse. Blood was oozing from both ears in tiny trickles. Jacques wasted no time and carried the body out into the night . . . round the back of the house, and down the earth 'cut' to the canal bank. He weighted it with stones, and slipped it silently into the dark, oily water. As he walked back he stared at the ground to eradicate any sign of blood dripping on the path. What he found he wiped clean before he slipped back into the house, and there carefully wiped the two large drops from the tiled floor. He looked about him, checked that he had the sealed envelope taken from Lecau's pocket before he dumped him, and was about to leave when he heard the sound of a woman's voice calling out, and the sound of shuffling feet.

'Marcel! Marcel! You should have gone. It is late!'

Jacques panicked momentarily and darted through the door. He pulled it shut after him, but did not notice the coil of barbed wire that Lecau had standing against the gate. As he flashed past barbs caught on his trousers and tugged. The cloth ripped, but it was enough to make him fall into the coil and the stakes beside it. Panic makes one stupid and precipitate, and Jacques was no exception to that rule. He leapt up regardless of his predicament, which somehow coiled the wire round a stake which dragged and then caught between two railings. They did not budge, but the velocity of Jacques' fearful flight pulled them tight, and that loop ripped across his left leg. It tore the skin and flesh as well as the trousers . . . and though he did not feel all that much pain for some seconds he writhed and kicked to remove the rusted wire barbs. At last he rushed off down the dark street. The whole thing had taken no more than six minutes, but it seemed an eternity, and he blessed the sleepy town for that very quality. No one had seen him. No one was about. Curfew was imminent and he had to make himself scarce. His curfew pass would not excuse the slashed wound on his leg which was now bleeding profusely. He made for his own home first, intending to reach de Grouchy as soon as he was able.

De Grouchy had reached his own barn and barred the door after he and Portales entered. She spun round, suddenly wary.

'Where is Major Gallagher?'

She was not given time to ask further. De Grouchy pulled the trigger on the silenced Luger pointing at her at a range of eight feet. She uttered a startled cry and asked something in French that he did not catch, before she sank to her knees and her eyes rolled into her head. She had died before she slid to the ground . . . the bullet straight through her brain, softened by the silencer rifling, had broken like a dum-dum as it entered her skull and made a very unpleasant hole. It was a sight that de Grouchy would remember for the rest of his life. A very lovely female face wearing a startled expression that seemed almost to heighten her beauty, suddenly surmounted by a red rosette distorting the upper head like a nightmare Picasso. De Grouchy had killed one woman before. He had not enjoyed that either. When he returned to his kitchen later Marie stared at him, the man who shared her bed, and did not know him. There was something about the face that filled her own bovine conscience with unease, as if she knew what had been done.

In the town Gallagher and his group moved through dark shadows little by little towards the wide street that housed the Hôtel de Ville. The great fourteenth-century church stood black and silent at one end.

Gallagher touched Macklin, and indicated he alone was to follow him. After a glance each way they crossed the street, and made for the side-door and porch of the eighteenth-century town hall. Macklin got to work on the lock immediately. Gallagher kept watch and waited. After a moment he turned and hissed, 'I thought you said it would be easy!'

The little cockney smiled at him and winked. 'These old locks are beautifully made. Nice and heavy. We don't want to spoil 'em, do we?' But he gave the spring steel a twist, and the door jumped open a couple of inches. Gallagher gritted his teeth.

'There could have been a burglar alarm operational there!' But Macklin gave him a pitying look.

'Do me a favour, squire. You do your stuff, let me do mine. I'm not new to the caper, am I? D'you think I didn't check?'

Gallagher nodded, and Cameron and Macaulay hastened across the dark and silent street. Macaulay went straight inside. Cameron exchanged a glance with his commander, and then stood back in the shadows, pulled the door shut that Gallagher had just disappeared through, and waited.

The three entrants ran up the stairs to the first floor. Gallagher indicated the direction to Macklin who moved ahead.

'You start on the ground floor and work your way up. Set the fuses for fifteen minutes and shorten slightly as you go up. Remember it is the top floors we *must* burn . . . the rest is a bonus.' Macaulay moved off, and Gallagher followed Macklin up the next flight.

The Surveyor's office was marked by a small brass plate, as it had been for over a century, and Macklin was already through the locked door and examining the fine old oak plan-chest, bound shut with one steel bar across the drawers, padlocked at the foot.

Macklin glanced at it contemptuously. 'They don't deserve to be safe. Look at that, it's a Woolworth's job. Galvanised crap. I thought they might have a nice old brass one.' He sighed and fiddled with his spring steel, the pointed end, this time, and the padlock sprang open almost as if at the touch. The bar was lifted out of its slot, and the drawers slid out one by one. The filing was orderly and well-regulated. The problem was to imagine what heading could possibly file the revived, old war plans that were half-secret yet recently unearthed by Frenchmen for German use.

The street was quiet. Cameron kept well into the porch shadows and watched, his ears alert to any sudden sound, or the approach of vehicles or pedestrians. About twelve minutes after entry he became aware of footfalls approaching. He turned and watched the street corner where it moved round into the small grassed area outside the mediaeval hunting lodge, now a town museum. A local girl giggling on the arm of a German Army Leutnant moved out from the area, where they had no doubt been using the bench and benefiting from the shadowed curfew hours. The young soldier saw his girl to what was presumably her home, then waved and walked away several yards before crossing the road. Crossing at a point that would lead him directly to the side door of the Hôtel de Ville. Cameron stiffened, and felt in his pocket for the cord garrotte that he carried, and waited. The fresh-faced, ruddy Leutnant pulled down his jacket, and dusted his breeches as he mounted the low kerb. It may have been something he heard, or a sixth sense, or simple curiosity, but the wretched man paused and looked at the porch. Cameron held himself back in the shadows, glanced at the door to see if it was ajar. It wasn't. He waited. The German swallowed an alcoholic belch, and had the grace to cover his mouth though there was no one about, then edged forward bending slightly from the hips and peering at the door of the Town Hall. Cameron bit his teeth and slipped the garrotte into his hands, waited. One step . . . two steps . . . the German was directly in front of him. He didn't know whether it was precautionary, or a sudden desire to kill the enemy, but Cameron stepped silently forward and whipped the cord round the man's throat and pulled. The knots bit into the throat and neck, and the German's eyes stood out from his cheeks as he snatched at the air and his feet kicked the door. And then a tighter pull, a shudder, and a slow slackening into limpness. Cameron was a strong man, and he used all the strength of his arms. When he unwound the cord from the dead German's neck there was a dark red ring, still embedded quarter-of-an-inch into the neck, and with two black hollows where the bigger knots had pushed the Adam's apple into a permanent swallow and stopped all breath. The eyes remained staring, and almost out onto the cheeks themselves, and there was a foam of mucus below the left nostril. Cameron lifted him gently into the shadow, behind the huge galvanised drum that held the Town Hall's rubbish every Friday and stank of unmentionable things.

Macaulay dashed up the last flight and set about his remaining charges. These would be two minute delays, no more. Those on the floors below would ignite at the same time, and the old dry wood of the building would burn swiftly. The evening had a slight wind from the south, enough to fan the flames into an eventual inferno.

Gallagher stopped at the fifth drawer and held up the sheet of mica that weighted the drawings in each drawer. The top set were in a brown paper folder, edged and stuck on two sides, and bore a label stating that the contents were the property of the French War Department and dated 1917. Half-overlapping was a second label, this time the recognisable pale orange colour of the Organisation Todt, and stating – this time in German – that the Augmentation and Reconstruction Enlargement of Requisitioned Government property (all in two portmanteau German words), were the exclusive property of the Third Reich and not for French dissemination, and dated 1944.

A quick glance told Gallagher that these were what they were after. He was checking possible additions when the sudden 'plop' and 'hiss' of the first detonation told him he had run out of time. Within one minute eight fires had started on his floor, and doubtless others were burning happily below. Smoke was beginning to fill the rooms. Macklin dashed across and opened one window to encourage the draught as Gallagher rolled the papers. Everything was quickly replaced, relocked, and the window reclosed, before they left the floor, now coughing into their handkerchiefs and trying to see through streaming eyes as they ran down the stairs.

Gallagher passed the documents to Cameron, and implied he was to push off with the others and he, Gallagher, would do the final checks. Cameron shook his head. 'You matter, I don't. I do the honours.'

Gallagher recognised the strength of his argument. Without Gallagher it would be back to square one. He didn't argue. He moved off on his own. Macaulay and Macklin acting as 'shotgun' wing three-quarters to his scrum-half. Cameron waited for a moment before he pulled out the dead German, and carried him over his shoulder into the smouldering building, up the stairs to the top floor, now nicely ablaze in the centre. Cameron, his heart pounding and his eyes streaming, tore off the German's uniform and his underclothing and wrapped them into a tight bundle. Then he dragged the body near the fast-burning floor, looked about him, and reached for the desk lamp. It was one of the heavy brass, lead-weighted, ornate type beloved of French bureaucracy since 1900. He was a tough man, and had seen much fighting and death, but he did not relish what he was about to do. Without looking too closely he brought the heavy base of the lamp down onto the man's face –

again and again until the entire jaw-area was a smashed, splintered mass of pulp, and there was no possibility of identifying the dental work of the dead man. Then he threw the body into the flames and picked up the clothing and staggered out, snatching his breath as and when there was some air to snatch.

21 May

Macklin moved as quickly as he could down the street. Macaulay was somewhere behind and Gallagher had gone on ahead. He could move silently and with supreme self-effacement, could Major Gallagher. Macklin envied that ability and would try to acquire it. You never knew when you might need that sort of skill. He was breathing well and moving comfortably, as his training had taught him when he saw them. Three Wehrmacht personnel . . . too dark to define . . . but they had seen him. One called out. 'Halt.'

Macklin bit his teeth, and his mind raced as the men approached, their machine-pistols uncocked and ready. Two were army personnel, privates as far as he could tell. The third was an SD junior officer. Macklin shuddered inside. This was a fine howdyedo and no mistake! Any one of the others might get away with it. A paper check, couple of questions. No problem. But with him it was a problem. His cockney accent was impossible to eradicate. His understanding of French or any other language was almost non-existent. Squires had given up on him and decided that, as a specialist with highly-qualified skills, he could skip the lingo stuff and concentrate on those areas that were within his competence. Shit! This would sink him. At least he wasn't carrying the flipping plans.

It was at about the same moment that Macaulay crossed the end of the street and saw what was happening. About the same time the three soldiers caught a glimpse of flames and glow above the silhouetted streets of the town. The connection in their minds was immediate as Macaulay intended it to be. He had seen Macklin's predicament, and knew the moment that he opened his mouth he was done for, and decided to create a diversion. Once he saw that he had become the object of attention he drew his revolver and fired in their general direction, then turned and ran for it. Immediately the Germans' attention focused upon him. They primed their carbines and fired after him. One ran forward and made to chase while the others, more faint-hearted, pressed themselves against the wall of the street-housing, and moved cautiously after their colleague. The clatter of distant footfall prompted them to hasty pursuit, and the chase was on. Macaulay carefully led them away from the little cockney, and exposed himself to keep them interested.

He did not notice the French gendarme standing in a shop doorway draw his pistol and empty four bullets into Macaulay's back and side. Mésange turned with a surprised look on his face, and then gave a silly, embarrassed chuckle as he dropped to the cobbled street, and sank into the dew-damp surface which quickly reddened with his sticky English blood. As the men ran up he shouted something in French that Choucas did not understand. The little man had been forgotten for a moment, though he had not forgotten his rescuer, and saw from his hiding place the one-time Captain of RASC breathe his last on the cobbles of Senlis.

The sight took the blood from his face, and he turned away and walked back towards the outskirts of the town. He was careful enough this time, but his mind was racing, constantly reviewing pictures of Nigel Macaulay, a name he did not know, for to 'Choucas' the man who had died was 'Mésange'. He thought it meant 'tit'. They joked about it for obvious reasons as Macaulay was such a womaniser . . . or had been. He could see the laughing, almost insolent face of the upper middle-class joker who put them all to shame so often by coming out with a bright idea of great imagination. He knew so little about him. He couldn't see him with a family. He didn't even know what he did as a job, a proper job that is, not the caper he was performing in Masham. And he was prepared, as he had shown, to give his life to save a little cockney twister. That realisation shook Macklin to his very core, and gave him a curious feeling of something he had never known in his life before. His parents wouldn't have cared if he had run away at the age of five. He almost had. Alice was happy enough to shack up with anyone else. His brother Tom he hadn't seen since he was eight. There was nothing and no one in Georgie Macklin's life who meant a sodding thing to him . . . except a young gentleman officer lying dead on the stones of a provincial French town – and lying there because of HIM.

Solange sent the 'Operation successful' signal as soon as Gallagher turned up with the plans. Cameron joined them quickly, then a pale and silent Choucas.

'Where's Mésange?'

'Dead. Jerries got 'im.'

The news was received in stony silence by Gallagher, and sudden horror by Solange. Cameron accepted it as the fortunes of war, though he was sorry. They all liked Macaulay. Gallagher was silent. He had not expected that of all things. Macaulay was too aware, too inventive to be caught napping. He was potentially the best operator Gallagher had selected, even allowing for his fear of heights. Not many had that imaginative flair, and he was angry that his support-elect had been taken from him. Macklin explained what had happened. With a lump in his throat as he told it, which they all recognised for what it was and said nothing.

Gallagher changed the subject quickly. 'Listen to me. The pick-up is scheduled for 02.00 tomorrow. Ferdy will be back from the town shortly. He will take charge. I have something I want to do. Choucas and Grive will return by Lysander taking the plans with them. Chardonneret and Ferdy will return by coastal pick-up as directed from London. Being French you'll have less trouble than anyone.'

They went back to the wood to sleep, but Macklin turned to Gallagher, and stood by the table.

Gallagher spoke quietly. 'It's not your fault, Choucas. Partly mine for not anticipating a patrol, but mostly his own. Because he tried to help you.'

'If he hadn't I'd be inside somewhere now having my fingernails torn out. He did that 'cos he knew I was a flamin' liability. What the 'ell's the good of draggin' me around when I can't speak the lingo? Time I was back in stir.'

'No it isn't! We entered that place with ease and without trace because of you. We expect to do the big job the same way . . . because of you. Mésange knew we needed you more than we needed him. He was also disobeying an order *not* to look out for lame ducks. It was his decision. That's all there is to it.'

Macklin digested it before answering. 'He was laughin'. Straight up . . . laughin' like he always does.'

'He was a good bloke. Don't let him down. Nobody's going back inside, Choucas . . . ever.'

Macklin looked at his boss and nodded quickly, then turned and went off towards the wood to join the others.

Lamboit had remained in the town, as a townsman, to observe the effect and report. The upshot was simple and as had been expected. The fire service – suitably alerted by de Grouchy – was none too quick off the mark, and the flames had a good hold when they arrived. By dint of careful activity, controlled as precisely as the operation had been, the fire completed the gutting of the top floor and the centre areas of the next two. The rest of the building was saved. Ten men saw to it that their Chief was the one to first examine the damage. He stepped through the smoking, charred embers, and looked up at the hanging, burnt rafters. There was no plan-chest left to be examined, there was no suggestion of arson for any eye to see. The police examined the doors and windows, and concluded that there had been no break-in. The fire had been caused by accident, possibly a cigarette end, or faulty wiring. The place had not been rewired since 1928 and much of the insulation was demonstrably perished. The man who had been shot by a German guard patrol seemed to have no connection with the fire . . . but there was a reported break-in down the street at the shop of Gaston Pelletier. The one that had belonged to Eli Dreyfus before they deported him on racial grounds . . . but then, why not, no one liked him – the slimy old Jew – and some said he was related to the Dreyfus of bygone days, and we all knew about him, didn't we? The little man had got away, but the dead man's papers implied he was from another Department and they would be contacted in due course.

Lecau's mother said her son was probably with his Milicien friends on an exercise. He had been threatening to go and leave her to her own devices for the two weeks involved. Obviously he had just 'gone'. There was one other thing reported, but not until the following day. Leutnant Schlemm had not reported for duty. His girlfriend said he had been 'with her' the previous evening, and had then walked away. Yes, he had been morose, but weren't all the Germans morose these days? She wouldn't be at all surprised if he hadn't deserted. He was sick of the war, and had said so many times. Perhaps if they looked in the back streets of some German city they might find him . . . with a tart, of course. Otto Schlemm liked his oats. Lamboit's report was satisfactory in every way. Marie de Grouchy had reported that her husband was anxious about his colleague, Jacques. They had found Portales to be treacherous, but in what way was not yet known as Jacques had taken the incriminating letter she had left with the Milice and he, de Grouchy had killed the girl himself, and buried the body. But he would report directly to Gallagher when he returned.

During the day Gallagher went off to recce the German complex once more. He wanted to see for himself certain details he did not remember, and the PR prints did not make clear. There are some things one cannot properly see from the air. You can't tell if a tree is solid or rotten, for one thing, and it doesn't say very much about just how impenetrable undergrowth really is.

De Grouchy was waiting for him when he returned. His face was grim and concerned.

'What happened to Jacques?'

'That's what I don't know. He got rid of Lecau, somewhere . . . at least that is what I conclude because there is no trace of him, of either of them.'

'Then it could be the other way round.'

'If it was, we would know. The Germans would be searching even if they didn't know what for. Jacques would not talk easily . . . but everyone talks in the end. No, they haven't got him. But I don't know where he is, or why. You said you wanted to go up to Picardy. You go now. We'll find him.'

'I need that letter she gave your Milicien. I have to know how much she knew about the job . . . and who she has passed it on to. I *have* to know, Pierre!'

He nodded. He understood how much hung upon that knowledge.

'Your farmers seem to be doing well enough . . . and there wasn't the same feeling in the town that I noticed three years ago. What's changed it all?'

De Grouchy looked him straight in the face, but his eyes were uneasy as well as unhappy.

'After three years of occupation everything has settled down. The Germans behave well. If you aren't a Jew or a Gypsy what have you to fear? That is all propaganda. The farmers make a good living supplying the German army. What if the currency is not all it might be? You can use it, no one knows the difference, and when there is no international market to concern yourself with does it really matter if the money is worthless? Who's to know? Many things are better than before the Occupation – Government for one!'

'So many of your young men have gone.'

'Of course, but after a while the girls begin to look at the Germans: they're young, handsome, smart . . . well-mannered. It is human nature. Soon they will integrate, there will be marriages and children.'

'*You* do not want to integrate. Why others?'

'I fought in the last war. I was young then. I remember. The young today have no memories, only the stories of their parents about the Boche monsters who eat little children. Pah! Look at them! Do these blond young heroes eat children? No! But they make good lovers.'

'And when the Invasion comes? Will you fight with us?'

'Oh yes. We are not all blind, nor all venal. France will be French once more, do not fear. I just want you British to realise it is not quite as you see it.'

Gallagher nodded. He knew that already, even if his countrymen did not, in the main. How could they? They were brought up with their own history books, not Europe's. They saw the world as their politicians wanted them to, and the Ministry of Information had done a miraculous job of propaganda. He knew that, too. If anyone could be said to have won the propaganda war it was the British. They were so much better at lying than anyone else. It was not, perhaps, a national characteristic the way it was with some people, but it became an art when properly applied, and one in which the British character could sometimes excel.

'The trains, are they running normally?'

'More or less, where to?'

'I have a call to make, beyond Amiens. Any problems?'

'You can travel well enough. Crowded as usual but they run.'

'Good. You cope for me, I'll be back tomorrow.'

It was daylight still when Gallagher arrived at the house. Once again he used the same side entrance, through the vegetable garden where no one seemed to go. It was just as well. There was a German Kübelwagen standing at the main entrance. As he watched from the rhododendron bushes he saw her come from the entrance and permit her hand to be kissed by the SS officer who bowed stiffly and beamed his pleasure as he departed. He thought the man was a Sturmbannführer but it was too far to see clearly, especially when your eyes are really only for someone who is eating your heart out anyway. His stomach told him he was experiencing the sick wretchedness of jealousy, now no longer vague but personalised. He did not know that the German was anything other than a billeting-officer calling to check a large house, or a lonely officer merely paying his respects to a local family. It didn't matter much, the jealousy was already gnawing away inside him, stupidly, indiscriminately, and like a teenager new to love's arrows, he could only suffer. He knew within himself that a man of his age, his worldliness, should know better and not be affected by such puerile emotions, but words are of no avail and self-admonishment merely an exercise in mental prevarication. It meant nothing and affected nothing. Hugh Gallagher was a slave to jealousy, and there was nothing he could do about it.

He waited until the car had left the grounds and until there was no corner he had not thoroughly observed, then he walked to the terrace and opened the French windows to the living-room. Claudine turned instinctively and saw him standing in the window frame and her face glowed for a moment before it dropped once again, perhaps a touch of apprehension across her eyes.

'Hugh!'

She did not move as he crossed into the room. He placed his hands on her shoulders as he bent to kiss her neck, and felt the slight tensing of the muscles that was the merest trace of rejection, and his heart cracked inside him. The upsurge of pain was as much as he could accept without making a sound. But he put a bold face on it and smiled weakly.

'Entertaining the SS these days?'

She saw the pain behind the eyes, and the bitterness behind the smile, and she felt her own brand of unhappiness for a moment. They would play their roles and be civilised and all the things lovers are who are no longer what they were.

'He was visiting on business. There are more units moving up towards the coast. He is looking for billets for his officers.'

Gallagher felt the lie down to his boots, and made the same smile come to his face once more. 'Did you send him packing with a flea in his ear?'

'What could I do? It is an order, not a request. They know most of the house is empty. They could turn us out if they wished.'

'But they won't, of course, not while there is someone to do the housework and extend some of the comforts of home. I shall have to be more careful when I visit.'

'No!' It came out too quickly and too vehemently.

'You would not be safe. You must not come, Hugh. It would be terrible for us all, if they caught you.'

Gallagher's pain increased inside him, and he moved towards her with a sudden sadness mingled with desire. She was so beautiful and he wanted her so much, and she was 'his' but she was in effect pushing him away. A rejection that was all the more ferocious because he knew the other side of that coin, and the soft eagerness and appetite she had shown hitherto. That rejection burned into him with the speed and intensity of acid in his system. He was about to react angrily when the door opened and Claudine's mother came in. She looked up at Hugh Gallagher and frowned for a moment, then smiled at him.

'Monsieur Gallagher, I did not understand it was you. There was another officer here. He was charming, you would like him. Claudine, ask him to come in here and meet M'sieur

Gallagher. Oh, you come to see us so little these days! Why are you not in uniform? I like the uniforms. They are so smart. My husband looked so splendid in his, you know. He was a tall man and could wear it with real dignity.'

'Mother, please . . .'

'You will stay for a few days, this time, won't you?'

But the doorbell rang and interrupted the invitation. Claudine hurried out and left Gallagher talking to her mother. She opened the front door and stood staring, fearfully, at Sturmbannführer Boehm. Gallagher laid his finger across the soft mouth of the older lady and pressed his ear to the door opening. The accent was unmistakably German, and the invitation to dinner painfully clear and succinct, as was the acceptance.

When Claudine's mother turned round there was no one in the room, but the French windows were open. Then she remembered they had been open since breakfast, and stepped out into the corridor and walked towards the entrance where her daughter was standing, her hand held by a man in uniform.

'Ah, that's better. I like you in uniform so much better. Claudine, ask Major Gallagher to stay for a few days. He used to stay quite often. I will see you later, Major.'

The confused Boehm clicked his heels and bowed from the waist. Claudine smiled at him weakly. 'My mother no longer recognises people, Sturmbannführer. You must forgive her. She is not well.'

'Of course. Then . . . until eight.'

He repeated the bow and click, and left. Claudine leant back against the closed door and breathed out gratefully, then hurried to the living room. It was empty. Hugh had gone. He understood, but she knew, fleetingly at least, the weight of guilt and unease that came with the inflicting of pain upon another. But it *is* fleeting, and not so heavy to bear as all that. Especially when the grass on the other side looked so green.

De Grouchy handed Gallagher the crumpled letter, still sealed.

'We found Jacques. He had got rid of the body all right, but his leg was torn open, and he had to find a doctor to attend to it. We can't trust the local doctor so he had to go to Aubin to see their man. You remember him, he attended to Lamboit.'

Gallagher nodded, and tore open the letter. He read it, and his face became grim.

De Grouchy glanced at him. 'Proof?'

Gallagher gritted his teeth, and lied to save the man's conscience. 'Yes. Conclusive proof.'

De Grouchy sighed with relief. 'Thank God. It is not a nice thing to kill a woman . . . especially one young and attractive.'

22 May

All the way back in the Lysander, he sat quite oblivious to the tight squeeze of the agent sharing the compartment cockpit with him, an attaché case and a WT set that needed maintenance. He was oblivious to the occasional searchlight that probed at the sound of their engine. Once they were caught over the coastline and coned, and the Flak made a short attempt to give them hell, but no night-fighters appeared. They didn't venture over the coast these days. They were too busy taking a deadly toll of the formations of Bomber Command laying waste to their Fatherland, city-by-city. He thought about Claudine, and his loss, and his jealousy and that pain did not leave him, but it was overbalanced by a new pain, by the intelligence he had not imparted to de Grouchy. The letter that Portales had left with the Milicien was totally without significance and blazoned her innocence for all to see. It was a simple letter to be delivered to her mother in Puy, explaining that she was well and engaged upon war work. It was circumspect and gave nothing away. It was loving and hopeful, and each word spelled out the total lack of substance in the accusations that had been entertained against her. They were just circumstantial and deadly. Gallagher had ordered the murder of a completely innocent girl.

Gwillim was looking at him with bland unconcern. 'The Free French admitted they had forgotten about her, and were as embarrassed as we were about the American enquiry. It turned out she had been the girlfriend of an American Air Force pilot.

When she started training with us he lost contact with her. He gathered there had been an attempt to contact him, but for some reason no phone number was given and he eventually asked a chum in American Intelligence to do him a favour and see if he could locate her. He's downstairs at the moment. The boyfriend. We have to say something, Hugh. Will you . . . er . . . do the thing?'

'It is my responsibility, sir.'

'Not necessarily, but perhaps it is better coming from you. It means our suspicions were groundless and now, from what you tell me, she is proved innocent. Terrible mistake, of course. But you did the right thing. There was no other possible action.'

Gallagher remained silent and without expression. He was still that way when Captain Jack Floyd was shown into the room and greeted him with a hearty handshake and a thick Iowa accent.

He lied, of course. Said she was on active service with Special Duties, which Floyd accepted easily as she had said how much she wanted to do her bit in that sort of way. It was agreed that she would be informed when she returned, though when that would be depended largely about the outcome of any possible Second Front, and the tall freckle-faced Captain left after another mighty handshake.

3

TRIBULATIONS

23 May
Tim Squires entered his office at 08.43, and found Gallagher standing by the window looking out across the gardens, no longer kept the way they once had been.

'Thinking of doing a bit of horticulture?'

Gallagher didn't move, he just grunted. 'Not really my forte. Never had time for gardens. Pity, I think.'

'I do agree. Everyone should have a garden and cultivate something. It imposes a sense of order and truth, and instils a respect for patience.'

Gallagher turned to him smiling. 'I never really saw you as a gardening man.'

'Alas, no.' Squires sighed. 'Like you I never had the time. Doesn't stop me pontificating, though. I know it's a good thing, even if I don't practise it. Like illicit sex.'

Gallagher managed a small smile, but the effort didn't escape Squires, who sat back in his chair and fingered his lower lip for a moment.

'You can't take it personally, man. We've lost two. I'm sorry, of course, but there *is* a war and that's what happens.'

Gallagher snorted. 'I'm not grieving for Macaulay. He was a good man and he did a good job. End of story.' He paused and breathed in, long and slowly. 'But I can't forgive myself for Rossignol. That bright, vivacious, lovely girl. I had her killed, Tim! I had her life terminated. No future, no kids, no anything. Jesus! People are hanged for that, and just because there's a war on I'm exonerated of blame.'

Squires handed him a cigarette which he brushed aside. 'There's a little matter of how to get into the wretched place still unresolved. If you don't apply yourself to it rather seriously you may find you have another half-dozen killed, then it *will* be your fault, Gallagher. Shall we get on with it?'

Gallagher looked at him coldly, then changed the subject.

'Did you manage to settle the enquiry, the American?'

Squires turned a blank and bland face to him. 'What American?'

He stood and walked towards the door before he turned and spoke again. 'By the way, Grive has asked to see us both. Any idea what it's about?'

'None.' Squires accepted the rude grunted reply. He knew Gallagher was blaming himself more than was necessary, but if he felt that way he had to be allowed time to work it out of his system.

When Gallagher crossed the hall to pick up his mess-bill from the rack he saw a folded local newspaper at Sergeant Dowding's elbow. Something had caught his eye. He picked it up and stared at the two column ad. A visiting circus was about to descend upon Masham. There were few enough about during the war, and many children had no idea what a circus really was, so the visits to small communities were doubly welcome. They were poor things usually. Even the circus had not escaped the war. Personnel either called up, or remained in those countries fortunate enough to be spared hostilities. More than half the British-based circuses were touring Ireland, permanently.

Gallagher stared at it blindly and something was triggered off in his mind, instantly to be forgotten as he stared at the crude black-and-white drawing of a trapeze artiste walking a high-wire with his pole. He walked away. Something in the recesses of his mind was bothering him, and what bothered him even more was that he didn't know what it was. But this was nothing compared to the revelation he was about to confront.

In Squires' office, Grive was standing to attention. There was something in the air, and it was not a pleasant smell, at least not by the look on Squires' face.

'I think you'd better hear this, Major.'

Gallagher listened as Grive unburdened himself about the German he had killed on the raid. He listened, slowly growing tense and cold at the possibilities. His stomach had turned over in the first moments. So much was in the balance. One slip . . .

'Why in hell didn't you say so at the time?'

The Highlander turned his racked face to him, patently honest and fully aware of his fault. 'I had gone against your orders, sir. I didn't want to blot my copybook. It was stupid, but I wasn't thinking.'

Squires watched the change in Gallagher keenly as his disappointment showed before the soldier took over and dispelled emotion.

'Right. It's done. Let's examine it. Was it avoidable?'

'Not in my estimation, sir.'

'Having made that judgment what did you do? How did you kill him?'

'Garrotted, sir. There was no blood.'

'What did you do with him?'

'Stuck him out of the way till everyone was clear. You'll remember I let you go first.'

'Then?'

'I took him into the town hall, up to the top floor, and put the body in the middle of the fire. He would burn all right.'

'Possible ID?'

'No, sir. I removed all his clothing, dog-tag, belt, weapon, everything. I took them with me and buried them all outside the town. They won't find anything.'

'Dental?'

'No, sir. I bashed his face in and broke up the jaw. They won't be able to identify him whatever they find.'

Gallagher was silent for some moments. Then he turned to Squires, 'I would appreciate a word with Grive privately, sir.'

Squires sighed and stood up, picked up his cap, and made for the office door. 'I shall be with unarmed combat if you want me.'

After he had gone Gallagher relaxed and sat down opposite Cameron. The latter was looking wretched and very sick with himself. He accepted the cigarette Gallagher passed to him, and they both sat and drew on the tobacco for some minutes before Gallagher looked up at him and spoke quietly.

'Where're you from, Cameron. I've forgotten?'

'Lochgilphead, sir, Hartside Road, it's a rough area. You learn to fight before you talk. It stops you being slashed up, you know? You can have a broken bottle on your neck before you can say Tam o' Shanter. It's instinctive.' He paused. 'I'm that sorry, sir.'

Gallagher nodded and sighed. 'At least you had the guts and the sense to come and tell me. You seem to have cleared up the mess you made thoroughly enough. That was good.'

'I don't want to be chucked out of the team, sir. It means a lot to me.'

'I don't want to chuck you out. You were going to be my backbone, Grive. I need someone tough and rough and ready, but not irresponsible.'

'I did what I could, sir. I won't make a mess again.'

Gallagher waited and ruminated, weighing the balance and always finding the same answer. At length he turned to the brawny Scot. 'Right. Get this through your skull. If I do take a chance and take you along you will obey orders to the letter. I won't jeopardise the operation and your teammates' lives for you or anything. I will do whatever is necessary. I mean that.'

'Yes, sir.'

'I want your hand on it, Grive.'

Cameron extended a huge hand and Gallagher held it tightly, his eyes never leaving the Scot's own. They understood each other.

As he left the Highlander gave an exemplary salute. 'Thank you, sir.'

Gallagher watched him go and sighed. Then turned his attention to the work on the desk. The top note was the start of a 'next-of-kin' letter to Macaulay's family. Gallagher stared at the paper then noticed the address: Great Coxwell, Oxfordshire, not more than eighteen miles from Masham. He decided it was churlish to avoid the issue, to take the easy way out and send a letter. And Gallagher needed to salve his soul by facing the music. The pain he had caused he would see for himself. Let the guilt be his and not avoided. He stood up and took his belt and uniform cap, and made for the door.

He found Squires in the Nissen hut that served as a gymnasium for wet days. The former eyed him with a stern look.

'I rather gather you've patted him on the head and said "don't be naughty". You and I are going to fall out one of these days, Hugh. I have no wish to rely upon rank, and I recognise you are the chap in charge of this operation, but I do have my say at this stage. I am OC Training.'

'Remark noted, sir.' Gallagher was stiff and formal. 'Have I your permission to leave the Hall? There are a couple of things I need to do outside.'

Squires nodded coldly and Gallagher left without a glance at his team working out.

The Macaulays lived in a pleasant, converted farmhouse on the edge of the village. He stopped his car some yards from the house, and walked down the path, recognised from its overgrown aspect that the front door was never used, and made for the side porch, shielded from prevailing winds by a small recess surrounded by roses and the first climbings of a newly-planted clematis. The door was open, and he knocked several times before any reply was forthcoming.

'Hello! Hello! Anyone in?'

After some moments a female voice called back. 'Sorry, can't come to the door. Do come through.'

Gallagher removed his cap, and entered the long, stone-paved passage that led into the old farmhouse kitchen. In the centre of the room was a large pine table at which a woman in her fifties was scraping the dregs out of a large brass pan. Before her on a tray were twenty jam jars and all the accoutrements of jam making. Elastic bands, waxed circles and larger cellophane circles, and neat pink gingham tops. The woman humped the huge brass pan over to the Aga cooker before she turned and beamed at him. A fine-looking woman with soft, unkempt hair, and blue eyes, and a very-much-in-command voice.

'Awfully sorry to be inhospitable, but you see I'm in the middle of an emergency. Can you lend a hand? Shove the empty ones towards this end.'

Gallagher obediently shoved the empty jars towards her for her to fill from the cooling jug. 'Must get it in while it's hot, you see. Not too hot, mind, but we need the vacuum or something as it cools and sets. Probably a lot of rot, but mother did it this way. We're all creatures of habit, aren't we? Last one! there. Would you be a darling and stick this on the draining board while I do the tops? Thank you so much.'

Gallagher did as he was bidden, and returned to the table to watch the tops being placed, sick at what he had to say in the next few moments.

'Can't offer you a drink. The village shop's run out. Place is quite dry. This war really is the end! Do sit down, if you can find a chair. Not that one. It belongs to the cat and she doesn't like boarders.'

She beamed at Gallagher. 'You must be a chum of Nigel's.'

'From the same unit. Yes.'

'Don't worry, shan't ask. All frightfully hush-hush, I know. It's awfully kind of you to drop in. We don't meet all that many of Nigel's friends. I should say *I* don't. Daddy's not with us now. He was a bomb-disposal boffin . . . Shall I make us some tea? I could do with a cup.'

Mrs Macaulay crossed to the sink to fill the kettle noisily from the elderly tap.

'Are you from the same unit as Nigel? Of course, you said so. How silly of me.'

'Actually I'm his CO.'

Mrs Macaulay turned off the tap and swung round, suddenly aware this was not a social call.

'Oh dear! Has he been posted overseas or something?'

Gallagher mentally took a deep breath, and spoke quietly but firmly.

'I'm afraid he was killed in action, Mrs Macaulay.'

Macaulay's mother gave a sudden sharp exhalation of breath. Gallagher heard the tiny whispered 'Oh God!', and saw her eyes fill with sudden sharp tears. Her mouth and chin trembled ever so slightly before she closed her eyes to blot out everything, and gather herself together again. Gallagher waited in silence.

'Is it possible, I mean, can you tell me how . . .'

'I am not at liberty to tell you very much. You must have known he had volunteered for special duties. It was a special assignment in Occupied territory. He was killed instantly saving the life of a comrade. I was there. I saw it. He was a very courageous young man. I am so sorry.'

Mrs Macaulay cleared her throat, and stood silent for some seconds. Her face had turned suddenly rather masculine. Fine-featured like her son.

'Thank you for telling me, and for taking the trouble to come and tell me yourself. It can't be easy for you . . . and I'm so grateful. Truly, it's a sort of contact.'

She started to melt into the tears that were welling up inside her.

'I'm so sorry. Please forgive me.' She rushed her handkerchief, grubby and crumpled, from her pinafore pocket and blew into it before she looked up at him. This time there was a heart-gripping look in her eyes but her voice had regained its strength. 'Daddy would have been so proud. Oh dear me, I didn't think I would go to pieces like this. It wasn't so terrible when Robert died. At least I had Nigel, *now* . . .'

Gallagher spoke quietly. 'I'll arrange for his things to be returned.' He stood up and took up his cap from the table.

'Yes. You didn't have any tea. I suppose there is no chance?'

Gallagher saw the pathetic hope for a second in the eyes, hope that he had to dash once and for all.

'None at all, Mrs Macaulay. I'm sorry.'

Gallagher turned, and made slowly for the doorway, conscious that she was following him and that her heels clattered and rang on the stone floor. At the doorway she spoke, very quietly.

'I wonder, if you're going through the village . . . could you pop into the Post Office and ask Diana if she could come home? That's my daughter, she's helping out before she goes into the WAAFs.'

'Of course. Goodbye, Mrs Macaulay.'

She didn't reply. Gallagher left knowing there was a totally shattered lady alone in a huge empty house. When he reached his car and sat at the wheel he found he was trembling ever so slightly from a nervous tension, nothing more . . . but it made him question his own reactions for some moments before he turned the ignition key and let in the clutch.

It was on the way back, driving towards Masham, that Gallagher had his brainwave. He had just passed the post on which the village name sign had faced incoming traffic before a careful government had decided that place names, boldly displayed on the roadside or on signposts, should be removed so that a potential invader might experience greater confusion. Whether or not it would have made a great deal of difference is a moot point. Britain's road system is tight and well-established and had been totally reliable for decades. However, removed they had been, and Masham's post now bore a simple board bearing a pale blue poster advertising the visiting circus, again with the crude drawing of a tight-rope walker prominently displayed. Gallagher found the circus site without much trouble. It had been pitched in the long pasture which ran down behind the church. He left his car by the church entrance, and wandered round the churchyard while he mulled over the scheme he had stumbled upon.

Mr Bainbridge's circus was a tatty affair. It had certainly not received a coat of paint since the outbreak of hostilities, and the canvas tent was badly patched. The caravans in which the company lived and travelled were a motley lot. One, presumably the owners', was a converted bus and rejoiced in a livery of pre-war extravaganza not extended to its lesser brethren. They were no more than lorries or vans pulling trailers, generators, and a small collection of animal cages whose stench drifted and hung over the village.

The artistes were practising and paid no attention to the uniformed officer who wandered through their midst. The big top, if that is not too grand a term to describe the tattered and twice-extended marquee in which the acts were performed, stood at the end of the field. The ticket booth was unattended, and Gallagher sauntered into the large tent and looked about him.

A juggler was trying to make his left hand, apparently recently damaged, as he wore a blood-stained bandage around it, perform its wonted task with its customary agility. Twice he dropped his metallic-blue clubs, and cursed in some language unknown to Gallagher. Above his head, along a wire stretched tightly between the main tent pillars, a man was practising. He carried a long pole and was wearing the woollen tights that dancers affect. He was a small man with a cheerful, Slavonic face. Someone called up to him 'Andy'! So, his name was Andrew, or Andrej, or André. Gallagher would see in due course. He sat down on one of the tiered bench-seats and watched the man perform for twenty minutes. He was good, better than Gallagher had expected from such a secondrate circus. Better than he had seen for many years, though his comparisons were of necessity coloured by the eyes of childhood. At least the man was competent and very sure of himself. Gallagher stood up and made his way to the bus-cum-caravan of Mr 'Colonel' Bainbridge.

The proprietor turned out to be a portly man in his late

fifties, and for a self-advertised 'Colonel' spoke with an accent that would have been out of place in any officer's mess known to Gallagher.

'But what can you tell me about him, Mr Bainbridge?' (Bainbridge had not pushed his 'Colonel' title when faced with Gallagher's uniform.)

'Not a lot. None of my bleedin' business, is it? Well, I mean, can't be too fussy these days, can you. There's only four circuses operatin' in Britain and believe me it's no joke. Can't get a bleedin' thing, no replacements, nothing! Here, d'you know I'm employing local blacksmiths to make new rings? How about that! Not even chromed! There's no farriers to replace harness, not a bleedin' thing!'

Gallagher ignored this and pursued his enquiry with restraint.

'This man, Soltysyk . . .'

'Andy? Oh, yeah, well, 'e's been with us since '41. Invalided out of the Polish Forces. Bit of a mess, 'e was. But he's good, oh yes. Very good! I think his old man worked the rings in Europe. Don't say much, nice enough bloke, willing to lend a hand.' Then he suddenly took on a shrewd tone.

'What's all this about, Mister . . . er, Major?'

'Nothing serious, Mr Bainbridge.'

'Not in any trouble, is he? I told him not to give his sweet ration to the kids! 'Ere, hasn't been messin' about, has he? I mean . . . well . . . kids. You know. Foreigners are a funny lot.'

'Nothing at all, Mr Bainbridge. How much d'you pay him?'

'Hang about! You want to pinch him, do you? Got a bleedin' show of your own, is that it? Well, hark to this, mate . . . I've a bleedin' contract with Mister bleedin' Soltysyk, and I don't bleedin' want no bleedin' opposition poking their bleedin' noses into my bleedin' business! Savvy?'

Gallagher held himself back under the barrage of words and stood up and sighed.

'Mr Bainbridge. There's no problem. I'm not in the circus business, and I've no intention of starting a fight with you.'

Bainbridge glowered at him as he left, vaguely conscious that he was being 'got at', then retired into his bus wagon to restore his poise with a large gin, muttering something about 'Bleedin' army . . . who the 'ell do they think they are. . . .'

Gallagher had decided. He had his total plan in his mind for the first time. The problem of getting into the complex was difficult enough in itself, but getting into the place carrying enough plastic explosive, detonators, and weapons for their own defence, was an area he had not solved and he was beginning to despair of ever doing so. Now he had it. After a call to the duty-sergeant informing him of his proposed whereabouts Gallagher left Dotheboys Hall behind and drove to London as fast as his Armstrong Siddeley would take him. He stopped once to telephone ahead and make appointments.

The Polish Armed Forces HQ was not far from Gwillim's office, but Gallagher decided that, for the moment, he would keep his own counsel. No point in anticipating without all the information available. The door he was shown to bore the small nameplate 'Major O. Piernjk'.

Once the pleasantries were put on one side, and a good measure of vodka put inside them, Major Piernjk got down to brass tacks.

'After you telephoned I consulted our records, Major, and I have obtained authority to cooperate from the Polish Military Authority in Exile. How can I be of assistance?'

'This man, Soltysyk, what do we know of him? What is his background?'

Piernjk opened the file before him and stacked the papers neatly with his flat hands before he spoke; a habit he had formed while an advocate in civilian life.

'Andrej Ignaz Soltysyk; born Sandomierz, 4 October 1907. Trained as a trapeze artiste and high-wire walker with the Circus Sambor. Volunteered for Polish Cavalry in April 1939. After basic military training commissioned as Lieutenant in 17th Cavalry Regiment at Katowice. Wounded in action at Ceranow, and escaped to England in January 1940. He was invalided out of the Polish Forces in March after several attempts to rejoin active units serving in France.'

He looked up at Gallagher, with a certain pride in his voice.

'It would seem that he sustained considerable wounds from shrapnel which entered his body from behind. His Discharge Medical examination indicated that, although his general fitness was more or less unimpaired, his internal condition was such as to make periods of active service quite intolerable.'

'What they're saying is that he's fit enough, but liable to internal haemorrhage under certain conditions, am I right?'

'I think that is what is implied, yes.'

'Security risk?'

'If you are asking me if you can trust him I would say "Yes". Major I have no idea what you have in mind for him, nor do I wish to know, but I do not think you will find him reluctant to help.'

'I am greatly obliged to you Major. Are there any formalities to be gone through before I approach him?'

'Not exactly formalities,' Piernjk was his pedantic, advocate self again. 'But there are certain procedures to be observed. A meeting will be arranged officially here, at Polish HQ, at which one Polish officer will be present, probably myself. *Bona fides* will be established, and introductions made, together with a statement of conditions. Thereafter, assuming all is agreed, the matter will be between Soltysyk and yourself, alone.'

'Must it be so formal and protracted? The man is, at this moment, less than five miles from my training establishment.'

'There is no other way we can permit this, Major. This brings up the question of a pension, possible disability rights, temporary re-enlistment, and the general rights of dependants. He has a wife in Poland, if she is still alive. My job is to look after the rights of Polish expatriots in the Free Polish Forces. I am sure you understand.'

Gallagher sighed, he understood, of course, and accepted.

The meeting with Soltysyk was arranged for the following day when he would come up to London for an interview. Gallagher decided to stay the night in London, and found himself a room in a modest hotel in Bayswater from where he telephoned to secure a meeting with Colonel Gwillim. Gwillim seemed anxious to talk to him, and they met for dinner at his club in Piccadilly.

The club was well patronised. The stuffy atmosphere of pre-war days had been replaced with a certain sense of bustle and it was full of officers from many regiments, though Gallagher noted very quickly that he was possibly the only man present below the rank of Lieutenant-Colonel. Gwillim was friendly and relaxed as they wandered into the lounge after their sparse, wartime dinner to take coffee.

'You been here before?'

'Once, with Tim Squires when we felt like a break, after a protracted meeting in town . . . with you, as a matter of fact.'

Gwillim grunted, and nodded to one of the stewards that they would take coffee. They found a large leather settee unoccupied and away from other ears.

'I use it quite a lot m'self. Food's no better than anywhere else, as you've just seen, but they still have a cellarful of decent brandy. They've recently removed the sandbags round the entrance. Premature in my view, as we know better than most. Still can't very well say anything.' He turned to face Gallagher, 'What did you want to see me about?'

'I want your permission to conscript a new member of the team. He's an ex-member of the Polish forces.'

Arrival of coffee and brandy stopped the flow for a moment but once the coast was clear and coffee had been poured, Gwillim asked, 'What's so special about this Polish chap?'

'He's a tight-rope walker of considerable skill. I need him.' Gwillim looked distinctly unhappy. 'I hope this isn't a forerunner to fire-eaters and snake-charmers. It would look decidedly odd on paper. We've already got a safe-cracker.'

Gallagher didn't say anything. Gwillim bit into a rich tea biscuit.

'Why him?'

'I can't think of another way of getting over the wire the explosives and stuff we need. We can't take it through the front door, can we?'

'Tunnelling?'

'Not on, sir. There's thirty to forty feet of tunnelling, and there is a guard every fifteen minutes, the minefield itself and solid rock about two feet down.'

'Tell me about your Polish tight-rope walker . . .'

24 May

The following day's meeting at the Polish HQ was initially formal and correct. Piernjk went through the formalities before leaving Gallagher alone with Soltysyk.

The Pole looked anxiously at Gallagher.

'Do you smoke, Andrej?'

'Of course,' the little man laughed. 'I do everything that is bad for me.' They lit up and then the Pole squinted at Gallagher.

'What do you want with an old soldier who now works in a circus?'

'Exactly that. I want an old soldier, a good experienced soldier . . . who just happens to be a tight-rope walker. They aren't all that thick on the ground.'

Soltysyk's face slowly beamed with a delighted, childlike joy.

'I do this thing. Is dangerous?'

'Very. I never thought to ask, can you do your act in the dark?'

The Pole stared at him puzzled, then scratched his head for some moments. 'I don' know. I never try.'

He burst out laughing, but the smile on Gallagher's face was suddenly weaker than he intended. He *had* not thought of that until this moment.

Gallagher informed Squires of his arrangements when he got back to the Hall, anticipating the shocked silence that greeted his statement. Squires faced him in disbelief.

'You can't be serious!'

'I am, Tim. I don't think there IS another way.'

'Good God, man! the whole thing is preposterous! I flatter myself that I'm slightly imaginative, even if I do go by the book as a general rule. But this? No. I can't take it seriously. We'd be laughed out of court, and rightly so.'

Gallagher stood up to him. 'Gwillim didn't laugh.'

'You mean, you've actually proposed this charade to the Colonel?'

'I did. He said, "Go ahead".'

Squires was suitably deflated and crossed to his desk, and sat down. Gallagher followed him and leant over the desk.

'Look. There's no way we can tackle the minefield by the book. There isn't time between guard checks. Even if we could, how do we get our stuff over the wire? We can't touch it, the alarm system would wake the dead and give away the whole show. I had thought about the possibility of tunnelling but there isn't time. It's solid rock underneath. That's why they built the bloody thing there in the first place. Don't be so damned stuffy. Answer me. What is there left?'

Squires didn't, or couldn't answer.

'Do you realise I even thought of the possibility of pole-vaulting. I was that desperate.' He straightened up. 'That's his file.'

Squires touched it without opening it. He sensed he was not only beaten, but there was also the likelihood that Gallagher was right. It might be the only way. He ruminated in silence for several minutes then he eventually stood up and walked towards the office door, muttering.

'Why do we bother to train these people into a tight, welded team if we are to just pick up another one out of a hat? It's not the way, you know.'

But he had given in, and Gallagher knew it.

25–30 May

Most of the trainees were having a pre-prandial drink in the mess when the taxi drew up outside the Hall. Moffat made for the door, and was seen carrying in a large, battered suitcase, followed by a short, broad man wearing the uniform of a Polish Cavalry Officer. The conversation stopped as they all watched the Pole look about him. Moffat returned from the desk, and picked up the case again.

'Mr Warsaw. I'll show you to your quarters.'

All eyes watched him as he walked up the stairs with a jaunty step. Ellen Robinson leant forward to the others.

'He's Polish! I wonder if that is the replacement they told us about.'

Macklin, now thoroughly at home, even proprietorial, scoffed, 'Nah! They wouldn't stick another foreigner in with us lot. What? A couple of Frenchies and a Scotsman . . .'

When Corporal Moffat descended the stairs, and entered the mess proper he was grabbed by the Cockney.

‘’Ere . . . What’s goin’ on, Miff? Who’s the comic-opera wallah?’

‘He’s your new recruit, sir.’

‘Christ! You mean ’e’s joinin’ us?’

The silence that held after Moffat went to the bar was something new. It wasn’t until Lamboit descended the stairs bringing the Pole with him that they properly accepted the state of affairs.

Soltysyk responded to the introductions by a series of short bows and heel-clips, as they made room for him round their table.

Lovell leant forward. ‘You’re joining us rather late, Warsaw. May one ask what you do that is so special?’

Soltysyk had spied the folded newspaper on the table rack, and fished it out. It was still folded at the place showing the advertisement of the circus and the block of the trapeze drawing.

‘Is special purpose. Is me! Is tight-rope.’

Solange gaped at the little man. ‘You are a tight-rope walker?’

Soltysyk beamed delightedly and childishly. ‘Very good! Best wire man in Eastern Europe, maybe Western Europe, too . . . maybe in whole world.’

He laughed loudly at his presumption as Moffat came to the table and presented the Pole with a bottle of vodka.

‘Major Gallagher’s compliments, sir, says there is no more where it came from so you are to guard it with your life.’

Andrej Soltysyk beamed happily and took the bottle, breaking the seal and unscrewing the top. ‘I like this Major Galley. More glasses . . . yes?’

Moffat brought a collection of clean glasses, and Soltysyk started to pour large measures into every one. Macklin grunted disapprovingly. ‘He never gave me no bottle when I joined up. What’s so special about you, mate?’

‘Maybe I am so pretty, like these ladies.’ He beamed at Solange and Ellen as he handed them their glasses. ‘I think I like this place. So, now we drink together.’

He emptied the last of the vodka into the last glass and passed it to Cameron. Then held up his glass for a toast.

‘*Na zdrowie!*’

After their drinks Lamboit showed Soltysyk round the Hall. They ended up in the unarmed combat class that Sergeant-

Major Gidney gave in one of the black Nissen huts. As they entered an argument was in progress. Lovell was flushed and facing Gidney angrily. Gidney, equally annoyed, was trying to keep his cool.

'Come along Mr Hibou, sir, it's all part of the course.'

'I will *not!* I go along with this course because I have to, but I am not going to become an assassin! There I draw the line. Is that clear?'

They all became aware that visitors were present and Lamboit introduced Soltysyk to Sergeant-Major Gidney. Cameron, who was standing by awkwardly, tried to change the tension, and turned grinning to Soltysyk.

'Fancy a bit of a fight, Warsaw? Here . . . catch.' He chucked the knife he was holding to the Pole, who caught it with dexterity. It was obvious from the expression on the little man's face that he did not want to fight, but realised that – this being his first moment with the team – he could not back down and save face. Quietly he took off his jacket and handed it to Lamboit, then faced his Highland opponent grimly. The two men circled and weighed each other up. Suddenly Soltysyk lunged, but it was a hard, bunched fist that hit Cameron sideways on his forehead. The Highlander sat back, pole-axed for a moment, but only for a moment. He made a quick grab for Soltysyk's legs, with every intention of toppling him. He got a sharp, fast kick in the chest for his pains. Cameron went backwards, shook his head, then grinned up at the little Pole.

'The streets of Poland aren't all that different, are they, lad?' He hurled himself at the little man, and a real brawl ensued. The two men, so different in size, were well-matched and fought like tigers, until Cameron threw him, at the same time holding one side of his shirt. As the little man flew the shirt ripped off his body. The Pole lay winded, face-down on the floor, but all eyes had suddenly gone to his back. The muscled surface caved in two places, deeply scarred in themselves, but merely the centre of a mass of appalling weals and scar tissue. There was a general gasp. Cameron's mouth dropped open.

'Oh Jesus!' He bent over the Pole and lifted him to his feet. 'Agh, Hell, man! I'm that sorry. I did no' know.'

Soltysyk smiled broadly, and took the offered hand, then

neatly threw the big Scot into the corner with a sudden jerk. Then he sprang into a circus pose and laughed loudly. The two men shook hands and clapped each other on the back.

'I'm real sorry about your shirt. I owe ye a new one. You'll do fine, laddie, just fine. You did no' get that in a circus.'

After they left Cameron blew out his cheeks, and raised his eyebrows. The others smiled to themselves. Cameron, their sometimes overbearing 'Grive', had met his match. The one who didn't notice was Stephen Lovell. He wasn't there. He had left.

During the afternoon Gallagher took Soltysyk into one of the unoccupied Nissen huts, and suggested he use it for his own private practice. Rope and stands, mats, and one NCO attendant were waiting. Soltysyk looked round the place and nodded. Gallagher told the NCO to go for a smoke for ten minutes, and then sat down facing Soltysyk.

'Sit down a minute, Warsaw. I ought to tell you in principle what it is I want you to do, but – for the moment – it is between *us*. The others do not know, and will not know. Clear?'

It took slightly longer than ten minutes to outline the plan and answer the Pole's questions. There seemed to be no problem, except the final question.

'What about doing it in the dark?'

'I don' know. Soltysyk never try this thing. Why should I? People pay to *see* my act, I try this now.'

Gallagher recognised that Soltysyk would do it if he was even remotely capable of it, and smiled, slapped his knee as he stood up.

'I'm glad I met you, Soltysyk.'

Later the same evening Colonel Gwillim turned up at the Hall with some rolls of paper under his arm. He laid them out on Squires' desk top.

'I had some dye-lines run off from the original plans. They tell us what we need to know. Viardot was not stringing us along. It bears out all he said. As I read it, this air-shaft still exists and leads down to the power-generator room.'

'Do we know if it's sealed off?'

Gwillim turned to Gallagher's questioning face. 'No, my boy, we do not.'

That was yet another unanswerable question for Gallagher. It meant taking the chance that it was still open, or could be opened. If not, they had a problem. The other problem he raised immediately.

'The electrified wires atop the fence. If our initial shot with the grapple misfires or the end trails and touches the top wire we've blown the whole thing. It isn't likely, but there is that tiny chance. The job is too important to risk it. I want that wire inoperative for one whole minute.'

'And how d'you propose to manage that? I agree it is essential.'

'I had thought of getting de Grouchy to throw the switches, but it would alert the Jerries. It's not on. There is a way. The main grid is disconnected automatically when the air-raid warning souhds, and switches the underground complex onto its own generator. It takes fifty-eight seconds for that to happen. I have checked it with an identical system. For fifty-eight seconds the wire is unelectrified. I want you to lay on an air-raid to coincide with the operation.'

Gwillim looked at him stonily.

'Don't want much, do you?'

'It matters, sir, it's worth it.'

Gwillim thought rapidly then nodded. 'I'll get the PM's approval and authority to lay it on. Anything else?'

'No sir, that's about it. I don't want an air-raid with bombs and that sort of thing, just enough of a presence to make the warning happen.'

Gallagher left later. It had registered with him that Gwillim had said he would get the PM's approval. The Prime Minister? Not the Joint Chiefs of Staff?

Nor had Squires missed it, and confronted Gwillim when Gallagher was out of earshot. There are questions colonels can ask each other that majors cannot.

'Surely we can blow our noses without asking the PM's permission or is Downing Street taking over?'

'Ordinarily we would go through our own channels. Not at this moment, Tim. As you know the Invasion's been put off again. I can't make up my mind if God is on Jerry's side or ours, and Eisenhower has a congenital inability to make up his mind about anything. Great mistake appointing that man. I know he's a good admin chap and all that, and he is patient and good at smoothing troubled waters, but the Supreme Commander needs a bit more than that. Monty's straining at the bit. Tedder's playing it safe. Patton's skulking somewhere in the North. Bedell-Smith's saying whatever anyone wants to hear, and Leigh Mallory is just a permanent pain in the arse, as he's always been. The Navy says it's up to the weather men, but they don't advise it. Poor old Winston is getting very uneasy.'

Squires didn't press the matter. Gwillim would tell him what he felt he could. There was nothing to be gained by prying. The next subject was Gallagher himself.

'Gallagher all right? I thought he was under-the-weather a little.'

'He's getting on with it . . . using his brains, but there is something not right. He's taken the loss of the girl Portales and Macaulay very badly. Blames himself. He tries not to show it, but it's very much there.'

Gwillim was silent and concerned. He sensed something of the sort in his Club earlier in the week. Now he was faced with a situation he would rather avoid if he could. An unhappy officer who blames himself for mishaps is very rapidly an indecisive officer. That Gwillim could do without. He was also beginning to feel wary of the whole enterprise.

Gallagher was indeed carrying a burden inside himself. He did blame himself for Portales' murder and Macaulay's death. He knew there were thousands of similar homes to the Macaulay one all over England, all mourning their lost loved ones. But these two, and those he had lost on the Brest raid the previous year, they went down in *his* book. *He*, and no other, had lost them, and it did not sit well upon him. That he was tired and strained and overworked did not seem significant. Guilt is the most useless of emotions, and its effects the most horrendous and harmful.

The moment of truth came when, during a mine-defusing exercise, Sally Birkett was badly shocked by a heavier than normal explosion. The dummies they practised on were old German S-35s and had a tiny charge inserted to 'teach' them when they had not done the job properly. They were not supposed to blow your head off! When Squires admitted that he slipped high-charge mines in to keep them on their toes it was too much for Gallagher and a flaming row ensued. It reached a pitch of home-truth stating on both sides, and left Gallagher only one possible course of action, unless he chose to back down – which he couldn't.

The next day he left for London, and handed Gwillim his resignation. Gwillim told *him* a few home-truths and refused to accept his resignation. Gallagher returned to the Hall with his tail between his legs. Solange commented upon his absence very solicitously, and Gallagher recognised that, had he wanted a liaison at that time, the French girl would have been very happy to accommodate him. There just wasn't time to make anything out of it, and there was still Claudine.

The final arrangements were put together when de Grouchy reported that a new batch of Todt workers was to be moved into the complex in three days' time. That was it. No further delays were possible. Gallagher collected his team together in front of Squires and Gidney, and announced his selection: Cameron, Soltysyk, Lovell, Macklin, Lamboit and Solange, with Ellen Robinson as contact at base. She and Solange had worked as a WT team so often that they were not only the best at the job but they had the necessary rapport. Squires beamed like a happy schoolboy and produced their sealed bet from his safe. Gallagher handed over two fivers without murmur. He was just relieved to be getting on with it.

1 June

The rejects were posted to other units to finish their training, and Gallagher got down to briefing. The chosen few were very silent as he took his place in the briefing room before them. Under a cloth, and guarded by Sergeant Dowding, was something that everyone recognised as a model of something. This was IT. They all tensed up as they waited.

He dismissed the Sergeant, and removed the cover from the model as they all gathered round and stared at the object they were to destroy.

Gallagher outlined the nature and purpose of the German storage complex. He laid it on the line with as much back-up information as he had. If they were going to risk their lives they had a right to know that it was worth it. He stuck to generalities for the first hour of the morning, making sure that everyone recognised the basic plan, and that any objections or comments could be raised and dealt with before he moved on to a detailed briefing. That much was essential, as once accepted and agreed in principle, the future acceptance of detail was a matter of course. They would do the job because they were ordered to, that is standard military procedure and accepted the world over. But a job that *had* to be done, no matter what, demanded just a little more than blind obedience. Gallagher knew many of his superiors would argue that point. The entire German General staff, possibly even the Wehrmacht itself, would. It changed nothing. He wanted his team to go in believing that what they were about to do was not merely a good thing militarily but that it was essential. There could be no failure, because the result of that failure was too terrible to accept.

They all recognised the destruction that more than one thousand of these rocket bombs per day could unfold upon their London, their country, and their fellow British. It was not to be contemplated, just as the possibility of military reversal was not.

These thoughts were racking the mind of Lovell as he listened to the briefing. He had revolted once or twice during the course. It was not that he did not understand the significance, nor that he had less motive than anyone else to pull his weight. But he wanted to do it his way. All his life he had turned from killing and cruelty of any sort. He had spent his childhood looking after hurt animals and keeping out of school fights. He wasn't a coward. At least no more than the next boy. He just did not like violence. Even at the tender age of ten he had refused to take part in house-games that always ended in a scrap. It was deeply engrained in him, and adulthood had changed that into a reasoned and convinced philosophy. The war had placed him in a quandary. He was too intelligent to simply place the hostilities on one side as no concern of his. He knew what the Germans stood for, and the dark deeds going on within Occupied Europe. He would do his share. Some had to fight with weapons hand-to-hand and face-to-face, to draw blood and take life. There were others who were just as necessary who worked behind the lines, making, experimenting and inventing. Stephen Lovell worked all the hours God sent, and completed four times as much as anyone else he knew. It was his way of making up for what he was unable to do.

He had been thrust into this job because they needed his expertise. He had accepted that and the accompanying para-military training and combat tactics. It had all seemed remote from reality but now it was *here*, and *real*. He was going to have to kill, with his hands. Take life, directly and personally, and his nature revolted against it.

Gallagher's voice rang in his head.

'. . . we go in as Todt workers posing as specialists in gyro-compass and guidance devices. We have been working at the Deauville launching-site, and are transferred to Senlis for final assembly before they are dispatched to the launching platforms.'

'Wouldn't it be safer to go in with a bunch of ordinary workers? Five people will be so conspicuous?'

'Yes. That's why we are specialists. Five top engineers would have separate transport. Our papers will be in order, and we will be expected. We could not risk being herded in with a crowd. We might not be able to separate and get out to do our jobs. This way, we should have that chance.'

Solange spoke in a quiet voice that showed no sense of strain.

'Major, when Warsaw has gone over the wire with the equipment what do I do with the recovered wire and things?'

'Nothing. It's too risky. I'll chance discovery. You leave everything where it is. Don't recover it. Keep your eye on the guard. Then disappear. You will eventually get back to de Grouchy's farm, pick up your WT, and go into the wood and send the success signal. After that go to bed and sleep until we get back.'

'*If* we get back.' Macklin's customary moan.

'Sergeant!' Gallagher called out. Dowding entered and marched to the table as Gallagher covered up the model. He indicated to Dowding that his duty was to guard the model.

'Back in one hour everybody. Detailed briefing.'

While they were sitting in the mess silently stirring their coffees, and thinking through what they had been told, Corporal Moffat came up to Ellen Robinson and said that the colonel wished to speak with her. Squires was relaxed and friendly and offered her a seat.

'Merle, I asked you to come and see me because there are one or two things I would like to discuss.' He paused and looked at her. 'Tell me about Grive and Hibou.'

Ellen sensed that she ought to feel flattered. The colonel was asking her opinion, almost advice, which argued that he respected her judgment and that pleased her enormously. She did not react as a schoolgirl asked to snitch on a comrade. She knew it was too serious for anything but honesty.

'Grive is a rough, tough soldier who enjoys his job. He's a good fighting-man. End of story, I think. He won't spoil your job by being too keen, if that's what you're thinking. He *is* responsible, Colonel.'

'You're very perceptive. That *was* concerning me. You bear out Major Gallagher's assessment. I am delighted to hear it.'

He paused and waited a moment.

'The next one presents a more serious problem – Mr Hibou.'

Ellen took a deep, slow breath, and knotted her forehead slightly. The question was one she had been avoiding asking herself.

'He's a liberal intellectual, none the worse for that. He doesn't like physical violence. None the worse for that either. If you are asking "Will he opt out?" I don't know. I doubt it, but I don't really know. Behind all that gruffness and irritability is a basically nice man. He is much more down-to-earth than people think. He just needs to be convinced that what he is supposed to do is *demonstrably* necessary.'

Squires was silent for some moment, then nodded.

'That brings me to you, Mrs Robinson.' He used her real name and it almost came as a shock to her. 'I have noted that your relationship with Monsieur Lamboit is very close. He is a fine man and a patriot. He is therefore more likely to be killed than most of his countrymen. I hope you recognise this possibility.'

'Yes, Colonel. Thank you for your concern.'

'No need for thanks. I am not a married man, as you probably realise. If I had chosen that path I rather think it would have been someone like you. Thank you for your help.'

Ellen smiled and started to rise, then hesitated.

'Is my relationship with Lamboit the reason why I am not actually going on this job, into France I mean?'

Squires looked at her. 'Yes . . . and no. No, because we need you here to accept the contact with Chardonneret. It had to be someone who knew her touch intimately. Yes, because I could not risk your personal concerns for Ferdy taking precedent over the job. It could happen. I'm not saying it would, but it could. We can't chance that.'

Ellen nodded understandingly, smiled again, and left his office.

Immediately after the break Gallagher issued the WT code-names to the two operators, and then got down to brass tacks while his team stayed glued to his every word.

'Chardonneret and Ferdy leave tomorrow night and will be put down by Lizzie approximately ten kilometres outside of Senlis, at 03.00 hours. You will be met. I will brief you both separately before you leave. I want to pass on to the main job. The operation proper commences on June fifth. We will be parachuted into the immediate area at 22.00 hours. Once again we will be met and regroup at de Grouchy's farm, where he will have our transport waiting.'

Squires meanwhile was finalising his arrangements for equipping and kitting-out, double-checking paperwork and so on. Gwillim would be handling the actual transport factor, and would by now have laid on the intruder raid as planned. Squires had posted Birkett and Wilson immediately the team was selected. They had gone to swell the ranks of Eastern Command on a temporary posting until the operation was completed. After which they would rejoin, and complete training. *His* training, not the scratched together make-shift thing they had just been through.

'The German guard passes the position at 00.15 hours. Chardonneret and Warsaw will be in position by 00.13. At 00.16 and no later, you should be ready to rig the wire. Wait until the air-raid warning sounds, then go. You have fifty-five seconds. If the first grapple shot fails we have a problem, so it mustn't. If that line drops into the minefield we can forget the whole operation. I am allowing three minutes to rig up the wire. We did it in two minutes fifteen seconds yesterday.'

Gallagher went on to elaborate in detail every aspect of the job. They rapidly began to understand why they had been chosen for the job in the first place, and their confidence grew. Only Macklin seemed unhappy. His brow was furrowed and his face had fallen.

'When does my bit come in? Or am I just there for the ride?'

'Not for the ride, Choucas, you can be sure of that. About here –' He pointed to the model. 'There is an old air-shaft. We know it still exists, even though it isn't on the model here. It leads down just off the generator room. It may have doors that need opening. We don't know that.'

'You mean I'm insurance?'

'No. Your job becomes positive and imperative once we are inside.'

Gallagher lifted off the top layer of the model revealing the complex bays, passages, and storage areas underneath.

'We devised this from the plans we pinched from the Hôtel de Ville at Senlis.'

The team muttered and murmured, 'So that's what that was all about!'

'We enter the complex here. In this corridor are the offices used by the technical staff, researchers and engineers. Inside this one is a safe, Liedke Mark 207/D. Built around 1936.'

Macklin's face changed instantly. He beamed his pleasure, and nodded that he was familiar with the safe.

'Your job is to open it and let Hibou go through the papers. That's what *he* is really here for. We take those papers with us. In the long run they are probably more important than destroying the place.'

Finally Gallagher explained that, in the likely event of their not being able to get out the way they entered, they would have to play it by ear, though he personally favoured the long sloping shaft used by the wagons that both took in, and sent out the rockets. It was the one contingency that it was not possible to plan in detail. It all depended upon so much. All Gallagher could do was outline possibilities and indicate preferences. They all realised that it could turn out to be a suicide mission. The quantity of explosives they were to plant, would set off a chain-reaction and because of the war-heads in store and the fuel contained within the bunker complex it would be one very large explosion. If they were caught inside they would never see daylight again. It was a sobering thought but they all accepted it without murmur.

When the briefing was finally over Gallagher returned to Squires' office, and found the colonel seated at his desk with whisky and water and glasses waiting for him.

'Cheers, old man! Two things: one, you are relying upon the RAF to ensure that your electricity supply is deflected for the grapple shot. Two, I must alert you to the *possibility* of intensive military activity at the time of your operation. Comments?'

'I assume the points are connected. The RAF say they will lay on the raid. If they say so . . . they will. If they are delayed we sweat it out until it does happen. This military activity, what is it?'

'Can't tell you, Hugh. Use your imagination if you will. By the way, the Met reports are not very encouraging. Doesn't sound at all like summer.'

He smiled and raised his glass to Gallagher. The latter nodded and returned the smile.

'In case I forget I want to say "Thank you" for your help. You got these people into shape, not me. I really am grateful.'

'Just remember me in your Will, dear boy. Post-war retirement looms large, and I can't spend all my life fishing. Odd jobs-about-the-house are not my forte. Might have to find a rich widow . . .' He sighed. 'Not my forte, either.'

Gallagher stood up to leave and put down his glass.

'Spare me your maudlin sentiments, Colonel. I just can't see it myself.'

In the lounge area of the mess Lamboit had collared Ellen Robinson, and was telling her briefly that he had no one in France, and asked if she would marry him. Ellen looked at him sweetly and smiled her agreement.

'Of course. I would have asked you if you hadn't asked me. You realise this makes for problems. I don't think they will let either of us stay in this unit.'

'Then we say nothing until I come back, yes?'

Further intimacies were stopped by Gallagher recalling them for a second run-through in which he fired questions of detail at them. The replies came quick and fast . . . and correct. He smiled to himself. He had his team . . . and they knew their job.

It was during the late evening that Gallagher came down into the mess to find the place deserted. They had all decided to turn in. All except Solange. She was sitting playing patience as Gallagher crossed to join her. Corporal Moffat had closed up the bar and most of the main-hall lights were out. He sat down beside her, interfering with her game by making conversation. He was on edge, yet at the same time mentally relaxed, as if the briefing had relieved him of a burden. The die was cast, there was nothing he could do to change it. It was now simply a matter of carrying out what had been decided for right or wrong. They talked a long time. Gallagher felt able to talk to the girl freely, something he had not done for longer than he cared to remember. He talked of private and personal things. She led him gently to talk about himself, and his pathetic affair with Claudine. She sensed his pain and sense of loss which obviously had been a traumatic experience. She realised that, for all this hard, experienced military man might have seen of life in war, he knew little of other things. He was, in many ways, a simple man, and a nice man. She had long since liked him instinctively. She had even recognised that, given half a chance, she could fall in love with him. He liked her, she knew that. He was also loyal and would not 'betray' his own love until he knew beyond any shadow of doubt that it was over and gone. She respected that. It wasn't all that common these days. War had uncovered latent promiscuity in more people than would hitherto have acknowledged or even suspected it. The world would not be the same again, after this war.

They sat long into the night and talked. She tried to make him understand a woman's feelings as she saw it. She tried to dispel the myth he had created for himself about Claudine, even to the point of antagonising him. But he was not irritated. In himself he knew it was all a delusion and that he had got his whole relationship wrong. It was simply not on. When he eventually went to his room to sleep he had calmed down considerably. He did not sleep, just reviewed their discussion and what Solange, as a woman, had helped him to understand and be aware of in his own antediluvian attitudes.

2 June

The morning brought him his biggest headache. Squires sent for him, and told him directly that Stephen Lovell had turned it in. He was opting out for reasons of conscience. They had no power to make him go . . . but they realised that one half of the operation ceased to exist without his expertise, and they both knew it to be the important part. Gallagher telephoned Professor Evans who was in London with Lindemann and Zukerman. Everything was mounting, and only an idiot did not sense that D-Day was imminent. Gallagher knew that already it had been on and off and on again and off again. Even the Germans were aware that Nemesis was about to knock on their door. But which door?

Evans agreed to come to the Hall and talk to Lovell. The interview was not stormy. He did not try to dissuade him. They talked about the air-to-ground missile that Lovell had put together after he had been given the bits in Cyprus the previous year which led onto the V-weapon situation on which the Germans set so much store, which, in turn, brought the dispute out into the open. Lovell was immediately on his guard, and refused to discuss it until stung by a comment of Evans'. They parted in some dudgeon after Evans had plainly told him he was a 'freeloader', expecting other people to do the unpleasant things for him. Lovell had not given in.

Squires himself tried later during the day when he found Lovell packing his things in his room.

'I've come to ask you if you would be good enough to brief Major Gallagher upon what he has to look for when he gets into the German emplacement.'

'If he gets in.'

'Oh, Gallagher will get in. I have no doubts on that score. What I *have* doubts about is in knowing what to select from Ali Baba's cave. The "Open Sesame" bit is taken care of, I assure you. There must be *some* easy way of recognising what is important and what isn't! Can you teach him?'

'If he can lay claim to something like an honours degree in Applied Science, the same in Applied Maths, and will give me eight years of his life to absorb by experiment and experience he might just be able to recognise the gold from the dross.'

'Exactly. The job needs you, Stephen Lovell. I'm not the sort of man to get down on my knees and beg. But we do need you. The devastation these will cause is terrifying to contemplate.'

'That's not fair! Principles stand or fall on their own. They must!'

'Of course it isn't fair! Is there anything in life that is? You accept death as part of life. We all murder bacteria because they are inconvenient for our life-support system. Is your aversion to killing merely applicable to creatures over a certain size? Surely you haven't the effrontery to confine it to your own species. That would be highly-suspect élitism, wouldn't it?'

'Shut up, and leave me alone!'

Squires ignored the discourtesy and regarded him solemnly, before he turned on his heel and left the dormitory.

After he had gone Lovell remained in his room. He had not yet organised transport to return him to his lab, and the Hall staff were not volunteering to do so. Probably because no one, as yet, knew of his decision apart from Squires and Gallagher. He stared out of the window, then watched Solange and Lamboit boarding the covered Land Rover that was taking them to the airfield for their part in the job. Somehow it irritated him and depressed him. It was the feeling of guilt that irritated; it was the sense of not belonging that depressed.

Macklin, his room-mate, came up later and lay on the bed, and lit a cigarette. He was quiet and thoughtful for once, not chatting and quipping as was his wont.

'What time is it, Choucas?'

'Don't know, old son. Lent my watch to Ferdy. It's a French one, you see. 'Bout late afternoon I reckon. Bit like the old stir, this. Sittin' about on your bunk waitin'."

'You're supposed to rest.'

'You too, mate. I dunno, I can't settle. Bit edgy, you know! Hope that Frog's lookin' after my watch. Came out of a job in Norfolk, that one did. Lovely timepiece! Shame to deprive someone really.'

They fell silent for some minutes before Lovell turned on his side and stared at Macklin inquisitively.

'Why're you doing this, Choucas? You could be safe and sound in wherever it was you were. It's not your line of country. Why?'

'It got me out, squire. If you haven't been inside you don't appreciate what that means. Believe me! B'sides . . . time I did my bit. Got into the old war. I never really belonged anywhere, you know . . . not really. It *was* my war . . . I didn't like Hitler any more'n the next man, but they wouldn't let me share. Know what I mean? Then this little lot and suddenly I was part of something. Like a family. Don't know about you, cock, but I like it here. Nice class of people.'

Lovell listened to him, almost open-mouthed. Here was a criminal, albeit a charming, likeable man when you got to know him, wanting to belong to a war he could well have escaped. The need to belong to something did not take much imagination to understand. We are all amateur psychologists these days. Lovell turned onto his back, strangely moved by the little man.

'What about that minefield, once you are inside?' Squires never missed an opportunity to question Gallagher. He had taken the whole operation deeply to heart and was as much part of it as any of them. Except that he was staying at home.

'You're acknowledging that I might just get inside, are you?'

'Do it by the book. You have the time.'

'We don't even know if there is one.'

'No, but if there is, play safe. That is the way of the book. Have my boffins come up with portable stuff to satisfy everyone?'

'Yes, first class. Thank you.'

'Could you make sense of those notes of Professor Evans?'

Gallagher sighed. 'Not a lot. But I'll grab what I can.'

The voice came from the open door. 'No need, major. I've

decided my place is with the team. I'm sorry I was so pig-headed.'

Both soldiers stared at Lovell for some moments. Finally Gallagher spoke, 'Welcome aboard, Captain Lovell.'

5 June

June the fifth had very little to commend it as a day. When Gallagher awoke it was drizzling and the sky showed it would be a cloudy and muggy day. He deliberately did not go through anything with his team. Their orders were to rest, and rest, and rest again. The mess had been instructed not to serve anyone with more than one measure of alcohol during the day. Gallagher spent an hour with the model in the side office. He avoided Squires. He didn't want to talk. Not until he went on his way. The day moved slowly, and the weather remained the same. Met reports were not encouraging. There was a front moving across from the north-east. If it did not change they were in for a wet night. Parachuting in the rain is no different from making dry drops, except you get wet and drop a little quicker. The silk soaks up water whatever they said about it being repellent. A chute can hold a lot of water, and can more than double your weight.

But it didn't rain. By six they were all moving out to make for the airfield. Packs were loaded into the waiting truck, and one by one the team made their appearances. Cameron was first . . . of course. Macklin second, walking out with a sheepish Lovell. Lamboit and Warsaw came out last joking quietly.

Gallagher went to Squires' office and found him standing by the window. They passed a few pleasantries.

'I can't say I enjoy departing from the manual, but your imaginative innovations might just work. Give it all you've got, Hugh. It rather matters.'

'You coming to their airfield?'

'Good God, no! I never kiss my nephews and nieces goodbye. Why should I change the behaviour patterns of a lifetime?'

Gallagher chuckled as he walked to the door with his bag.

'I'll say one thing. You're a hell of a good training officer.'

Squires watched Gallagher go without a flicker of emotion, but there was a tiny smile at the back of his eyes.

They made the airfield in good time, drank cups of strong tea, and picked up their kit. At 9.40 they walked out to the tarmac where the Dakota was waiting for them. Ground staff helped them to stash their gear and climb into the hatch. The door closed and the engines started one by one and eventually roared into life. Their wheels left the ground of England at exactly 10.03.

4
THE OPERATION

5 June 1944

After skimming the Channel and the French coastline well below German radar the Dakota climbed to reach a satisfactory drop-height for the Dropping Zone.

Gallagher handed them paper cups, one by one, containing very sweet tea, very hot from the dispatcher's large thermos flask, and a curious blue-brown in colour.

'Bloody hell! It's hot!'

Macklin swopped hands quickly, and back again. The throb and roar of the engines was loud and sounded 'loose' and rattling inside the aircraft. Daks rattled. Everyone said so, but they kept on flying. They were reliable. Lovell stared at him without humour.

'There wouldn't be a lot of point in a cold drink, would there? It's cold enough! Isn't there any heating in these things?'

The others glanced at each other and smiled. It wouldn't be Lovell if he didn't complain. He caught the look, and grinned shyly. He knew he was a pain in the arse.

Macklin bent to his ear.

'You were right, squire. What *am* I doing here? Eh? I could've been tucked up nice and cosy sittin' out the 'ostilities . . . no threat to life and limb. 'Stead of which . . . look at me! A bleedin' officer! About to be dropped into Occupied Europe to do a peter job that I can't be nicked for. But I've swopped the old coppers for ruddy Gestapo, an' that won't bring me any hot dinners. I must be stark ravin' . . .'

Gallagher checked his watch. Eight minutes to drop.

Gwillim had decided to sit out the operation at the Hall rather than at one remove in his office. The radio contact would be with Masham. He couldn't be bothered with telephone calls and third-hand information. Squires seemed happy enough to accommodate him. He obviously didn't intend going to bed. They would sit up together, with Evans if he could manage it. The Welshman was more concerned than anyone it seemed. Perhaps he knew things the others did not.

'What time is he likely to turn up?'

'Said he would leave after his meeting with Lindemann. My guess is that he should be here just before midnight.'

They made themselves comfortable in chairs. Squires

brought his silver tray with whisky and glasses to the desk where they could help themselves as they felt like it.

'I suppose they've got a chance of pulling it off.'

Gwillim's insecurity was showing for once. He would take the can ultimately, whatever he said. Squires kept his end up, and assured him that it was all well prepared and had every chance of success. He looked at Gwillim for a moment.

'You don't really expect them to get back, do you?'

'Let's say the job is just a possibility. Someone actually returning would be an unlooked-for bonus.'

It was the bland acceptance of other people's deaths that always stuck in Squires' throat. He could never just 'accept', which was why he was such a damn good serving officer and would never make staff brass.

'There is a callous acceptance of loss about High Command that I still find makes me uneasy. Don't you feel anything for these people?'

'Can't afford to, Tim. And you ought to know that. A surgeon shouldn't know his patient under the knife. It makes for bad incisions.'

'Well I find it somewhat different. I trained them. I'm responsible for them staying alive. I also know them.'

But the sentiment was lost on Gwillim. He was a cold bastard like all the others on General Staff, and Squires was irritated. It was not a good beginning for a long night.

The dispatcher moved to Gallagher and whispered in his ear. Actually he was speaking loudly but the effect was that of a whisper, he had learned you cannot fight Dak engines without an effort. Gallagher nodded and moved towards his team while the dispatcher unfastened then swung back the hatch door. The slipstream was felt inside but not desperately so. Less so than they had expected. It seemed as if they had felt it more during the training, now it was nothing. Nobody was going to be sucked out or fall out.

They stood and checked their gear yet again. The red light came on, and gave the aircraft interior a strange appearance that reminded Macklin of Christmas in Cell Block 'D': one perishing red light and a sprig of holly. Mean bastards!

They took their jumping positions in line, all of them tense and scared. The dispatcher moved to the hatch and stared at the red light. Cameron kept his eyes on the black outside. He could see the colour change out of the corner of his eye. Better than staring at it. Soltysyk saw it change to green the moment he brought his eyes from greedily staring through the night outside. Down there was France. Down there were the Germans.

Macklin jumped. Soltysyk jumped, all he could think of suddenly was a street in Katowice with a house, painted cream-and-pink and a broad-faced girl at the door waving goodbye as he left to join his unit. He saw her wide eyes, her soft brown hair: he had not seen his wife since that day. Perhaps she was dead.

Cameron jumped, the dispatcher sent out the canister. Gallagher watched it disappear and stepped forward.

Lovell jumped. Before Gallagher now there was only the black shape of the hatchway. A tap on the shoulder and he leapt out.

De Grouchy received them as planned, he had met Solange and Lamboit almost as they touched the ground. It was a very efficient operation. The Lysander turned into the wind, and waited as its passengers leapt out and made way for the man who was being picked up. Already the flarepath was extinguished. The pilot would remember his landing in reverse, he had done it many times. De Grouchy and his helpers collected the team and soon they had disappeared into the night. The Germans seemed unaware of their existence. But there had been an accident, the handle on the WT case had caught on the Lysander hatch and broken. The case had dropped seven feet, and by sheer bad luck fell onto one of the three stones in the field. The result had been a smashed bracket.

Lamboit was hard-soldering the bracket when the others arrived. Solange opened the door, and de Grouchy led the team into his kitchen. After minimal greeting and an explanation of the current state of play, including the mending job Lamboit was doing, de Grouchy passed round a jug of red wine and some tumblers. Like most farmers he had half-a-dozen wine-glasses he kept for best and wouldn't dream of using them except maybe for funerals and marriages. They drank out of the simple tumblers. The wine was new, last autumn's, and sharp on the palate, but it wasn't worth laying down. It had not been a good year, and what little wine was produced in the area was poor stuff anyway. It had too alkaline a soil, too little sun to ripen the grapes and give them sugar. But they drank it. There wasn't much else.

'It takes eleven minutes exactly to drive to the checkpoint, I timed it. The first of the Todt trucks is due to arrive at 11.40. That means it will get to the checkpoint about 11.33. The schedule makes us number two in line. The other workers are coming from Picardy and the Beauce. You are the specialists from Deauville as we agreed.'

'Will it check out?'

De Grouchy nodded. 'It will if they make a check before six. We have our own man handling the telephone calls at the military exchange.'

He opened the drawer in his table and brought out a sheaf of papers, in the centre of which was an envelope. In that envelope were their papers, he passed them out.

'This is the Occupation Ausweis, this one the Department Identity card for civilians. Your Todt Organisation directive papers, and Todt worker ration-card.' Gallagher looked at them closely.

'They are not forgeries, Major. They're real. You people exist . . . that's why we need our man on the phone.'

'Clothing situation?'

'As you suggested. Todt employees leave their work clothes in their place of work, they get a new issue, probably used, when they are transferred. The overalls never leave the establishment.'

They talked for some time as they sipped the wine. Soltysyk held out his glass for a refill, but Gallagher shook his head. Soltysyk shrugged and beamed, then crossed to Solange and patted her bottom. His way of doing it was simply to show his pleasure in a pretty girl. Somehow it was neither lascivious nor offensive. She laughed at him, and Gallagher was suddenly conscious that he was watching her. When their eyes met and they exchanged a smile it was a personal greeting as well as a military recognition. The clock on the wall said 11.07. A little time to wait.

Ellen had paced her room for half-an-hour. It was still long short of midnight but she couldn't wait any longer. One never could be sure. She walked down the staircase and across the hall, out into the courtyard and across the gravel path to the Radio Shed. Actually it was not a shed at all. It had once been a games room built outside the house rather than onto it, probably to keep the children at arm's length when they were noisy. Now it had been gutted and restocked with radio equipment, RT and WT. There was a training area which took up more than half of the room, and was where they had all done their advanced training after the days of a portable key-on-a-block and a patient alphabet instructor. She and Solange had been spared that as they were both already advanced operators. The rest of the room was for high-powered equipment used by receiving operators acting under Gwillim's aegis. From there they kept in touch with over thirty agents operating within Occupied Europe. The range of the equipment was never stated, but Ellen knew enough about the job to make a fair estimate that, given reasonable weather conditions, they would expect to be able to operate in a thousand-mile radius.

She did not expect anyone to be there this evening. They had no scheduled transmission for the next thirty-six hours apart from her own team's signals. She would cope with them herself. Corporal Moffat entered not long after her carrying a tray with a thermos, cup and saucer, sandwiches, and two tomatoes.

'Hot tea for later, Miss, and a nibble to keep the wolf from the door. Will you be warm enough, Ma'am?'

'Yes, thank you, Miff, that was very thoughtful.'

Moffat left with a tiny smile on his face. Nice lot this bunch. He liked Merle, she always had a sweet smile and a friendly word. You sort of knew she was a nice person. Bit like his sister who'd copped it during the raids on Liverpool, 1941 that was.

Ellen checked her equipment. It was functioning properly. She glanced at the clock again: 11.18, and sat down to wait.

Squires smiled tiredly at Evans who was taking his coat off

and hanging it on the stand. Gwillim had dozed off, and was not aware of his arrival. Evans indicated that Squires shouldn't wake him, and sat himself down in the battered easy chair, closed his eyes, and seemed to drop off instantly. Squires looked from one to the other and switched out the light . . . all except his desk-light. But he wasn't going to sleep, he couldn't.

6 June 1944

The car that de Grouchy had organised for them was a 1936 Citroën, it was a roomy, three-litre saloon, which at the beginning of the war had been commandeered by the Army, then it was given up to the Germans after the Occupation and subsequently stolen and repainted. It was slightly rusty, but the engine was well-tuned and serviceable. It was the sort of car the Todt Organisation used for their collaborator engineers. De Grouchy switched off the headlamps when they reached the intersection, where the road crossing them was the approach road to the complex. Two kilometres down to the right was the checkpoint. The head-lamp masks did not give much light spill, but it was enough for wartime purposes. Now it was out, and they sat watching and listening. Gallagher next to de Grouchy in the front, Cameron, Lovell and Lamboit, with Macklin squeezed between the latter two, sat in the rear. At their feet, under a blanket, were Solange and Soltysyk with their gear. Gallagher's watch was at 11.30 when they heard the sound of a truck approaching. It was a German 3-tonne Opel 'Blitz' with a canvas cover. As it passed they could see two heads lolling against the metal frame. Doubtless there were many more in the shadows inside. The moon had appeared on schedule. The Met boys were right in that, and the weather was clearing from the north. Little clouds obscured the moon, and what there was moved swiftly in the breeze.

They allowed a minute for the truck to be out of sight, then de Grouchy turned on the ignition and let in the clutch. The Citroën pulled out into the road and turned right. Minutes later they saw the checkpoint ahead, the truck was just moving off, and the bar lowered.

Gallagher turned. 'Right, get your heads down.' The occupants of the rear spread themselves into feigned sleep, put their feet on top of the blanket, and rearranged their own suitcases to best advantage. Gallagher leant his head against the door frame and closed his eyes. The car drew to a halt, and the German guards moved in. De Grouchy handed them his sheaf of papers as the guard held out his hand and switched on his torch to read them.

'How many?'

'Four in the back, asleep. One here.'

The guard shone his torch across the recumbent forms. His companion opened the boot and shone his torch over the spare wheel and the rubbish, then closed it and said something in German that Gallagher couldn't catch. The guard nodded, gave back the papers, and walked forward to raise the bar. De Grouchy edged the Citroën forward. So far so good. Once through they went half-a-mile down the road to where it turned to the left, then stopped. Solange and Soltysyk nipped out quickly with their gear. Gallagher leant out of the window.

'Good luck.'

The two disappeared into the wooded undergrowth, and de Grouchy put the Citroën into gear once more.

The main gate to the underground complex was obvious from a distance, if only because of the light glow from the floods round the loading-bays. They apparently kept their lights operative until air-raid warnings sounded. There was some activity, but less than Gallagher expected. He checked his watch, 11.41. The guards put up the bar, and the Citroën drew to a halt at the place the guard indicated. The team piled out, feigning emergence from sleep and a long uncomfortable drive. The papers were handed over to the guard who passed them to his leutnant standing idly by the gate-house. Suitcases were quickly gone through by another guard as the first one frisked them all for weapons, or anything that might be suspicious. The leutnant crossed to them, and compared each face with the ID photo on the cards. Apparently satisfied he handed back the papers individually, and muttered to his sergeant to get them into their bunkhouse. They marched off after the guard, eyes taking in everything as they walked, noting gun and pill-box emplacements, number of men, position of lights, and so on.

Solange led the way through the undergrowth, then stopped and brought out her map and pencil-torch.

'Easy from here, Warsaw, keep your eyes on the ground.'

They moved cautiously until they reached the tall trees that Gallagher had marked. So far so good, again. Soltysyk now took the lead, it wasn't gallantry. He knew that, all things considered, he was more important to the enterprise than Chardonneret. He also knew that his eyesight was, if anything, sharper than hers. Despite his greater age this was just the case – it usually was. He produced his own pencil-torch and crawled forward on his knees, Solange following exactly where he led. After some moments he stopped and grunted.

Solange looked up and peered into the gloom where the torch-beam was probing. It flashed across the red-and-white sign with the skull-and-crossbones and the warning '*Minen*'. It settled upon four wire tines standing up just proud of the turf.

Already Soltysyk felt the perspiration running down his temples. These were not training mines . . . they were real . . . and they were lethal. They had come as far as they could. He waited and glanced at the sky. The cloud skimming across the moon would have gone in a moment. The trees were on his right, Gallagher had been correct. They were strong enough to hold his wire without giving. Then the moonlight shone forth. It was enough to see the wire perimeter fence quite clearly, ten, possibly twelve yards ahead. Then he felt a hand on his back and froze. Solange's ears had picked up a sound. They tensed, and waited. The footfall approached, then the moonlight glinted on steel, and they saw the perimeter guard, inside the fence, walking slowly on his beat. He passed them, and Soltysyk looked at the phosphorescent hands of his watch. Dead on time!

They were taken past the first blockhouse, and then ordered into the second doorway, concealed by a wall of sandbags, and round the corner facing the loading-bays. The model was accurate and Gallagher breathed a sigh of relief. On the door a paper sticker, headed 'Todt Workers', gave regulations in German, French, Hungarian and Czech. The Germans assumed with good reason that any minorities would speak at least one of the main languages. Inside the building an ablutions area led off the entrance on one side. They were shepherded into the shower-room where galvanised showers set in the ceiling looked like so many large horticultural watering-cans, they were operated by individual string 'pulls', while those to be washed stood over a metal grill. They were all obliged to undress completely, their clothing being chucked into a composition box, and tied, then chalked upon with an ID number, as they were stood under the lights, and a man in a grubby white coat examined them for lice, puffing their anal and genital areas with some vile-smelling powder. They were then thrown their buff underwear and blue overalls which bore the 'OT' on the sleeve below the shoulder join, and an identification number sewn over the left breast pocket.

They had all had the sense to remove their watches, and conceal them as they undressed. All except Lovell, who tended to be unduly trusting and frighteningly naïve. The guard with a small moustache relieved him of the watch and slipped it into his pocket. After they had dressed they were pushed into the main hut, and told to wait until called. The guards left. Macklin crossed to Lovell and handed him his watch back.

'You got to be careful, mate . . . I can't spend my life pickin' pockets. I got war work to do.'

Solange and Soltysyk had their gear unstrapped, ready and waiting. The grapple gun was loaded. Warsaw checked the coil that there was no tangle, no possible snag to impede the flight. Solange looked at the luminous dial of her watch, any minute now. She looked into the sky and listened.

De Grouchy turned the Citroën off the road and drove it under the heavy shrubbery less than quarter-of-a-mile outside of the checkpoint. He had no trouble passing through, though they did check his empty vehicle. He hastily cut branches of trees and thick hawthorn, and proceeded to camouflage his car. When he was satisfied he made off into the woods. He knew the area well enough, and there was just enough moonlight to let him see his position.

Lovell had crossed to the noticeboard on the wall as the others sat on the nearest bunks. The bunkhouse must have held in the region of a hundred workers in double-tiered bunks. The place was spartan but clean. Lamboit was nervous and impatient.

'What time is the raid scheduled?'

Gallagher swung round to glare at him. 'You were briefed like everyone else!'

'I just can't remember.'

'Then you're lucky you've got us, aren't you?'

Lovell joined them. 'The notices imply that there are four bunkhouses. This seems to be hut two and the shift-roster says they're working at this moment.'

'Then our information is correct.' (Gallagher checked his watch yet again.) 'Warsaw should be in position and ready to move out. If the RAF's on time we should have a siren in about seven-and-a-half minutes.'

'Cut it a bit fine, didn't we, guv?'

'Couldn't risk anything else, Choucas. We had to fit between the Todt workers' arrival time, and the new shift start. That's in fifteen minutes. If we are caught in here or get hauled into reporting for work we could be in trouble.'

Cameron grumbled about feeling naked without a weapon of any sort. Macklin started talking to Lovell, when the latter stiffened and stared over the cockney's head. They all turned.

A small, unshaven, tattered man was standing by the side of a bunk just staring at them in silence.

Soltysyk was unwrapping his telescopic pole that they had made up for him, it was lighter than he liked but it would do. He extended it, and stood it against the tree. Picked up the spring-loaded gun, like a Very pistol to look at, and cradled it in his arm. He waited. Searchlights probed the western sky a long way off, and there was the very distant coughing of Flak batteries.

Lovell stared and cleared his throat. 'We've been speaking English.'

Gallagher nodded to Cameron who needed no second urging. He swept round to behind the little man and waited, tensed as Gallagher approached him. There was just a touch of fear in the little man as he spoke, and more than a touch of curiosity.

'Angol?'

No one answered, but Lamboit offered, 'I think he's Hungarian. Magyar?'

The question brought forth a smile from the man who nodded happily. 'Igen! Igen! Magyar.'

He felt nothing as Cameron chopped him behind the ear with a sound that they all heard and shuddered at.

Gallagher lifted his shoulders as Cameron went for his feet.

'Put him in the bed. You haven't killed him?'

'Och, no. But he won't work on the next shift.'

Lamboit was covering him up when the siren sounded. It rose from a throaty groan into the wail that brought panic to so many hearts. The lights instantly went out. Gallagher spoke with the report of a gun.

'Let's move!'

Soltysyk waited for one second, saw the light-glow doused, then took careful aim – very, very careful – and fired. The pop was little more than the sound of an air-gun. The grapple shot out from the barrel, and its tines spread themselves automatically as soon as they left the confining tube. The coil of wire-rope trailed gracefully behind it like the tail of a kite. A tail that Soltysyk grabbed just before it became extended. The grapple soared over the wire and fell between the branches, just near the bole, as he intended. Immediately he hauled hard on the rope and it jerked tight, but it held. Quickly he mounted the tree and climbed to a height of twelve or thirteen feet that he had earmarked as being the best place. With solemn and concentrated rapidity he wound the rope round the tree once as Solange held up the ratchet against the tree. Soltysyk threaded the rope-end, and the wheel picked it up. He stationed the sharp claw feet against the rear of the tree so that the rope just passed the main trunk, over the shoulder of the main branch. Quickly he turned the well-oiled ratchet, and heard the peg slip over the cog as he tightened it more and more.

Gallagher and his team left the bunkhouse while the lights were off and the siren still wailing. It covered any noise they made, though there was some action and pounding of feet by German guards taking up their positions by the raid bunkers. Flak from the surrounding area opened up as searchlights probed and coned. There was a throb of engines in the sky, but Gallagher's people paid no attention, and raced for the perimeter walk on the inside of the fence, throwing themselves onto the turf and hard ground as they reached the mound before descending to the perimeter fence.

Solange watched Warsaw in silence as he tested the wire and saw it flash for a moment on the other side of the perimeter wire where moonlight caught it momentarily.

'It's dipping too much, you'll touch the wire.'

Soltysyk bit his lip and considered. It was not possible to tighten the wire without endangering the stability of the branch. It might well be as thick as his leg but the tension on it was enormous. The ratchet end was no problem, the feet stretched against the bole of the tree. It was the far end. The grapple would hold – it was well lodged. But the branches it had grasped were arm-thick and no more, and it was not possible to go and investigate. Warsaw had to decide, and immediately.

'I make two walks!'

He handed one pack back to Solange and braced himself.

'Twelve minutes-eight seconds. Good luck.'

Soltysyk nodded and balanced his pole. Then set off, one foot sliding forward, never losing contact with the wire he could only just see.

Gallagher led his team down the slope to the perimeter path. The lights were extinguished, and would remain so until the All-Clear sounded. There was still the throbbing of aeroplane engines above somewhere in the blackness, but they were hardly aware of it. All concentration was for the job in hand, and they were listening for different sounds. So far so good . . . no one on the path. There had been no warning bells, no pounding of boots in the direction of the crossing-point. Either it had been successful, or nothing at all had happened. Gallagher glanced about him at the others. They were tense, aware, silent, and apparently cool. Squires had done his job well. They were ready.

Eight hundred yards down the perimeter path Egon Lueger

paused in his slow solid tread and looked up at the night sky. The damned RAF were back again, and those idiots on the searchlights had not yet found them. If they were all as incompetent then it was no wonder that Germany was being reduced to ruins. His own home no longer existed, and his wife was in hospital. Stuttgart had been raided at least fifteen times, and Egon had no liking for the Allied Air Forces. He continued on his perimeter walk, shifting the Karabiner 98b on his shoulder. Why couldn't he have his old Bolt-operated Gewehr 98 instead of this damned thing? The cavalry-type sling at the side instead of underneath as on his old rifle made humping the thing on your shoulder for hours at a stretch painful. It made your shoulder ache. Any day now there would be the Invasion . . . everyone said so . . . and Egon would almost certainly be sent to the beach to die for his Fatherland. And Egon didn't want to die . . . not for Hitler, not for Germany . . . not at all, in fact.

Andrej Soltysyk was half-way across the wire when he chanced a look down at the ground. It was surprisingly clear and focused considering the sparsity of the moonlight. If he could see the couch grass, even the mine-tines with such clarity, then he, himself, would be painfully obvious to any German guard who was making his round. But there was little point in thinking of that. Concentrate! Concentrate! One slip and one fall was all he had available to him. That slip would cost him his life, blown to bits by one of those frightening mines. It would also mean the end of the operation and his comrades.

The wire sagged under the slow-moving weight. The grapple fastening rubbed against the tree bark with a curious soft squeak. Solange tried to make out just how much the tight-wire was sagging, and decided that at the moment of Warsaw's crossing the perimeter the clearance was no more than four inches. She knew that the Pole would be aware of that, and that he would be sweating and mentally urging himself to a levitation that was almost superhuman.

Gallagher and his team reached the last hump in the ground and saw the clump of larger trees before them. Gallagher recognised the place he had selected. From their position nothing untoward was visible. Neither tight-rope walker nor German guard. They moved carefully down the slight rise, and into the undergrowth surrounding the copse. It was then that he saw him. Touched with pale grey-blue light the figure of the little Pole was suddenly alarmingly visible, poised in the air on a wire that was not. It looked strange and unearthly. The little man looked about him anxiously.

Gallagher slipped forward and put up his hand to receive the pack. 'Right here, Warsaw.'

The little man's face smiled in simple relief, and he slipped out of the pack-straps and passed it down to Gallagher by bending his legs at the knees. Without a word he turned and walked back along the wire. Cameron had joined his leader and stared at the retreating back.

'What's he going back for?'

'I didn't ask him. But there is only one pack here, my guess is the sag was too great with the additional weight.'

Behind the bush cover Macklin's eyes stared wildly.

'Blimey! He's goin' to do it twice!'

'Three times, actually.' Lovell, accurate as ever. 'He has to get back.'

Lamboit said nothing but his eyes spoke eloquently of the little man's courage. That was an expression echoed by the two waiting for him at the other end. De Grouchy handed him the pack in silence. Warsaw slipped into the straps, supporting himself against the tree as he did so. Solange touched his foot.

'You have only three minutes left.'

Soltysyk nodded and started off immediately, then felt her hand grab his ankle. He looked down. She was handing him his boots, tied together by the laces. He slipped them over his head, and moved off without a second's pause. His speed was quicker this time. Either he had gained confidence or he was becoming anxious about the time factor – with good reason.

Gallagher looked at his watch, and bit his lips. He motioned the others to take cover, and looked back at Soltysyk half-way across the minefield.

Less than one hundred yards away Private Egon Lueger trod the springy turf between the patches of foot-flattened mud that formed the perimeter path.

Soltysyk knew the second pack was heavier than the first, and he knew that the sag had dropped another inch or more. It was dangerously close to the electrified wire. He glanced down and saw them almost touching. Then he heard the approaching footfall . . .

Gallagher glanced round quickly . . . then back to the Pole willing him to make that last few feet. Otherwise he would be forced to kill the guard, and that would, seven-and-a-half minutes later when he was due to report in, ruin their whole operation.

Soltysyk continued without stopping over the fence, and reached the other end, and flattened himself against the tree. They were fortunate in that the moon had clouded over momentarily. One of life's little bonuses. He heard his heart pounding so loudly within his chest that he could not believe the German would not hear it.

Cameron slowly and silently drew his commando knife, then felt Gallagher's hard grip upon his wrist. The Highlander remembered their conversation in the office at the Hall, he relaxed and smiled slightly as Gallagher's hand left his arm. Private Lueger did not see the wire, nor notice anything amiss. His thoughts were elsewhere: how to evade being sent to the coastal defences when it all started to happen. That was what mattered to him.

Soltysyk had put on his boots by the time the team came out of their hiding place and advanced to take the packs. They unloaded and distributed them quickly. They assembled their weapons, loaded them, pocketed additional ammo, and left the explosive and detonating equipment in the packs, then made their way back up the rising ground to wait. Soltysyk, now with his boots on and pleased with himself, checked his automatic weapon quickly before he hurried to join the others. Macklin had started to break up the sausages of plastic explosive into eight-inch lengths, convenient for each of the team to secrete about his person ready for the moment when they would be required to stuff it into a crevice, bend it round a drum, press it to a support, or whatever was convenient for the job in hand. It was the great beauty of plastic. Like a log of child's plasticine it could be easily moulded into whatever shape one wanted.

All that remained to be done was to insert the appropriate detonator and affix the timing device and battery that would provide the 'spark' to set it off. Whatever remained would be kept within the webbing pack they were to carry with them. The broken-down Sten guns were also carried in the bag.

Solange watched them disappear into the darkness and turned to de Grouchy and gave a wan smile that told him of her fear and concern for her comrades. Briefly and quietly he told her the details of 'Plan B' that Gallagher had instilled into him. They were to remain where they were at the outer end of the wire and keep watch. Gallagher knew that sooner or later a German guard would notice the wire crossing the fence and minefield and raise the alarm. In that event they were to make quickly for the *réseau* rendezvous point, previously arranged by de Grouchy and less than two hundred metres from the German outer checkpoint. They would then attack that same checkpoint. She, Solange, would make directly back to the farmhouse, pick up her WT gear, and head for the woods in order to relay her 'entry success' signal to England.

There was a smothered crackle behind them as of a ground twig being snapped by footfall. Both froze where they crouched and de Grouchy's hand drew the long knife from his boot. They waited, tensed. A whispered French voice broke the silence.

'Pierre?'

'Batiste?'

De Grouchy did not relax for one second as the dark figure approached through the undergrowth.

'What's the matter? Why aren't you with the others?'

'There is a message from Marin. You are to go back to the farm immediately. Something has happened. It is important, Pierre! I keep watch here. The plan remains the same.'

De Grouchy hesitated and exchanged a quick glance with Solange before he nodded rapidly and indicated she was to go with him.

'Hurry. There is not much time if you are to get back again. I don't want to start the war without you.'

Marin chuckled at de Grouchy's expression as he left the

perimeter position and made back towards the village followed by Solange.

In the darkness, no great distance from the German checkpoint, four dark shapes moved silently into concealing positions. They were the only members of de Grouchy's *réseau* who he called upon – however rarely – to assist him in anything. It was seldom more than making a flarepath for a visiting Lysander. He did not welcome anything else. Even so he would not draw upon the others of his *réseau*. There were more than a dozen of them unused, and they would remain unused until the necessity was paramount and France was due for immediate liberation. They were married men – family men. They were no good to France, or their families, dead. And dead they would most certainly be if de Grouchy had not refused, guarded, and husbanded his resources adamantly. It was 1944 and his local patriots were still alive – ready for the fray that was soon inevitable.

'You're a careful man, Pierre.' Solange made the observation as they hurried through the night.

'Aye. But I'm still alive.'

Ellen Robinson looked up from the book she was reading as Corporal Moffat entered the radio room bearing a small bar-tray with a full glass upon it.

She looked up at him and smiled questioningly.

'I remembered it's gin-and-tonic you drink, Ma'am . . . Colonel's compliments.'

She smiled widely, 'How lovely! Please thank the Colonel for me. I could really use that.' Then she paused. 'Miff, I suppose that *is* the right time?'

Her head indicated the clock on the radio room wall, a brass chronometer of the ship's type which bore the maker's name 'R. D. Beckwith. Bristol'.

'Yes, Miss Merle, on the nose.'

Ellen sighed and smiled again. Miff departed leaving her to sip her gin-and-tonic and wonder what was happening to her comrades.

Solange followed de Grouchy into the farm kitchen and promptly sat down by the table. She found herself shaking uncontrollably and was ashamed of the fact. De Grouchy lit the lamp and replaced the glass, and looked at her sideways.

'All right?'

She nodded and sighed quietly, but there was a tiny sob in the exhalation.

'What sort of people send girls like you to do this job? It is not girl's work.'

'I think it is, Pierre.' She was firm in her reply, and her eyes were clear and direct. 'I think it is time my countrymen stood up to be counted. It is now or not at all. You know that, surely?'

De Grouchy was silent for a moment. 'Yes, I know that. And I don't need a girl to tell me. But there have been too many killed for no purpose. The British play too many games. They cannot lose in the end. Only Europe loses.'

She stared him out. 'That isn't true, Pierre. I used to think like that. When I left France and saw the British living as if nothing much had changed I was angry. I hated them for it . . . for being so secure. But it isn't like that. Europe blames them for *not* being occupied.'

'They think only of themselves.'

'And what was my France thinking of when it capitulated? Was she thinking of her allies then? You tell me, Pierre! I want to know!'

Further altercation was prevented by a knock on the door. It was Marin, a member of the *réseau*; he was strangely excited, and at the same time his simple concern was evident for de Grouchy had not been there the hour or so earlier when he had called. Clearly it had to be important to risk the curfew twice in one night.

'You'll get yourself killed, Marin. What is it?'

'The signal came, on the radio from England. . . . It's today!' De Grouchy stared at him not fully understanding what he meant.

'The second part of the message: "*Blessent mon coeur d'une langue monotone*".'

Slowly it dawned upon de Grouchy's consciousness. He didn't speak for some moments, then his eyes filled with tears.

'I didn't think it would ever come. You were right to bring me back. Break out the heavy weapons. Round up the full *réseau.* They are to meet me by the three oaks, near the German checkpoint.'

When he had gone, the farmer explained to Solange what the quotation signified. She felt suddenly elated and went off into the wood to send her first signal.

In one sense the French were ahead of the greater part of the Allies. Their BBC messages had given the first part of the quotation several days before. The French Resistance knew then that the invasion was imminent. The second part told them it would happen within twenty-four hours. France trembled and waited for liberation.

At Masham Hall three men sat drowsily through the small hours, unaware as yet of several momentous events, though their talk nibbled round the fringes of it all.

Gwillim was grumbling, 'These delays with "Overlord" are becoming intolerable. There's fidgeting all down the line. Eisenhower is becoming dangerously indecisive, and Monty isn't helping the situation.'

Evans grunted and scratched his head. 'I wouldn't have his job for all the leeks in Gower, I don't mind telling you. But you know, my friends, our little problem may *seem* small beer by the side of the Invasion, but it is as important to get at these new weapons and stop them as it is to fight it out with the German forces. I haven't told you before, but there is mounting evidence to suggest that they are not all that far away from some form of nuclear device. If they manage that we can all go home. It's over.'

The knock stopped further exchanges and Ellen came in. She handed him a signal which he read and passed to Gwillim.

'Phase two completed. They're inside safely. Well done! Thank you, Merle. Er, is this quite certain?'

'Oh yes, sir. I recognised Michelle's touch on the key. I have no doubts.'

After she left they decided it was worth pushing the boat out and having a small celebratory drink. Squires poured, and heard the sound of an approaching motor-cycle, followed by distant exchanges and a clatter of boots on the staircase.

He crossed to the door and waited for the actual knock, then flung the door wide to reveal the dispatch rider about to rap on the wood.

'Colonel Gwillim, sir?'

'Inside. I'll give it to him.'

'Sorry, sir. Personal delivery only.'

Squires stood back to invite the messenger into his den.

The man saw an officer in colonel's uniform wearing the red flashes of Staff and crossed to Gwillim.

'Colonel Gwillim?'

'Yes.'

'May I see your official ID, sir?'

Gwillim produced his card and the dispatch rider examined it carefully before he took the dispatch from his sleeve pocket and handed it to Gwillim, saluted, turned, and left.

Gwillim frowned and tore open the signal envelope and read rapidly. After a moment he turned his head to his colleagues.

'It's on! At this moment our invasion force is on its way to Normandy.'

D-Day was nothing more than a nickname as far as the five inside the perimeter wire of the German underground complex were concerned. They had spread out and were moving across the uneven terrain above the old quarry, trying to find the old air-shaft marked on the plans they had purloined. It was Lamboit who came across its overgrown entrance, covered with hawthorn and nettle. He snapped his fingers and the others moved towards him. The shaft was little more than a wide chimney built of brick, that had once been painted white, most of the paint having now peeled away and blown into Picardy. Gallagher and Soltysyk mounted it immediately and shone a torch into the opening. It dropped some eight feet, and then there was a 'floor' of mud, grass and general rubbish. There were even old, hard fox-droppings in one corner. Gallagher dropped into the hole and scratched about on the floor with a stick, dragging the mud off the flat metal surface underneath.

'Choucas!'

Macklin dropped down beside him and bent to examine the floor that Gallagher was uncovering.

'It's a cast-iron door!'

'Can we open it?'

'Dunno, mate. It don't have any lock. That means it's a bar fastening. That could be tricky. The 'andle's bust off.'

Lovell's voice came from above into the chimney.

'The bar would surely be on the inside only? If it's rusted we may never shift it.'

'Dead right, squire.'

'If there is no lock, why is there a keyhole?' Gallagher wasn't happy with the turn of events.

Macklin shook his head. 'It isn't a keyhole, it's an air-hole. There'll be another of these doors at the far end of the shaft. When you close 'em tight you can create an air-lock – a sort of vacuum effect. Can't open them. So they drill a small hole to let air in. Happens with safes sometimes.'

'So?' Gallagher was getting impatient.

'So we find out where the bar is, don't we?'

Macklin moved forward and tried to see through the air-hole with the narrow beam from the pencil-torch, he then tried his finger through. Then he produced a bit of wire (he always seemed to have a bit of wire about his person even when wearing clothing that wasn't his). He felt, and gently twisted.

'Right. The bar's about here. We can blow it away.'

Gallagher looked at him as if he was mad. Macklin held his eyes and leant towards him.

'Got a better idea? If we had a power-drill we could drill it if we had some power. Just a detonator, guv, no problem.'

He stretched upwards and was given a detonator by Lovell, who seemed fascinated by the whole proceeding. 'It won't work, you know.'

Macklin smiled to himself. 'Leave it to Georgie. We just want to move a rusty bar what ain't fastened to nothing. All it needs is a bit of a shock.'

'That's all Jerry needs, too.' Cameron's Gallic pessimism was showing, but he handed down the small battery just the same. Macklin took 67 seconds to set, muffle, and blow the charge. It was, as he anticipated, a small explosion, and muffled as it was both by the muffling cloth and the chimney itself was scarcely heard much beyond the chimney opening.

Macklin used his wire again, but it bent under the weight of the door. He tried again with a cord and the toggle of a duffle-coat he found in the rucksack. The door lifted. It was heavy but the bar had moved enough to clear the jamb. They swung it back and stared down into the blackness.

'How do we know the other end is not blocked up?' Lamboit wanted to know. It was Lovell who answered him.

'Feel the air rising. It's warm. If that shaft was sealed it would be dank and cold. I think we're in business.'

Less than five hundred yards away, nervously glancing up into the night sky as the sound of the Intruder Mosquito could be heard returning to resume its nuisance, Oberschütze Ferenc Reiter walked towards the clump of trees against the perimeter fence where he usually chose to relieve himself. It was out of the wind. This night was warmer than the two previous ones. It was his third night in the complex and he'd been on dog-watch guard duties every bloody night. His company had come to the complex from Amiens as a temporary relief for the Guard Detachment who had been in Senlis for almost a year.

Ferenc Reiter didn't much like France. He was a German Hungarian whose father had settled on the shores of Lake Ballaton just before the First World War. The son had not expected to be involved in any war, but the German Führer thought otherwise. Ferenc was musing about his native land when he thought he saw something above his head. He peered closer and recognised the wire stretching out across the minefield for what is was . . . a tight-rope.

One by one they lowered themselves down the air-shaft after Gallagher. They found an enlarged area at the bottom. Soltysyk stayed above ground for the moment. He had held the rope for the others, now there was no one to hold him, and nothing to tie it to. He fumbled in his pack and brought out the collapsible, telescopic pole he had used for balance. The spring-loading would keep it extended against the sides of the chimney, leaving three or four inches on either side of the aperture to act as bearers. He tied off the rope to the centre of the pole and laid it across. A whispered word from Cameron came echoing up the chimney-shaft to warn him to remain where he was for the moment. There just was not enough room in the open area to accept another person.

Macklin loosely held his knife against the metal door leading out of their chamber. It vibrated, smoothly and gently; Gallagher murmured to him, 'The generator room is out there.'

'Dead right, squire, there's a hefty motor goin'. I can feel it.'

Together he and Gallagher put their weight into lifting the bar across the iron doorway. It opened without much difficulty and Gallagher peered into the room. It was the generator annexe, a storeroom with little stored in it. There was no one about. Gallagher slipped out and through to the open doorway to the generator room. Inside the huge turbine whirred and throbbed, unattended except for one white-coated supervisor on a metal-bridge platform at the far end. Gallagher signalled to the others to come out and they did so, quickly and silently. They already wore their Todt issue so had no need of the spare overalls hanging on pegs in the annexe. Thoughtfully Cameron picked out one and took it to the air-shaft cupboard. He hissed for Soltysyk to descend and left the overalls for him. He was still wearing the French civvies in which he had crossed the wire.

Gallagher waited until they were all ready to move out then he picked up a clipboard and some papers he found lying by the door, and walked down the catwalk beside the generator towards the operator on the bridge. The latter heard nothing above the machine's drone until Gallagher was almost upon him. He looked up and suspected nothing. Gallagher smiled, and fell into conversation with him, carefully manoeuvring him to face in the opposite direction while his team sidled out one-by-one through the door into the corridors beyond.

Oberleutnant Küpper entered the guard house that served as the complex telephone exchange and walked to the operator, taking the offered receiver.

'Ja? Was ist los? Wire with grapple . . . across the minefield. Ja, ja . . . continue your round. I will send a squad. Reiter . . . which box?'

As Küpper lowered the receiver thoughtfully the telephone operator turned his narrow head. 'Shall I get the Kommandant, sir?'

Küpper tapped his thumbnail for a moment with a piece of card.

'Not yet. Feldwebel!'

The shout brought a response in a clatter of boots.

'Take a squad of men and comb the area between posts five and ten. A possible intruder. Schnell!'

Küpper grabbed a jack-plug and pushed it into hole number nine, and spun the small metal handle.

'Waechter? Get up here at the double. We may have a problem.' Küpper turned to the operator. 'It takes more than an hour to get the dogs here from the Hauptamt. Are there any in St Estephe?'

'No, sir, we tried that once when there was a false alarm.'

'Stand by to go to Black Alert . . . but not yet.'

He met Leutnant Waechter at the top of the ramp that led down into the complex, and explained the discovery.

Shortly afterwards Gallagher joined them in the side cutting. He took in the structure of the complex. The old stone workings had been reinforced with concrete and steel girders. Most walls and ceilings had been faced with cement and plaster, and carried rows of conduit, and a few newly-hung cables. The telephone wires were set apart in parallel lines and were easily distinguishable by their mauve-coloured, rubber sheathing. Gallagher quickly consulted the small plan he had had copied. They oriented themselves accordingly, and walked stealthily towards the main corridor. As they neared the thoroughfare they heard the sound of something approaching, a car or electric vehicle by the sound of it. Pressed back into the shadows they watched a battery-driven transporter pass the end of the side tunnel in which they stood. They made their way to the intersection and looked out cautiously. Two battery transports, one with trailer, were parked in a lay-by on the right. Gallagher indicated they were to brazen it out and use it openly. Lamboit led them forward and climbed into the driving position with Gallagher, still holding his clipboard, beside him. The rest climbed aboard, and chucked their packs into the trailer. Lamboit moved off and out into the corridor.

Gallagher had his map clipped under the top papers of his

board and consulted them as they moved. Lamboit kicked his ankle as a checkpoint appeared before them. Gallagher made to get out, and thanked Lamboit for the lift, walking with his clipboard directly towards the guard who had emerged from his small sentry-box. The box Gallagher noted, was connected by phone, and the guard was armed with the Schmeisser MP 38. Gallagher thought that probably all the MP 43s and 44s had gone to the Russian front leaving the old 9mm ones for other duties. This was good as they tended to jam if fired for longer than five-rounds. The guard was now concentrating on the man walking towards him, and didn't bother the transporter that moved away down the concourse. Gallagher spoke to him quickly, firing questions which only confused the poor fellow, then nodded, left, and walked down the corridor muttering. The guard went back to his sentry-box convinced that all boffins were slightly mad. How did he know where the whatever-it-was-he-asked-for were kept? It was not his business.

Gallagher turned the corner and found the transporter and his team waiting for him. They continued on their way, glancing into the open storage areas as they passed, areas stockpiled with components, wings, ram-jets and housings. He nudged Lamboit, and indicated they were to take the next side-turning on the left. Once secluded in an alcove Gallagher nodded to Macklin to accompany him. They walked back to the corridor and rounded the corner towards where several offices gave off into the concourse. Gallagher made for the first of the doors and tried it. It was locked. He nodded to Macklin and stood talking to him as the little man fiddled and played with his skeleton keys. Within seconds it was open, and they stepped inside.

The office was basic. Draughtsman's tables, angled drawing-boards, and files; both metal and wooden cabinets stretched down one wall against rough-hewn stone. There was a door at one end that led into a simple washroom and lavatory. Next to that a second door, latch-locked but no obstacle to Choucas, led into the inner-office of what was presumably the superintendent engineer's domain. There in the corner stood the Liedke safe. Macklin walked to it and looked at it carefully, turned, and gave Gallagher a brief nod. Then he knelt down and got to work.

Across the corridor the others waited impatiently for this most important aspect of their task to be settled before going about their demolition work. Lovell walked back into the recesses of the alcove store and stopped dead in his tracks. Staring at him in equal surprise was a German gefreiter, the top button of his uniform undone and his helmet pushed back. He was looking guilty, and Lovell registered something in his hand behind his back before he noticed two flattened cigarette stubs on the concrete floor. The man was dodging out for a quiet smoke in a forbidden area. Forbidden for damn good reasons, flashed through Lovell's mind at the same time as he realised what he had to do. But he just stared at the man's face. All he saw was the ruddy complexion, the dark hair, the thick, shiny nose with a blackhead on the right nostril. What went through the German's head was anybody's guess. Suddenly he seemed to stand on his toes and bite the air with a sharp gasp before a large hand clamped his mouth shut. The helmet fell to the floor with a clatter as the man sank in Cameron's arms, and he withdrew the commando knife from his ribs. Soltysyk helped conceal the body and the helmet behind the crates at the rear of the alcove. As he came back he looked into Lovell's face curiously.

Gallagher appeared momentarily in the doorway of the office and hissed that Lovell should join him immediately. The young man crossed the corridor in a daze, and entered the office. Macklin stood by the open safe, not exactly smug, but certainly with a touch of professional pride in a job well done. Gallagher pointed to the stack of filed papers inside the safe.

'How long?'

'Half-an-hour, maybe more.'

'You've got forty minutes *only*.'

Macklin accompanied Gallagher to the door. Three German troopers and a Todt foreman were approaching. They flattened into the doorway and watched as they approached.

Macklin looked into Gallagher's face.

'When you talk to those geezers . . . what the hell do you say to 'em?'

Gallagher peered through the side window. 'I ask them if they've seen the last delivery of Laclanché cells.'

'An' what's that when it's at home?'

'Don't really know, bit like a dry-cell battery if I remember my schooldays. I act on the not-unreasonable assumption that guards and labourers know even less about this little lot than I do. It seems to work.'

He darted out of the door followed by Macklin, who closed it after him.

Once aboard the conveyance again they moved down the main corridor, obviously entering the central area where there were many Todt workers, more guards, and activity of all sorts. To the left they found the main assembly area. There were at least forty benches in the open-floor area with three workers to a bench. Others manoeuvred the trolleys and overhead chain-pulleys as wings were fitted and the whole rocket assembly took shape. Another work-area showed the sections being unloaded from the trucks that fed the underground workings with the deliveries from the factories.

Oberleutnant Carl Friedrich Feldheim had been Kommandant of the complex for fourteen months. He had supervised the final amendments to the old workings, watched over the first deliveries, and made several intelligent comments about the *modus operandi* which OKW (Ober Kommando der Wehrmacht) had approved. Feldheim had been seriously wounded in Norway in the early days of the war, and his subsequent short spell on the Balkan front had convinced his superiors that, young though he was, active service was no longer a possibility. They gave him the responsible, but desk-bound job in the complex. He was a practical officer and the spartan appearance of his office indicated that creature comforts were not essential to the Oberleutnant's well-being. Küpper respected him and made his report without nonsense.

'Then what do you think it is, Leutnant?'

'I think it is a tight-rope, sir. I sent two men to observe the outer end of the wire. There is a ratchet device. I estimate it is light-weight dural specially prepared for a Commando exercise.'

The Kommandant considered and looked directly at Küpper.

'In your estimation is this a saboteur's entry, or an advance recce before a main attack?'

Küpper did not hesitate. 'The latter, sir. I know of no way a saboteur could have gained entry to the underground complex.'

The Kommandant was also decisive. 'Go to Black Alpha Alert.'

By the outer checkpoint de Grouchy and his *réseau* stared at the guard post and the three German guards. Heads nodded, shadows moved between trees, soft whispering footfall was heard – then silence.

'Let him make telephone contact and report *first*.' Batiste Pelletier nodded and moved off into the blackness.

Thirty seconds later that attack opened with much noise and mayhem. The German guards, taken by surprise, fired aimlessly into the night while the Corporal grabbed the post phone and spun the activating handle. He had reported the attack before he felt the hard rough arm round his body and the almost imperceptible touch of a sharp knife against his throat. Then the sudden hot gush of blood flowing down into his collar, coupled with the heart-stopping realisation of what was done to him. A moment's terrified panic and struggle . . . then a quiet choking death, like drowning.

The signals office at the complex understood the reason for the sudden silence which followed the hasty report of attack, and sped with the information to the Kommandant. The reaction was swift and military. Operations HQ at District HQ was informed and reinforcements requested before anyone realised they were talking to a dead line. The contact had to be remade by wireless, but there, too, they found a problem. The air was full of Allied jamming on all operational wavelengths. They were effectively cut off.

The main intersection of the end corridor was the pivot of the underground labyrinth and showed them the long descending ramp that gave onto the main entrance where the winch-house and truck-bays were. The winch operated the cable set into the floor that the bogies and hoppers hooked onto to be raised and lowered, to accept or make deliveries at the surface. This was the artery, and the place that mattered most as far as escape was concerned. Gallagher had already mentally written off the air-shaft through which they had entered. It would take too long to get back to and the ascent would be a slow business at best, and even then it brought them out onto a surface they were about to blow-up, and there was still the perimeter-wire and the minefield.

The essence of the operation was speed and simplicity. This was the way out. They would probably have to fight all the way. This way they had a chance. The other way they had not.

Further careful examination showed Gallagher that one room held crates of boxes each of which contained the giro-guidance mechanism complete and ready to fit as a unit with minimal connections. The transporter shunted into an open housing alongside other vacated battery-cars. Under the pretence of serious discussion Gallagher briefed his team on their individual jobs. The explosive plastic and detonators, timers, etc., had already been divided up into four and the weapons were left in the trailer under a folded tarpaulin. They operated in pairs, apart from Gallagher. Macklin and Cameron followed Gallagher into the assembly area. Openly, and with the utmost seriousness and self-control, Gallagher indicated where they were to place their explosive charges. Macklin had seen some cool customers in his time but Gallagher took the biscuit. There he was, walking about bold as brass waving his clip-board, nodding to the foreman, ordering them to do what they had to, and climbing over piles of material to show exactly where he wanted things. No one seemed to notice or bother. They were all busy and working against the clock. Once they had been instructed Gallagher crossed to the foreman and talked with him for a moment or two, then went on his way. The burly Highlander and the little cockney looked at each other and shrugged, then got on with their job.

When the Kommandant and Hauptman Klockner reached the head of the main ramp leading to the steel-door exits they were met by Leutnant Waechter who reported excitedly.

'There is no activity elsewhere, sir. Just the attack at the main gate.'

'You deployed the Reserve Force?'

'Round the entire complex inside the perimeter wire, sir.'

The Kommandant led the way as they moved out into the warm summer night. The sky was not studded with stars, it was a muggy, overcast night with almost no moonlight and black as the ace of spades. They made their way quickly towards the Main Gate where the sounds of sporadic firing could be heard. Major Schaffner saluted his Kommandant and reported on the conflict so far. The enemy force remained in the dark and fired sporadically from several positions . . . mostly mortar and grenade-launched explosions without any obvious pattern. They watched the attack for some time, returned equally sporadically by similar weaponry on the German defence side.

Küpper walked briskly towards them and saluted.

'I think it is time to reconsider the possibilities, sir.' Hauptmann Klockner swung round upon his junior and frowned.

'What do you mean, Leutnant?'

Küpper held up one gloved hand and pointed to each finger as he enumerated. 'One: the perimeter guard reports he has discovered what appears to be a tight-rope. Two: at that precise moment there is an air-raid that is not an air-raid. No attack, no bombs, merely nuisance – or diversion. Three: the checkpoint reports an attack by a superior force, then the line goes dead, *but*, the attack begins *after* we are alerted to the crossing wire, and they were foolish enough – or clever enough – to allow the report of the attack on the checkpoint to reach us before the wires were cut. They are either badly-trained commandos, which I doubt, or they are deliberate.'

Klockner was about to interrupt when the Kommandant held up his hand.

'Moment! I agree with the Oberleutnant. I have been watching the attackers' fire. It is a small force, and they are not commandos. The whole deployment is unmilitary. They are a diversion. You are right, Küpper. What are you getting at?'

Küpper sighed slightly. 'In my assessment, sir, there are saboteurs already inside the complex perimeter, they crossed the wire we found.'

'And the electrified fence?'

'They got over it. Someone had to fix the bolt in the tree that held the wire. That could not be done, barring miracles, without touching the electrified alarm wire on the fence top.'

Klockner shook his head. 'No . . . I don't believe that.'

'There was a suspicious air-raid at exactly the right moment.'

The Kommandant had narrowed his eyes and stared at him. 'Make your point, Küpper.'

'The electric wire is without current for one minute as the mains switches over to the generator. The air-raid siren is automatically triggered off and would give anyone waiting audible warning that the supply was dead for one minute.'

The silence indicated that all agreed the possibility was beginning to come together as a likelihood. Oberleutnant Feldheim spoke quietly.

'Where do you imagine they would be, Küpper?'

'Exactly where they wanted to be, sir: inside and underground.'

Feldheim thought for one moment and then turned to Hauptmann Klockner. 'Put the complex on immediate Red Alert. I will speak to District by radio if I can and request reinforcements . . . just in case.' He turned to Küpper. 'Feldpolizei units to scour the complex. Examine everyone's papers. Todt workers and military personnel not known to them personally. I realise a whole company arrived two days ago as our relief so it will be a long job. Waechter, take out twenty men and disperse the attacking force. Clean them out, then report back.'

He walked smartly back towards the complex entrance, then turned again to Klockner. 'Hauptmann, keep your men deployed on the surface. I think Küpper is right, but let us be secure.'

Gallagher hurried down the corridor to where Soltysyk and Lamboit carried their explosive gear hidden in a tray of tools through the entrance of the big storage area which was filled to the ceiling with rocket-planes ready for transportation, but still without the guidance mechanism. Gallagher frowned and went up to the guard and Todt supervisor and asked where the completed ones were. The Herr Direktor wished to come and inspect them before they were released for launching. He was directed down the corridor to the end chamber. On pretext of stencilling numbers on certain batches of the stockpiled missiles, Lamboit and Soltysyk got on with their job of laying explosives. The detonators were inserted, and the timers set.

Gallagher hurried down to the end chamber. Time was running short. The explosion was set for 02.18. There was still much to do.

When he arrived back at the office Lovell was still going through the files. He had extracted much of value, but not what he was really looking for.

'You've got roughly thirty-four minutes. In that time we have also to collect the guidance mechanism from one of the completed rockets. I'll be back for you.'

He stepped out into the corridor and passed some Todt workers en route for their break in the lower level canteen. Gallagher had noted from the map provided, which was proving accurate in every significant detail, that the fuel store for generators and presumably vehicles was down the end of the long corridor. That was his next port of call, then there were the garrison quarters and the drivers' rest rooms.

One by one they realised that something was afoot. Gallagher understood the implications as soon as the Red Alert sounded over the Tannoy system. Lovell understood it from his position in front of the safe. Soltysyk understood the implication because his German was good enough to translate the announcement in its distorted booming. Telefunken didn't manage the problem any better than Tannoy. Out of the corner of their eyes they noted the background activity of Feldpolizei, the questioning, the producing of papers, and quietly went about their business with a sharpened awareness. Gallagher knew it was bound to happen sooner or later. Someone had to spot the wire, and, just as long as de Grouchy was on his toes and saw it happening, plan 'B' would swing into effect by the planned diversionary attack. The thinking was that it would keep the Germans convinced that a commando surface assault was imminent until it was too late to do anything else. He had not known that Oberleutnant Küpper was a policeman in civil life, and put two and two together very frequently. Seldom was his answer anything else than 'four'.

Gallagher knew they had one thing really going for them. A bonus that was, at the time of conception, totally unlooked for. The confusion and anticipation of the long-awaited Allied

Invasion happening at the same time would throw a spanner into the works and, with any luck, would make mayhem in such a way as to cover the operation. Even so, that Plan 'B' diversion would be the saver for Gallagher's team objective, and might make the difference as to whether any of them actually made it outside before the whole place blew sky-high. The next half-hour would answer all the questions . . . for everybody.

Squires got up from his chair and made a small adjustment to the minute hand of the wall clock. It had irritated him for days. Three minutes was, after all, three minutes. In years to come wars might take no longer than that to be effective.

'Why is it that time spent waiting seems so much slower than any other? Bears out Einstein's Relativity on quite a different plane. I wonder if that was what gave him the idea?'

Gwillim sighed. He too was tired and, though used to lack of sleep, he found sitting about tedious. 'I doubt it. These chaps live in a constant equation, not normal at all. *He* does too!' He pointed a finger in the direction of the slumbering Evans. 'Can't make head-nor-tail of what he's talking about half the time.'

Gwillim sighed and fingered his nose. 'We aren't going to stop the rockets coming, you know. If we're successful we'll put a spoke in the wheel and render them less effective . . . but we shan't stop them coming.'

Evans stirred as if on cue, then sat up and arched his back.

'What's happened? Have we heard anything?'

'Nothing further, Dafid. Go back to sleep. Be a couple of hours yet.'

Evans pulled the blanket round his knees again.

'I can't stand these everlasting nights. The war's been full of them.' Then as an afterthought. 'What about Overlord?'

Gwillim became testy, and almost snarled at him.

'What about it? Nobody's going to give us a running commentary on the landing progress! We'll hear soon enough.'

Evans rocked a little and mumbled. 'The little knowledge we have has made me very concerned. But it's what we *don't* know that frightens the life out of me.'

Two-thirds of the way across the English Channel the greatest armada the world had ever known was moving towards the coast of Normandy. Under the blanket of night and by countless ploys of deception the Allies had so confused the enemy as to their aims, the exact time and place for the Invasion that so far it was totally undetected. The first wave of airborne troops had already gone in. Eleven thousand aircraft provided an umbrella, the scale of which was unimagined by the once victorious Germans who had stood on the chalk cliffs of France and gazed greedily across at the shores of Albion. Shores they were destined never to set foot upon.

The Allied High Command's strategy involved scattered but heavy air-raids on targets throughout Northern France, scattered enough to confuse the Germans thoroughly as to what area was objective designate; heavy enough to keep Area Commands uncertain as to whether this was part of a softening-up process in *their* district prior to Combined Operations assault in force. At the same time Airborne troops, mainly American, were being dropped in considerable numbers again in scattered areas of Northern France, mainly in Normandy and the Beauce plain, hopefully achieving the same objective in the eyes of the enemy, but in reality no more than an advance, behind-the-lines disposition to augment the breathtaking armada fast approaching the shores of Normandy, which was, so far, totally undetected. The nervous anticipation of German units throughout France, but particularly in the northern coastal regions, was a calculated factor in the probable confusion which would occur in the underground complex that was the target. The calculation was fairly accurate.

Lamboit finished setting his charges before the Pole, and moved out of the huge chamber with his box of tools. He hurried down the corridor. Cameron and Macklin had more-or-less completed their own sections. Soltysyk turned the knob of his timer-setting, and stood up to leave. Twenty or more Todt workers had gathered in the area and stood about, obviously waiting for their next directive. Soltysyk considered his move. He had two alternatives. One, was to brazen it out and walk through them.

The other was to stay put and be blown sky-high with the rockets. There was no real contest. He stood up and advanced towards them.

'Who are you? What are you doing?'

Soltysyk looked at the broad-faced man who had addressed him. A face familiar and his words had been in Polish.

Soltysyk beamed widely. 'Did you not see the new intake? Fifty or sixty Poles – they're coming into this section to work. Why don't we go and greet them?'

He slapped the man on the shoulder but spoke loudly enough in Polish for them all to hear. Immediately there was an excited response and they all started to walk to the entrance. In the confusion Soltysyk slipped into the corridor and melted away.

Gallagher stood at the base of the long, sloping ramp, and watched the truck-and-trailer being lowered by cable ready for unloading at the base. He clutched his clipboard to his side, and started walking up the incline, skipping the odd step, then taking two-at-a-time until he reached the surface. Before him the winch was stopped until someone rang the bell to start it. On the far side were the loading-bays. One truck was busily unloading, and still well-laden. By the first bay stood a three-tonne truck. Gallagher walked over to it and peered inside, it was empty. He called to the guard on duty by the door.

'Where is the driver of this truck?'

'Down in the canteen, sir. He is having his supper-break. There is no loading until 04.00.'

Gallagher frowned and turned on his heel, crossed to the glass-fronted guard post and peered inside before knocking on the door. He was watched by the first guard he had spoken to as he questioned the duty officer. All the guard saw was the Todt official asking questions and the officer being very helpful. He did not notice that the man was examining the telephone switchboard quickly as he talked. Nor had he noticed that the same man had also examined the exit, and the immediate blockages outside the loading-bays while he pretended to look inside the truck. These Todt foremen were all alike – worried about their jobs – frightened they might get sent to the Russian front that was collapsing day-by-day. He, too, was frightened of that. He had heard the stories.

Gallagher tripped quickly and expertly down the long line of white-painted stone steps alongside the rail-ramp that carried the trucks and trailers. He had learned what he needed to know but there was little time left and still much to do. The others had probably completed their tasks and were doubtless waiting for him. Most of them were. Lovell was not . . . Lamboit was not.

The latter had found the garrison area and the canteen areas. One for military personnel, one for civilians, such as drivers or visiting experts and the Todt workers. He had planted charges by the doors. They wouldn't get out very quickly, if at all.

Gallagher passed the door sign which read in German 'DANGER – Fuel. Highly inflammable' to check the coast was clear. It was. He rapidly set his charges against the underside of the two, huge, black-painted diesel-fuel tanks. When he arrived at the office and entered he found Lovell facing him with his Walther pointing at his chest.

'Found what you wanted?'

The thin man nodded, and touched the rucksack he carried under a pile of folded paper.

'We've got eleven-and-a-half minutes. Move it.'

They hurried out and down the corridor towards the main concourse area. The others were there – all except Macklin.

'I thought he was here. Where did he go?'

'Wanted to make extra explosion. Is not safe! I tell him. He speak nothing very good,' Soltysyk replied.

That was the understatement of the year. Choucas had learned a little French at the Hall but his accent had to be heard to be believed. Gallagher gritted his teeth in anger, and glanced down the corridor. Sure enough there was Macklin hitching a lift on a battery-transporter. He dropped off by the end of the intersection. Gallagher heard him.

'Ta, mate. Mercy bowcoo . . .'

He returned smiling cockily. Gallagher snapped at him. 'I thought I told you to shut your trap.'

'S'all right, squire. They're Poles or somethin'. Don' understand a flippin' word. Real ignorant. That's the lot, then?'

'Except for the guidance mechanism. Hibou!'

The two of them walked quickly to the rough-hewn stone areas where the completed rockets were stored. The pile of cardboard boxes stood empty and carefully husbanded for re-use. Gallagher picked one up and studied it, noting the name of the supplier: 'I. G. Farben – Eindhoven'. That information alone would be worth a thousand bomber raids. But all the boxes were empty. They would have to dismantle a rocket to get one. Gallagher walked up to the guard who was eyeing him with suspicion.

As he approached a young fresh-faced Leutnant stepped from behind a column. In his hand was a Luger. In his eyes a question. Gallagher did not wait to be asked.

'Leutnant. We think the saboteurs have been in this section and an explosive device is already planted in one of the rocket casings. Please get your men to take cover. We shall attempt to remove the device but if it detonates it will take us all with it. There could be a chain reaction from one rocket to the next.' He glanced round the huge assembly of upwards of five hundred completed flying-bombs.

Waechter was impressed but still hesitated.

'There is no time, Leutnant. You know we are on Red Alert. Let this engineer find and dismantle the detonating device . . . *please*!'

Even Lovell had to admit that the British theatre had lost a very convincing actor in Hugh Gallagher, and smiled grimly to himself.

'Yes, sir . . . of course . . .'

It was then that Küpper appeared. It was then that they recognised they were face to face with their prime antagonist. It was not the Feldpolizei uniform, nor was it the Luger in his hand. It was the professional policeman's air of intimidation and authority that implied and communicated guilt.

'What is going on?'

Gallagher sensed the moment of truth had arrived, and knew he had to play it for what it was worth. There was also something inside him that accepted the challenge of wits. He clicked his heels and gave a quick head bow.

'I am explaining to the Leutnant that there is an explosive device planted by saboteurs that we *must remove* . . . and quickly!'

Küpper's face did not move a muscle as he looked stonily at Gallagher.

'Has the device been located?'

'Not yet, Oberleutnant, but we have reason to believe it is in this section. Kindly permit us to proceed.'

Küpper did not move. His cold fish eyes moved quickly to regard Lovell standing with the innocent, bemused air of the born boffin.

'So. Your papers please, Bauleiter.'

Gallagher obliged but edged forward and became just a shade quieter and more urgent in his speech.

'Please, Oberleutnant, while you are checking identity may we proceed. We have no means of knowing how rapidly the timers have been set.'

Küpper nodded and handed the identity papers sideways to Waechter.

'Check with Heeresgruppe Vierzehn.'

The young leutnant hurried away replacing his automatic in his holster. Gallagher and Lovell hurried to the nearest stack of rockets and exchanged a glance as they moved. Both men produced screwdrivers and commenced to remove housing cover-plates as speedily as they could . . . and in silent concentration watched by Küpper and the fascinated stares of Waechter's helmeted squad. The two men moved rapidly from one rocket to the next.

In the corridor checkpoint Waechter swore at the telephone operator, then read out the identity details.

Küpper moved forward a pace to look slightly across at Lovell as the latter gasped and stood rock still peering into the newly-opened housing.

His voice was hoarse and thick as he spoke. Bauleiter.' Gallagher hurried to his side and peered into the casing as Lovell carefully attached a cigarette box he had previously wrapped with black insulating tape to the guidance mechanism and crudely twisted two ends of fuse wire to anything available . . .

Küpper moved forward but Lovell barked at him the way no mere worker however brilliant would bark at an army officer. It worked.

'Keep still, damn you!'

Küpper froze. The men's eyes stared as at a Second Coming. Lovell continued, this time quietly.

'Please . . . no movement at all . . . none.'

It was at that moment that Waechter chose to clatter into the area brandishing the identity papers. Küpper it was who bawled at him.

'No moving! Quiet!'

It was this acceptance that clinched the subterfuge. Küpper had said it and it was, therefore, true. He turned quickly to the trembling Leutnant.

'Well?'

'There is still no telephone communication with outside, sir. But the name is listed on the new intake as Bauleiter, and specialist.'

Lovell pretended to ignore all the conversation and spoke as to a colleague in science. Gallagher played up to him.

'There is a secondary device, Herr Bauleiter. I must get it away from these rockets before I dismantle it . . . it is too dangerous.'

'Can you get the mechanism out in one piece?'

'Yes, I think so . . .'

Slowly and with exaggerated care, as if a trembler was already sensing the disturbed ambience, Lovell gently removed the guidance mechanism.

Gallagher spoke over his shoulder, tense and pale.

'Oberleutnant, can you get your men to clear a path through the complex, please. We must get this up to the surface as quickly as possible.' Then to Lovell. 'Careful . . . easy now . . .'

The whole pantomime was convincing and worked like a charm. Within seconds, Küpper had organised his men to clear the path down the corridor towards the ramp. The guards stared uneasily as Lovell and Gallagher moved swiftly, but with infinite care towards the ramp preceded by Küpper himself speaking with authority and command. Waechter, acting under orders, had alerted the ramp guards and the guard house operators. It was then that Lamboit decided to make his move. He was spotted, commanded to stop, and turned with a borrowed Schmeisser to fire at the interrogating guards.

The sound of firing echoed down the corridors of the complex. Küpper nodded to Waechter, now convinced that *his* people were genuine and the saboteurs were apparently elsewhere.

Out of the corner of his eye Gallagher saw Soltysyk and Macklin walking up the ramp exit, and then glanced at the watch on his wrist. Two minutes less eight seconds and the whole thing would erupt. He muttered to Lovell who reacted by an alarmed shout.

'It's started to tick. The mechanism has been activated, we must run, sir, now.'

He and Gallagher started to move up the ramp as fast as they could. Küpper overheard the remark and raced ahead to clear the path of descending *Schützen* answering the call to the emergency in the corridors below. The firing continued. Gallagher could only guess that Lamboit was holding his own. Still the firing continued. A descending officer shouted an exchange at Küpper who shouted back something about saboteurs that Gallagher did not catch.

Gallagher' glanced at his watch. Thirty-five seconds to detonation. The ramp top was near and their breath coming hard with hearts pounding against their ribs from the hurried ascent.

Then it happened. At first an almost distant rumble that opened out into a still-muffled blast, accompanied by a rush of warm air and a trembling of the ground. Soltysyk and Macklin opened up with their Stens at the guards through the glass-doors of the guard houses. Küpper turned open-mouthed as Lovell hastily put the guidance mechanism under his arm and Gallagher reached inside his overalls for the dismantled Sten hanging about his person. For a moment he stared at Gallagher, then the sick realisation of being duped crossed his visage and he raised the Luger. He was dropped by raking fire from behind from a Sten. Cameron grinned through a ruddy face and very black moustache.

'Sometimes you just *have* to kill them, Major.'

They were rocked and thrown to the ground as the second, third, fourth explosions followed in quick succession.

In the corridors below the explosions sent clouds of dust, followed by billows of flame along and through the winding complex. Then came the debris and within seconds the cracking of concrete. German guards and Todt workers turned and looked, knowing they were trapped and finished as their wide eyes stared at the advancing roaring clouds of flame and oily smoke. Gallagher chucked Soltysyk two grenades. He caught them expertly, like the circus performer he was.

'First truck!'

Lovell led them as they made their way, Soltysyk dodged as Cameron opened up with his Sten gun, and riddled the two guards who had remained up on top; the rest had gone down to answer the alarm. He mentally decided that Gallagher was nobody's fool. He thought of every bloody thing, just as he was doing now. He watched Gallagher cross to the glass-windowed guard house and rake the area with Sten fire, then he shot-up the telephone switchboard before turning to run for the truck. Lovell had rammed a screwdriver into the ignition switch but it wasn't working. He tried and tried . . . nothing! Gallagher ran towards the truck, then caught his foot in a loose length of the truck-cable and fell forward, at the same time as Lovell kicked the panel and the motor roared into action. He put it into gear and edged the truck forward, one eye on the rear as Cameron dashed to help Gallagher onto his feet.

'Don't you ever learn a bloody thing!' He swore at Cameron as they bolted, and leapt aboard the truck. The Scot had taken his place at the tail-board with his Sten gun pointing over the panel. Macklin and Soltysyk both without guns were unpinning their grenades, and holding them tight, ready to throw them if necessary. The truck roared into the small yard, and headed straight for the exit and the sentry-post bar.

By now the explosions behind them were coming thick and fast. Great clouds of smoke and flame belched up from the earth, and they sensed but could not see that in several places the top of the quarry had blown off. Lovell headed straight for the bar, and bashed through it, ignoring the bullets that spattered against the truck and windscreen, shattering the glass. Macklin and Soltysyk threw their grenades, one into the sentry-post, the other into the tower-entrance. The explosions were lost in the general noise and mayhem as the three-tonner roared out into the night. Lovell switched on his masked headlights to find a Kübelwagen heading straight for him. For a second he glimpsed the frightened face of the Hauptmann driving the car, and they both swerved. Machine-gun fire raked the truck as they passed the post. The unit in the tower had got one good burst in before they were out of range. Most of the bullets had hit their target, and Lovell felt a sharp pain in his upper-arm, and a sudden sense of warm stickiness running down his overall sleeve.

What he did not know was that two bullets had entered the radiator low down, and the water that cooled the engine was draining away rapidly.

From the farmhouse they heard the explosions although it was almost nine kilometres away. Solange and de Grouchy stepped outside into the dark night and listened to them, then the skyline lit up suddenly and an orange glow was seen behind the hill and the trees of the copse by the barn.

Lovell felt the whole thing shudder slightly and he sensed something was amiss. They had come about two kilometres and were nearing the checkpoint across the road. He stopped the truck and turned to Gallagher.

'I think we have to ditch. We're running dry. It'll seize-up any minute now, and we ought to conceal it somewhere.'

Gallagher nodded and they climbed over the side and dropped to the ground after a glance to the rear. There seemed to be no pursuit. Lovell then drove the truck off the road into the undergrowth of the wood where it was thick and lush. He switched off and flopped back into his seat.

Gallagher opened the door for him and he almost fell out, still cluthing the box of the gyro-mechanism.

'I'm sorry, I think my arm's gone to sleep.'

Gallagher glanced quickly at the torn and bloody upper-arm, bent down to find a suitable stone and pressed it under Lovell's armpit to form a tourniquet, then bound the arm to his body with a piece of webbing found in the cab.

'Bookworm!' He smiled at the pale young scientist.

Cameron and Soltysyk lifted him down as Gallagher went round to the back of the truck to check for pursuers, but there were still none.

'What about the checkpoint?'

'De Grouchy's men will have knocked that out. We chance it.'

There was no sign of life by the guard post, merely three

German bodies, all with several bullet holes in the uniforms stained by recently congealed blood. Gallagher recognised that 'Plan B' had gone into effect. De Grouchy had done exactly as he had been asked. The cost was not yet known.

It was just turned 03.28 when the knock came upon the farmhouse door. Solange and de Grouchy froze, not sure if it was a survivor or the Germans. De Grouchy nodded to her to get behind the curtain while he answered the door. He opened it and Cameron entered, followed by Macklin and Soltysyk carrying Lovell between them. The door was kicked shut behind them. Solange came out and rushed to them. She was overjoyed to see them alive and more or less unhurt, but her face fell as she scanned them. Where was Gallagher? Surely he had not . . .

'No flowers needed. You haven't got rid of me yet.'

She spun round as he entered, and her face betrayed her relief, as did the sigh that just trembled on her lips. He went straight to de Grouchy, who asked, 'Any pursuit?'

'Not yet. That'll come eventually when they sort themselves out and get some troops into the area. Most of the garrison were down there, almost all.'

'Then my people will suffer heavy reprisals. I hope it was worth it.'

'We will broadcast the success of a British Commando raid. That should keep them off your back.' He turned to Solange. 'Send the Operation successful signal as soon as possible.'

Solange looked doubtful, and glanced at the grinning de Grouchy.

'Is there a problem?'

'You do not know, of course. The Second Front, the Invasion has begun.'

This was received in momentary silence before an outburst of joyful cries. Cameron laughed his short, hard laugh and hugged the diminutive cockney, Soltysyk clapped his hands together then opened them wide to embrace the whole world.

'Is Invasion? My country is saved! The end of the Nazis! Soon we fight the bloody Russians!'

Lovell looked bemused and managed a smile tinged with pain.

'Before we all light candles, you take these papers.' He passed a fistful of them to Gallagher. 'I can remember what matters, we might get separated. It is absolutely vital. I can't stress that enough.'

Gallagher nodded and put the papers into his overalls. He turned to Solange.

'Does this mean we have a problem getting a message out?'

She nodded. 'The air is filled with jamming. I've tried all our frequencies, they are awash with signal-noise. I'll try, of course.'

Gallagher scribbled a note on a piece of paper, and passed it to her. 'Send this, uncoded. Jerry knows it's happened, there's no point in trying to hide it.'

Cameron and the others were holding tumblers out to de Grouchy, who had found another bottle of wine and was pouring it liberally.

'We pulled it off!' He laughed again. 'And now the Invasion! Man, this is a hell of a day! Let's drink to it.'

'Cheers!' said Lovell limply.

'*Na zdrowie!*' from Soltysyk.

'First today,' rounded off Macklin.

Gallagher watched them drink, and moved into the scullery to wipe some dried blood off his hand. There was another distant explosion. De Grouchy joined him with the bottle and looked out of the window into the darkness.

'You did well, I think. Whatever you say, there will be hostages, my friend. The Invasion will have made them angry . . . and nervous.'

'It also works for *us*. They will move every available man to the beach-heads. Our little job may get lost in the confusion.'

De Grouchy grunted his doubts, but passed Gallagher the bottle. After a long swig he turned to the farmer and indicated his Todt overalls. 'We left our clothing in the bunkhouse. Any chance of some more?'

De Grouchy nodded. He would find some.

Dawn was just beginning to show over the fields as Gwillim turned back along the gravel drive from the radio room and made his way to Squires' office.

'The air seems quieter now. There's a security blackout. Only official communiqués.' He sat down and accepted a cigarette from Squires. 'Seems to be going all right. Too early to say anything. They won't land until first light, which won't be long now. Our people reported in yet?'

Squires squinted at him curiously.

'You don't expect anyone to survive this little escapade, do you?'

Gwillim hadn't a chance to reply. There was a knock at the door, and Ellen entered at Squire's invitation.

'Signal from "Michelle", sir.'

She handed it to Gwillim as the senior officer. He read it quickly and raised his eyebrows.

'Well, bless my soul!'

He passed the signal to Squires, but Evans had wakened at the sound of another voice and sat upright.

'Read it aloud. I can't stand the suspense.'

Squires read it quietly and coldly, without inflection or emotion.

'Operation carried out as planned. Complex destroyed. Guidance mechanism and specifications of FZG-76 in custody together with initial specifications for A-4 rocket and A-10 intercontinental missile.'

Evans spluttered. 'The A-10! It can't be!'

Squires continued – 'Hibou with flesh wound. Ferdy killed. Relay pick-up schedule s.a.p.'

There was a moment's silence. Squires was the only one who knew of the relationship between Merle and Ferdy, he glanced quickly at Ellen. She was looking directly ahead, giving nothing away.

'We have to get those details out . . . and fast!'

When she was dismissed Squires suggested kindly that she might like to go off duty, but she said she preferred to stay at the WT . . . it gave her something to do, and anyway, Chardonneret knew her, and she knew the touch. Squires nodded and let her go.

Once outside the door she leant back upon it, and her face showed she was ready to give way to her grief. Lamboit had meant a lot to her.

When Solange returned from the woods carrying her small WT attaché-case she found Gallagher bent over the gyro-mechanism with Lovell as the latter tried to explain the details to him.

He turned to face her. 'Any answer?'

Solange read out the paper in her hand. 'Delighted decay has been eliminated. Well done. Early extraction impossible due to other patients. New appointment in immediate future. Will advise.'

De Grouchy was anxious about how long he was to entertain his uninvited guests. 'How long is "immediate future"?'

Gallagher sighed. 'Usually about three days. They won't want us to clutter up the air right now.' He turned to Chardonneret once more.

'Leave your WT switched on and tuned. Wait till they contact us, but don't reply from the house.'

Solange gave him an old-fashioned look. 'I think I know not to do that, Major.'

Gallagher grinned his old cheeky grin. 'Just testing.' He turned to the farmer. 'Pierre, we won't embarrass you by staying here. We'll hole up in the woods. I want the girl to stay with the WT . . . all right?' De Grouchy nodded.

'And this one,' indicating the wounded Lovell. 'She can look after him.'

De Grouchy grunted. 'In the barn . . . not here. It's dangerous.' Gallagher nodded to the others who shouldered their gear and tried to look at home in the ill-fitting farm clothing de Grouchy had found for them. The Todt overalls had been burned.

Gallagher bent over Solange and spoke quietly to her.

'Can you cope till I get back? I don't want to explain to the others. Twenty-four hours at most.'

Solange's eyes clouded over as she looked at his face, and his dark perturbed eyes.

'Claudine?'

He nodded. 'I must. With the Second Front established the Germans could get nasty. If anything happens – don't wait.'

She nodded, and he bent over to kiss her cheek. Impulsively she kissed his mouth. When they drew back he looked at her . . . their eyes met and smiled. Within seconds he was gone.

News of the Invasion had not filtered through to the station at Chantilly and the local train left only six minutes later than scheduled. There were few travellers, and Gallagher was able to cat-nap in the corner before they reached Saint-Amand-de-Chauny. The early morning light filtered across the Picardy landscape and sparkled in the dew-touched spiders' webs and on the cropped grass at his feet. The house stood silent and damp in the chilled morning. When he rounded the garden wall he saw the Kübelwagen standing round the corner of the house. It caused the anguish he had anticipated to shoot through him. He walked carefully towards the building keeping out of sight of any windows until he reached the small grey car. He put his hand on the bonnet and on the roof. It was cold, and covered with dew. It had been there all night.

His belly weak and trembling, he reached the trellis against the rough-hewn coin stones and climbed up to Claudine's bedroom window. With one leg over the balcony he saw the French windows were ajar as always. He kept against the wall, and then looked into the room.

The large double bed was occupied and no one stirred. Gallagher stepped into the doorway and stared into the shadowed room. Claudine faced him, asleep. Her mouth open as she always slept. Next to her was a man Gallagher assumed to be a German officer. There was an SS Sturmbannführer's uniform on the chair. Gallagher gritted his teeth to bite back the jealous pain he felt. The urge to kill them both flashed through his mind, but only momentarily. What else could he expect? It was this wretched war!

Claudine stirred and half-opened her eyes. She thought she saw an immensely thin, ghost-like figure standing in the window. After a moment she opened her eyes again and sat up and stared, suddenly awake. But there was nothing . . . no one.

Behind her someone moved in the bed, and a guttural voice waid, '*Was ist's?*'

Claudine shook her head sadly. '*Rien . . . c'est rien*,' and lay back as a hard, rough hand was laid on her hip.

Gallagher stepped off the trellis and walked round the corner of the building, biting back his feelings, staring at the ground, for once not noticing where he was going until two shoes appeared in front of him and the shock made him look up quickly. Looking at him was Claudine's mother, staring like a wild thing, but he saw that she knew who he was. She said nothing. Her eyes were suddenly gentle where they had been bitter, and she stretched out a soft, loose-skinned hand to touch his cheek for a moment in infinite compassion. Then she was gone. Gallagher did not turn, but breathed in deeply and walked past the Kübelwagen. Suddenly he noted that it had four flat, slashed tyres. He smiled wryly to himself. The old girl was not such a cabbage as she seemed.

He was back by noon. Solange looked at him in surprise, and told him that de Grouchy was out taking food to the others.

'Anything happen?'

She shook her head and he crossed to the old coffee-pot on the hob.

'This hot?'

He didn't wait for a reply as his fingers told him it was, and he poured himself a cupful.

'Are you hungry?'

'No.'

She waited for a moment then found herself having to ask the inevitable question.

'Did you see her?'

He nodded and offered no more. That made her anxious, and unable to sit back and wait.

'Well?'

'That's *it!* It's over. She has a protector.'

Solange didn't answer, but she felt a warm comforting glow suffuse through her whole being. Inside her heart she relaxed and the female in her immediately started planning.

7 June

Gwillim telephoned Squires later the same day to say he had laid on the RAF Lysander pick-up for one person, with difficulty. The others would have to make their own way back, and, under the present conditions, it would have to be a Navy pick-up from Gibraltar, not even from the Midi coastal areas. The Germans anticipated an 'underbelly thrust' from the Mediterranean and had disproportionately defended the coastal areas. One of those phrases which so mesmerised Churchill. Ellen Robinson was asked to send the coded message. Squires recognised she was putting up a brave working front to cover her personal pain. He felt for her. He actually liked Ellen Robinson, and respected her. He didn't often like women.

That same evening, having sorted out the basic situation at the underground complex, or what was left of it, there was time to consider what to do about the saboteurs. The BBC was already crowing about a successful commando operation which had destroyed an underground installation of some importance north of Paris. The implication was that the raiding-party were already back in the UK. Obergefreiter Artur Greiser thought otherwise. He had four men he was able to deploy to make a search and he had available to him two police dogs – Alsatian beasts trained by Belgian police and 'borrowed' by the German forces for just such contingencies. All other able-bodied men in the area had been hastily recalled to their units, fighting units, that is, policing was to be kept to a minimum, and left wherever possible to the Milice and local Gendarmerie. Not a lot to work with. But Obergefreiter Greiser had been lucky and found the abandoned truck very quickly. The dogs had been given their scent, but one of the *Schützen* remarked that with such a stink of petrol in the truck the dogs wouldn't be a lot of help. As indeed they weren't. In any case the truck had been there almost a full twenty hours. They could be anywhere.

8 June
Gallagher assembled the men in de Grouchy's barn beside the palliasse made up for Lovell, who was recovering from the loss of blood and his wound without complications. The bullet had shattered one side of the humerus and one rib before proceeding out of his back. There was no bullet to remove and the wound seemed clean enough. The bismuth powder held back any infection that might be hovering. So far so good.

‘We’ve finally heard from London. There will be a Lysander pick-up to take Hibou and the stuff he has back to England. That is the number one priority. The rest of us are to make our way overland to Gibraltar.’ He turned to de Grouchy. ‘Can we organise a flarepath?’

The farmer thought for a moment, then nodded. ‘You realise that with the Germans looking for you, it is dangerous for my men.’

Macklin crossed to Lovell and grinned at him, lighting a cigarette and blowing the smoke into his face deliberately, but Lovell saw it as the curiously friendly gesture it was meant to be.

‘’s all right for some. I’ve got a flippin’ walk ahead of me. How far’s Gib, then?’

‘I would estimate something in the region of a thousand miles. The way you smoke you’ll never make it.’

Macklin’s jaw had dropped.

‘You’re ’avin’ me on!’

But Lovell shook his head slowly, and Macklin knew it was for real. He turned and spoke to Gallagher.

‘Here, Squire, I’ll ’ave me gratuity now. Sod that walk!’

‘You’ll walk and like it, my lad. I want you for my *next* job.’

Macklin looked at him, and realised he meant exactly what he said. For the first time in his life George Macklin knew he was wanted. He had made it. They liked him, they respected his talent, and treated him like a human being no different from themselves. Macklin swelled with warmth and pride inside.

‘Well, that’s different, then.’

Marin, the small, swarthy-skinned man from the village, arrived to say that the Germans had found the truck and were searching the woods.

‘It was bound to happen. I don’t like the sound of those dogs, though.’ Gallagher was concerned. Time was, therefore, of the essence.

‘I shouldn’t worry too much about the dogs. I found a can of petrol in the truck when we was on the scarper. Upset it on purpose, if you know what I mean. Them dogs won’t smell nothin’. I know. It’s not the first time I got clumsy with petrol.’

Gallagher looked at Macklin, and a tiny smile crept across his face. ‘Where would we be without criminals?’

Macklin fixed him with a stony stare, and pointed a 'watch-it' finger in his direction.

Gallagher turned to de Grouchy. 'We owe you a great deal, Pierre. Thank you.'

But in England there were snags. Snags of the sort that did not concern agents in the field, nor should they be told of them, for the petty bickering of staff and administrative bureaucrats was sometimes enough to get fighting men shot and civilians massacred. Squires' thoughts were with the men on the job, as always.

'What d'you mean we can't get them out?'

'They just said the Lysander had been called off. They had orders to stand-by for other things.'

Gwillim was slightly embarrassed that he had to return to the Hall with such news. Evans was about to go to bed in one of the dormitories. He wanted the papers and was becoming increasingly concerned that they come into British hands at the first possible moment: preferably into his hands.

'Damn it, Colonel, this isn't good enough!'

'Allow them something, Dafid.' Gwillim tried to be reasonable. 'SHAEF* can spare nothing. They do have several beach-heads to consolidate, and all their effort must go into that. The Americans have one of theirs in trouble. If it collapses or fails it could jeopardise the whole front.'

Evans swung round. 'Damn the Second Front!' Then he felt embarrassed at his vehemence and foolishness, and backed down. 'Oh, I don't mean that, but they're all living in the past, boyo. These missiles are the wars of the future, and the future has just become the present. Make them understand that, will you.'

'You think these flying-bombs are just the beginning?'

'They're not even the beginning, Colonel. They were outmoded before they began. Jerry saw this and took a new tack. We will have rockets raining down on us before you can say "Eisteddfod". Rockets, man! Not just these things, though Lord knows they're bad enough. What do I have to do to make someone comprehend? Can I use your phone, Squires?'

* Supreme Headquarters Allied Expeditionary Forces.

'Please do.'

Evans picked up the desk-phone and waited for the sergeant on duty to answer.

'Can you get me Whitehall 8424 extension 191. I want to speak to Duncan Sandys. Tell him it's Dafid Evans. Thank you.'

The squad of German soldiers under Obergefreiter Artur Greiser were having no luck. Always they drew blanks. Greiser was beginning to believe that the BBC hints had been well founded. It was possible. The saboteur-commandos *could* be back in England by now. But then Chantilly HQ had said they were picking up radio signals from Greiser's area as recently as one hour ago. No, he was sure they were still in the area and Greiser was determined to find them if it took him the rest of the week to do so.

He requartered his map, and pencilled out the areas searched. With only four men and two dogs it did not make it easy to cover the territory at speed. He didn't even have co-operation from the Gendarmerie. The news of the landings had made them reconsider their position rather hastily. Greiser would do it on his own. His father had been awarded an Iron Cross for a similar operation not thirty miles from where his son, Artur, now stood. Awarded and pinned on by the 'old man' himself, Field-Marshall Hindenburg.

Evans had finally got through to Sandys and urged him to help, explaining exactly what it was they wanted and why. Sandys was the right man, he understood the potential and trusted Evans. He also had Churchill's ear, and the PM still had pull even though the whole business was really in Eisenhower's lap for the moment. He had seen Churchill, and was now returning the call.

'Yes, I understand, so what did Winston say?'

Evans was clearly on edge, and scratching the desk-top with his finger nails. 'Damn it, man, it is the big one we are talking about! We must get them back *now!* What?' He put his hand over the phone and turned to Gwillim. 'Have we got RAF agreement?'

Gwillim put out his hand and accepted the receiver.

'Duncan? Gwillim. I *had* agreement for the pick-up. This clamp-down is quite ridiculous. Who? I don't care what Tedder said. This is quite a different matter. Duncan, *please*. Winston must over-ride the ruling. It is obviously misinterpreted. No, tomorrow could be too late! It must be now! Very well . . . I shall stay here at Masham until you ring.'

Evans glowered at the phone. 'It's like drawing teeth trying to get something out of them. I suppose they want to *win* this war?'

The team set out from the farm shortly before nine. It would take them an hour to walk to the pick-up field. Possibly longer as they had to carry Lovell some of the way. He tried bravely to do as the others, but after two kilometres the loss of blood showed, and he wilted. Soltysyk carried him first, then Cameron.

Obergefreiter Greiser's search party had narrowed their area down to the hundred-and-fifty hectares surrounding de Grouchy's farm. Not because they suspected de Grouchy. It just worked out that way. They had been spotted, and word had got about and action taken accordingly. Jules Marin, who made a speciality of appearing as the local village idiot openly confessed to Greiser that he had seen several men moving in an easterly direction. Greiser's men set out wearily towards the east. They had been walking all day, and half of the previous night. Even the master-race needed a rest now and again.

In the west Gallagher's group reached the edge of the long pasture which was to be the landing-field specified. The RAF had not used it before, and Gallagher decided to double-check. His team spread out across the field and walked carefully in a single line down the entire length, to ensure that there were no obstructions, which could so easily cripple an aircraft by smashing the landing-cart. The 'Lizzie' was a sturdy little lady, but an old, half-rusted carriage-wheel, or broken plough was enough to damage, and one really deep pot-hole could break the wheel-strut. There was nothing. It was clear for landing. The night was dark enough, with very little moon showing as yet.

Unaware of the battle that had been raging in the corridors of power over such a trivial detail in a highly important operation, Gallagher was not concerned *if* the Lysander was coming . . . merely would it be on time and without ground problems?

The ground problems started when they got back to their original position to wait. Cameron heard it first, the sound of a vehicle approaching, and without lights. Gallagher immediately deployed his people to defend the field if necessary. The sole matter of import was to get Lovell and his information onto that plane and away to England. The rest would happen as it fell out.

The lane was pitch black, and they heard the vehicle stop some hundred yards down the road, the sound of doors being closed quietly . . . then silence.

Gallagher heard the tiny click on both sides that told him his team had removed the safety-catches, and were ready to open fire. There was, out of the night, a hissed voice.

'Major Gallagher! Major, it's de Grouchy.'

Gallagher recognised the voice and considered. Possibly he was a hostage, possibly not. There were others present he knew. Years of operations had taught him to estimate from the feel of the hairs on the back of his neck. He guessed eight, possibly ten. Cameron was suddenly, silently at his side.

Gallagher whispered to him. 'I'll talk, open fire if you need to. Don't worry about me.'

Gallagher stood up and walked towards the voice.

De Grouchy advanced towards him holding a German Schmeisser .48. Captured, or – liberated – as the Resistance euphemistically called it. Behind him were eight Frenchmen, largely farm workers as far as he could tell. A quick glance told him that they were genuine. There was no German presence. He ordered his people to stand down, and walked up to de Grouchy, looking smilingly at the group of Resistants.

'I always knew there *was* a *réseau*.'

He nodded his thanks to de Grouchy and the men.

'The Boche are coming this way, Marin tried to send them the other way, but they must have sensed it was false. You haven't a chance of getting the plane away unless I lead them off. We'll create a diversion and get them to move away.'

Gallagher looked at de Grouchy and nodded again. The men shook hands, and de Grouchy led his men back to the farm truck. They heard the motor start, then it moved into the distance and faded out. Gallagher turned his head and listened carefully. Nothing. Where in God's name was that blasted plane? He checked his watch. Two minutes overdue! He joined the others and glanced down at Lovell sitting on the ground clutching his box. He smiled wanly up at Gallagher. No one spoke. They all were thinking the same thing.

It was Soltysyk who first heard it. He touched Gallagher's sleeve and looked upwards. There it was, the approaching sound of an aircraft flying low. Single engine. Rotary.

'Make a flarepath with the torches. It'll have to be a single line, there aren't enough of us. Hibou, stay where you are and use your torch when we do to imply which side of the line to land. Get cracking!'

They ran across the turf and made the line as the airplane approached in the black sky. Suddenly there was the sound of distant gunfire, Schmeissers, unmistakably, interrupted by the slightly deeper crack of the breech-loading rifle. De Grouchy was timing it perfectly. The enemy was engaged. The engine-roar throttled down, and they heard the additional swish of slipstream as the plane touched down on the field, and came bounding towards them out of the night. They momentarily turned their torch beams to show the terrain ahead of the Lysander and give away their own positions. The monoplane stopped and turned round into the wind, waiting. For once, no one got out. It was a one-way trip. Cameron and Soltysyk carried Lovell out to the plane as Macklin threw back the hatch-cover, and assisted them in putting the wounded man into the back seat. The box was placed on his lap. Gallagher looked at him and smiled.

'You know what to do.'

Lovell nodded. Macklin shouted up at him from the ground. 'Don't let anybody pinch my bed!' Lovell nodded once more, and the window hatch was lowered and secured. Gallagher slapped the fuselage and waved a finger at the pilot, who immediately revved the engine and taxied into the gloom, then roared forward into take-off.

They didn't wait to watch it rise. They couldn't see anyway. That was their contact with home gone now they were on their own, in Occupied territory with a thousand-mile walk ahead of them. The sound of distant firing continued, and was now noticeable without the plane's engine to mask it. The heads turned and hesitated.

Gallagher spoke briskly. 'Well, if we're going to Gib, we'd better start moving. I want to be back in England by the end of the week.'

'Shouldn't we go and help them?' Cameron turned a concerned face to Gallagher. Gallagher didn't reply, just held his eye with a look that said 'Don't you ever learn anything?'

'They've come into the open at last. They'll be on their own for a bit yet. Let them get used to the idea.'

He turned to Solange who was standing near him, smiled into her face. 'Collect up the weapons. Leave them against the field-gate. That's what I agreed with Pierre. They'll pick them up later.'

She and Macklin did so, and were joined by the other two where they waited for Gallagher. He came to them jauntily enough to give them confidence. He had done the journey many times. They had not. He turned down the lane, and headed towards the town and the nearest railway station. It wasn't all that different from England when you thought about it. Gallagher asked them all to synchronise their French-made watches. It had just become 9 June 1944.